PICTURES OF THE SKY

A NOVEL

WILLIAM MINTON

2015 Letters From Elsewhere Trade Paperback Edition

ISBN: 0692423559
ISBN-13: 978-0692423554 (Letters From Elsewhere)

www.lettersfromelsewhere.com

Cover photo by William Minton

Jacket design by Lauren Fischer and William Minton

For Adriana, gone from life too soon…

Summer

Year 5
Michael and Veronica

A bead of sweat forms on her brow and then slips, slides, and hangs for a moment at the corner of her eye before falling and splashing gently on the table.

"Are you all right?" asks Michael. "I always forget how hot it gets."

"Yes, I'm fine," she says. She turns her eyes to the ground and wipes the perspiration from her forehead with her fingertips. A soft breeze measures the silence. Veronica sets her hand on the table, takes a deep breath, and looks back toward Michael. "No. I'm sorry... I don't know what's wrong with me." She looks away and then back again. "We should do this another time. Forgive me. I'm being awful, I know. I'll call you."

Michael protests, but her posture is rigid now. She is leaning forward with her hand cupped over her lighter and pack of cigarettes. He realizes that she is waiting for him to let her go. "Alright. Call me. I hope you feel better."

"Thank you."

Year 1
Michael

On the first rocket, the bulls are let loose and then I wait to run. Why do I suddenly feel like I have to shit? BANG! *Jesus Christ!* The mass of people starts to jog around him, and Michael tries to steady his nerves. His breaths become short and chop with the beats of his heart. Somehow he finds room to run full stride. The shouts behind him melt into the air. *Holy shit!* A bull gallops by him in a blur. *I'm going to fucking die!* He darts to one of the wooden barricades that block off the side streets and as he jumps to climb over it a police officer clubs his head and shoulders from above. He looks back. The bulls have passed. *Damn.*

At an outdoor bar, Michael makes fast friends with Sean, from California. Sean is seven years older than Michael. Like Michael, he is tall with an athletic build and sharp features. They drink quickly and trade stories from the run.

"I almost tripped, man. Right when the bull was coming up behind me. My foot caught on one of the stones. I've never been scared like that." Sean thuds his hand against the counter, "Fucking intense man."

A half-drunk Spaniard spills beer on Michael's shoulder and the girl he's with apologizes before pulling him away. It's not yet 9 AM, but the street is loud, and Michael and Sean have to raise their voices to be understood.

"So, you're traveling alone?" asks Sean.

"I was with my friend Adam in Italy a few days ago when I heard this was going on. I think he's in France now."

Sean started traveling in Vietnam almost a year ago. He can hardly believe that Michael is just 18. With a slap, he rests his hand on Michael's shoulder. "You need to come to the bullfight tonight. We'll see those bastards we ran with face off against the matadors."

When Michael arrives at the bullfight, Sean and his friend Jeff are talking with a family seated in the row behind them, and eating from Styrofoam bowls.

"Yes," continues the Grandfather, "your Hemingway understood the bullfight. He knew that tragedy could be a context for art. He saw the sacrifices of the matadors. The matadors in his stories were never lucky men."

Should I say something about Hemingway?

The grandfather grins toward Michael and serves another bowl of stew.

"Take, take," he says. "The meat is from one of yesterday's bulls."

This place is incredible.

In the ring below, the ceremony commences. The grandfather narrates the fights while Michael shares his stew. When a popular matador descends to his knees Michael stands with the rest of the crowd. He watches the man raise his cape, jut his chest forward, and beckon the bull to charge. The bull kicks at the earth and rushes forward. The matador raises the cape and brushes his shoulder against the side of the bull as he passes. The cheer is thunderous. When he raises his sword, the setting sun shimmers in its blade.

After the last bull is killed and dragged away, people begin to pour into the ring. Michael, Sean, and Jeff follow, singing along, "Oh *le*, oh le oh le oh le, *oh le, oh le*." Standing above blood-stained sand, Michael turns his eyes to the sky. He hears a Spanish brass band marching outside the arena.

The three of them stride over cobblestone streets with bottles of sangria in their hands. "This festival is older than America," declares Jeff.

"Fiesta!" exclaims Michael. They throw their free arms around each other's shoulders and swing their bottles in the air.

Thousands of people in white shirts and red scarves course through the streets and squares. Music is everywhere. When they stop to regroup, Michael makes eye contact with a Spanish girl dancing on a balcony. They both smile. Michael moves his shoulders to the rhythm of the music. She gestures for him to come up. He gestures for her to come down. Sean and Jeff figure out what's going on.

"Well, shit. Let's get up there," says Sean.

The girl doesn't seem to mind that Michael can't speak Spanish, "Me llamo, Isabel, quieres bailar conmigo?" she says. Soon they kiss, and with Michael against the wall, she begins to dance for him. She arches her back and turns in a blur as she claps her hands above her shoulders. The wall seems to move behind him, and he realizes that he's gotten quite drunk. Soon he follows Sean back into the street. The music and drink escalate. They find themselves in an alley smoking hash and trading English for Spanish phrases. By fire escape, they end up on the roof of a building where they watch the city boil around them.

"I'm glad we didn't die this morning," says Jeff.

"It's good to be alive," says Sean.

Walking back to the apartment, Michael feels a sense of triumph. The sun is breaking over the horizon. *This is the life I've been searching for.*

* * * * *

A week later, Michael is on a train platform in Barcelona saying goodbye to some people he's met.

"And we hope you find your friend Adam."

From down the tracks: "Michael! Michael!"

"Holy shit. That's Adam."

Adam is running, his long legs kicking awkwardly behind him, an unrestrained smile on his face.

"I can't believe I found you!" he says, almost out of breath, "Cesky Krumlov was amazing. I met these gypsies, and I might have a chance to get rich. This Russian woman wants to look at some of my drawings."

"Does she know anything about your drawings?"

"She *knows* about *me*. Where are you going?"

"I'm going to Paris."

"*I'm* going to Paris!"

Adam lunges forward and thrusts his arms around

Michael.

"It's good to see you too buddy."

Michael waves to his friends from the hostel and follows Adam on board. Neither one is surprised to reconnect like this. Each day of the past several weeks, the unusual has become increasingly common. Now, two months out of high school, they are both convinced that life is destined to bend to their favor.

Once at their seats, Adam takes a small travel pillow from his bag and stuffs it, along with his head, into the gap between his seat and the window. He seems unbothered by the light against his face. Michael relaxes. Exhaustion seeps from his muscles and into his bones. He closes his eyes. *I guess we both should be pretty tired.*

At the hostel, it's clear that they've both gotten used to traveling alone. Michael finds a quiet table to catch up on his travel journal while Adam befriends a group of Australians and tells them about how he's moving to New York City when he gets back to the States.

The next morning they decide to do their own things. At a café by the hostel, Michael meets an attractive girl named Lindsay from Subiaco, Arkansas. She is one of the only people he's met who is also right out of high school. They talk about how surprisingly easy traveling has been. She is quick to mention that she has a boyfriend, and Michael can tell that she is used to guys mistaking her friendliness for something more.

They decide to go to the Louvre but soon find themselves lost. Michael is taken by how effortlessly Lindsay swings through her emotions. She is vocal in her frustrations but ecstatic at each sign they may have found their way. When they reach the Louvre, he takes a picture of her in front of the glass pyramid with her hands extended toward the sky.

The next day they take the train to Versailles. Michael has never heard of Versailles, but Lindsay has wanted to come here since she was a child. Standing at the rear of the palace, the royal gardens dominate their view. Michael is struck by their linear composition.

They walk side by side between the hedges. "Marie Antoinette," begins Lindsay, "was younger than I am when she moved here. She hardly knew anything else and then mobs came and threw her to the guillotine."

They approach the centuries old rectangular lake and are surprised to learn that they can rent a boat. Michael sits next to Lindsay on the front bench and then lies back to look at the clouds.

"My girlfriend would like this," says Michael.

"I didn't know you had a girlfriend."

"Yeah. Kelsey. She's the best part of my life back home."

Lindsay looks over her shoulder. Her face is drenched with sun. "So, I guess you'll get to see her tomorrow." She smiles suggestively and Michael looks away.

"She'll be at the airport. Her and my Mom get along pretty well."

The nearby fountains begin to shoot arcs of water into the air. Michael sits up and focuses on the palace above them, "You know," he says, "it would be cool to be a king."

For the third night in a row, people from Michael's hostel have gathered in a circle on the lawn in front of the Eiffel Tower. Michael cuts around groups of people while drinking wine from a bottle he holds by the neck. When he finds the group from his hostel, they cheer his arrival. He raises his bottle and cheers in return. *It's good to have people in Paris*. He notices that Lindsay and Adam are talking and moves to sit by them.

Adam raises his bottle in a toast, "Here we go Mikey. One more night."

"One more night."

Michael and Lindsay decide to take a walk to the base of the tower. He buys her a rose from a man who approaches them. Quietly, they drift away from each other and look at different parts of the tower. Alcohol warms his cheeks and the people around him blend into a blur. Michael decides that these past two months will forever bind him to what is beautiful in the world. Adventure is everything it promises to be. He stops his feet, looks up, and traces his eyes over the crisscrossing lights above him. He smiles, raises his arms level to the ground and begins to spin.

Year 5
Susan and Leah

Susan stands in front of the sink washing dishes. The radio behind her mixes with the sound of running water. She is at ease. Above the sink is a large window that looks out on a park where she can see a father teaching his son how to fly a kite. She is singing quietly to herself but stops when the father passes the kite and she watches the son, maybe six years old, struggle to get a grip of it in his hands. Susan smiles. She is tall, with long brown hair, and slender, slightly awkward limbs. She wonders if the boy will remember this day when he's older.

Behind her stretches the apartment. The tile in the kitchen gives way to dark hardwood floors that expand into the dining room before passing by a set of French doors and receding into a long, sparsely furnished room. A bamboo coffee table with a glass top sits on a worn down Persian rug. A couch is pressed against the wall, a wicker chair sits next to it, and a tattered recliner rests in the far corner. Plants fill the open spaces. A pair of large windows frames the light from the sun as it casts the shadow of an oak branch across the floor. Leah is sitting by the windows, reading. Steam rises from the coffee that she holds between herself and the newspaper. She blows on it gently and takes a sip. She sets the mug on the windowsill and begins to flip through the paper. After a while, she folds the paper, drops it on the floor, stretches her arms and returns to her coffee. She curls her fingers around its heat and sends her voice across the room, "I think we should have a party."

Susan looks over her shoulder, sets down the plate and sponge, and turns down the music.

"What?"

"I said, I think we should have a party."

Susan rubs a towel over her hands and steps into the doorway.

"When?"

Susan decides to take a walk to buy groceries for dinner. Her hair is pulled back into a ponytail. She wears a gray cotton tank top and frayed khaki pants that shape to her body just above the thighs. She's on her way to the door when she calls to Leah, "How many people do you think we can get to come to this party?"

"Let's invite everyone." Leah's voice ricochets from inside her bedroom. "We can talk more about it when you get back."

Thinking it better for her legs to take the stairs Susan passes the elevator to her right and pushes the door open to the stairwell. The air inside is stuffy and humid. Dampness rises on her chest and behind her knees. In the street, a breeze licks across her face. She tucks a few loose strands of hair behind her ear. The sidewalk is lined with small boutiques and cafes with outdoor patios. She makes note of a bakery she'd like to return to and congratulates herself on the idea to move to Shadyside. She thinks of Leah sitting alone in the apartment. At first she was worried about living with Leah. She didn't know how Leah would handle the transition from her life in France. But Leah's return has triggered something in Susan. For the first time in years, she feels like fate is on her side. Susan catches her reflection in a store window and smiles. She thinks about how her bedroom fills with light in the morning, and she savors the simple pleasure of walking to the grocery store. Susan imagines herself a bud uncurling its petals to the spring. A new act is beginning.

When she returns home, Leah is standing by the couch, "At the end of the month there's a full moon," says Leah. "We should have the party then. You know, to celebrate."

"I don't know Leah. Are you sure a party is a good idea?" Grocery bags hang from her fingertips.

"Why would you say that?" Leah scrunches her brow, "You're *always* trying to ruin my fun."

Susan smiles, steps into the kitchen, and sets the bags on the counter. The sun warms the tile by the window. The park is empty. For an instant, the veil of a familiar loneliness descends around her. She makes an effort not to be alarmed and turns on the radio. She opens the fridge and begins to unpack the groceries. A woman's acoustic cover of "Voodoo Child" begins to play, and Leah sings along from the other room, "I'm standing next to a mountain. Gonna' chop it down with the edge of my hand."

Year 1
Leah

Leah sits naked on the edge of her tub and passes her fingers through the water to test its heat. When the water turns hot, she plugs the drain and the sound of a running bath fills the room. Her imagination plays a montage of her recent flirtations. She feels a flush in her cheeks. Steam begins to rise from the water. Leah stands and walks out of the bathroom toward the full-length mirror propped against the wall beside her bed. She makes eye contact with her reflection. She hesitates briefly and then pulls up the corner of her mouth, turns her nose to the side and holds the pose. She flutters her eyelashes. Her face moves quickly through surprise and amusement. She looks down, lifts her chin and opens her eyes wide. This pose is for tall men at close range. She bends slightly forward to see herself from their perspective. She turns around and looks back over her shoulder. *I should run more often.*

It's night outside, and a chill begins to cling to her skin. Still, Leah continues through her regular review of her body's assets. Her hips may be too wide, but her breasts are nice. She likes the curve of her neck, and her shoulders go well with her height. She considers her hair and decides she likes it shorter. Overall she finds herself alluring and young.

The sound of water from the bathroom becomes muffled, and Leah knows the bath is ready. She steps slowly into the tub and savors the heat as it envelops her skin. She slides her body beneath the water and rests her neck along the curve of the ceramic behind her. She thinks of the yellow dress she's picked out for tonight hanging from her closet door and then slides her hand back and forth along her inner thigh. Her thoughts circle around the fact that she is a virgin. *Still a virgin.* The thought used to be a point of pride, but over the last few months, it's begun to feel like a weight. She feels, more and more, like life is leaving her behind. Still, she knows that she needs to wait. She's too beautiful to offer herself to someone who loves her less than completely. *Someday.*

She brushes the hair from her forehead and water drips down her cheek. *Maybe tonight it will begin.* She imagines meeting someone and feeling suddenly off balance. He's handsome but playful. She's charmed by his laugh. Their voices create a kind of song. He tells her that she's beautiful, and when he holds her she feels safe from fear. In time, they'll be together, and she'll offer him everything that he needs. Her heart beats quicker at the thought. *Love... Soon I'll be in love.*

Year 3
Michael and Susan

On the first Friday of each month, graduate students and young professionals, local artists and musicians, older couples and self-described punks, undergrads and local residents, hipster couples with small children, suburbanites, occasional critics of art, and always lovers of free wine, all gather on Penn Avenue in and between a stretch of low rent galleries, artist studios, music venues, and dimly lit bars, in an effort to unwind from the tensions of the week and remind themselves that they know how to have a good time.

A few miles away, Michael is getting dressed. Clothing is strewn around the bed. He picks through the undershirts, somewhat at random, and sniffs the armpits of each. He chooses the one with the faintest odor and slips it on over his head. As part of an effort to be more fashionable, he decides to wear his blue plaid blazer and grey fedora. He considers calling his friend Derrick, but decides against it. *Susan might be there.* He grabs his car keys from the dresser and heads toward the door.

Susan has been spending most of her weekends home

alone, writing, drinking wine and streaming old movies on her laptop. Occasionally she meets up with someone for dinner, but she always declines to get drinks afterward. When her friend Jane invited her out to First Fridays, she felt apprehensive, even though the event used to be something of a monthly ritual for her. On her way home for the weekend, she decided to buy a dress pattern and some fabric instead. She told herself she would finally learn to sew. At home, she unpacked the pattern, and her hands quivered with indecision as she cut and pinned it together. Now the pattern sits in front of her, but she can't summon the effort to do anything but stare.

She criticizes herself for going out of her way to stay in tonight. She stands and opens a window. The wind licks her hair and lifts it from the back of her neck. She closes her eyes.

Susan is surprised to find a dozen or so people sitting around Jane at the Quiet Storm. She approaches slowly and catches Jane's eye.

"Susan! You've made it." Jane stands and gestures toward her, "Everyone: this is Susan." Susan smiles softly and waves with a slight flick of her wrist.

Michael is driving slowly to better pay attention to the old Victorian homes along the street. The houses are broad with modest porches, large windows, and the occasional balcony. This is only Michael's third year living in Pittsburgh, but it is the second time that he has returned here after traveling somewhere else, and he is beginning to feel a special affinity for the city. A few blocks ahead, he sees groups of people crossing the street. He rolls down his window, and the sound of electric guitars wafts into the car.

Not long after Susan's arrival, Jane and company decide to move toward the galleries. The first one they find is a brightly lit rectangular room with a cello, trumpet, and keyboard trio set up in the corner. The female cello player is singing. The group moves toward the wine and cheese table in the back, but Susan steps toward a large canvas by the door and begins to make her way counter-clockwise around the room. Her feet assume a slow and steady rhythm; her eyes take time to trace over each piece. Many of the paintings are of brightly colored houses. Houses growing out of mountains, houses being carried on peoples' backs, houses in trees and a house on the trunk of an elephant that is reared up on its hind legs. At the end of the wall, a group of people are gathered around the artist. As Susan passes by, she hears her say, "and part of it is the idea that everywhere we've come from is with us everywhere we go." She picks up a glass of white wine and heads toward the opposite wall. She glances toward the door and sees Michael enter the gallery.

When Michael sees Susan, his breath stops, and he turns away. He's tempted to leave. He doesn't know if Susan has seen him. He finds himself staring at the musicians.

Jane touches Susan's elbow and suggests heading to the artist studios next door. As they approach Michael, Susan forces her eyes away. They pass him, push open the door and step into the nighttime air. Without thinking, he follows her.

"Susan!"

She turns. His heart is racing.

"Michael." She smiles.

"Hey, it's been awhile."

Susan introduces Jane, "We work together at *The Boulevard.*"

"Oh yeah? Cool." He should have put together something to say.

"What are you up to?" She moves her weight from her left to right foot and back again.

Michael is embarrassed to admit he's still finishing up his undergrad and finds himself laughing as he explains himself. Jane says that she's going to go catch up with everyone at the studio.

"Oh, I'm coming with you," says Susan. "Michael, it was really good running into you." She turns, and as they walk away, Jane slips her arm into Susan's.

"What was *that* about?" asks Jane.

"What?"

"You know what I'm talking about."

Michael considers following after them. Patience. Susan and Jane drift farther away. He turns and then stands still. He can't go after them and he can't seem to go anywhere else. He needs to keep occupied. *Was she flirting with me?* He spots a taco truck and walks over to stand in line. *I wonder if she'll come back out to find me?*

Susan doesn't understand how Michael can have such

an effect on her. The moment he called her name, she felt an uncompromising pull towards him. She was starting to enjoy herself, but suddenly Jane's friends seem superficial and dull.

The artists' studio is an old, high-ceilinged warehouse, with thick black outlines for workspaces painted on the ground. Some spaces are cluttered with easels displaying canvases. Some are converted into installations. Here and there artists are working, seemingly undistracted by the groups of people moving about and staring at them.

Michael scans the room for Susan but also tries to make an effort to look at the art around him. He finds a painting that is tall and thin and devoted entirely to a match. The tip of the match is scratched but unlit. The stem is broken. *Clever.* His anxiety begins to build. Michael picks up his pace and is soon hurrying through the warehouse.

Susan has found a side room that used to serve as a large storage closet. The art here is different. The colors are bold, and the brush technique is flawless. When she stands close to the paintings, she is stunned by the attention to detail.

The last painting she moves toward is the largest. Its shadows are set to put the viewer directly behind the sun. She steps close to take in each of its parts. Left of center is the edge of a cliff, which drops down the canvas to a shore where waves crash onto boulders and sand. Ocean covers the right half of the painting. Susan is struck by the painting's complexity. The water seems impossibly real and impossibly clear at the same time. In the back left corner, miniature compared to the rest of the painting but still about the size of her thumb, is a lighthouse. Its details are delicate and concise. Dozens of birds are suspended across the surface of the canvas, each one distinct in color and posture. Just below center is the focal point of the painting. A couple is frozen between the edge of the cliff and the rocks and sand below. They are holding hands as they dive, headfirst, toward the breaking waves. A group of birds beneath them scurry out of the way. The man is wearing a tuxedo. The woman is in a wedding gown. Susan steps back to take it in all at once.

Michael's voice startles her. "I think it was probably an accident."

Susan turns toward him. He glances at her, and they both look back toward the painting. "Seems unlikely."

"No. I think just over here, out of frame, is probably the wedding photographer. 'Little to the left. OK, now step back, little more, little more, one more step,' and then poof. Off they go."

"But they're not falling. They're diving."

"Then maybe that's the message. You have to make the best of things."

Susan laughs lightly, looks down and then up at Michael. She takes a half step toward him. "Whatever it is, I like it. I like all of the paintings back here."

The drone of conversation bleeds in from the main room outside. Susan seems nervous. Michael gives himself a count down. *Three*, he readies his right arm. *Two*, inhale, exhale. *One*, he bends his arm at the elbow and moves his fingertips to the small of Susan's back. When she doesn't flinch, he continues with his palm and slides his hand across her back. The touch is electrifying. She slides closer and leans her shoulder against his chest. He rests his hand on her hip.

"By the way," she says. "Nice hat."

"Oh yeah, I think it really brings out the jacket."

"Oh Michael, what have you done with yourself?"

They leave the room and meander through the warehouse. They make comments about the art and the people around them. Jane spots them from a few aisles away and flashes Susan an open-mouthed expression of surprise when Michael isn't looking. Susan blushes.

Outside packs of people flow in both directions down the middle of the street. Music from different angles blends together. They stand next to each other in jittery silence. Michael is tempted to kiss her. *No...* He shouldn't rush.

"Do you want to find some more art?" he asks.

"Not especially."

"What were you thinking?"

"Well, I kinda want to get home. I don't really go out much." She's surprised to hear an enticing tone in her voice.

"Oh," he says, not understanding, losing confidence, "Well, can I walk you to your car?"

She smiles. "You can walk me home if you want. I just live a few blocks around the corner."

Susan gestures to her house. They step onto her porch. This is not what she expected from her evening. "Um, you haven't seen my place have you?" *What am I doing?* "Do you want to come up?" It's like she's watching herself say these things.

"Sure," he says, straining to mute his enthusiasm.

Upstairs, Susan offers a brief tour of her three-room apartment. She apologizes for the clutter, but Michael assures her his place is much worse. Stepping out of the bedroom, he takes her hand. The reality of the evening begins to dawn on Michael.

They move toward the couch. He places his hand on her knee. She slides toward him.

"I can't believe I'm doing this," she says.

"Doing what?"

"I find you out in the middle of the street and before I can help myself we're back at my place with your hand on my leg."

"We don't have to do anything."

"I know." She looks up into his eyes. Her heart is pounding.

He leans toward her. They part their lips and close their eyes. Her breath brushes against his lips. They kiss. She grips his shoulder, and he moves his arm behind her back. Their lips press firmer together. Surrendering to each other's embrace, they fall sideways onto the couch. This is really happening. Their kiss softens and then escalates in intensity. There is no more thinking. Their bodies arch with approval as fingers explore under fabric and slide over skin. Her hands run across his back. She pulls his shirt over his head. She leans forward, and soon her shirt is gone. He unclasps her bra, and she lets it fall beside the couch. When she feels the skin of his chest press against hers, she sighs deeply. Their lips roam across cheeks, jaws, ears and necklines. His hands feel strong and gentle as they pass over her breasts. His fingers peak toward her waistline, and she takes his wrist.

"We should go to the bedroom."

He is perched above her with her legs to his sides. "Are you sure this is what you want?"

"Yes," she whispers. He sees a fire lick behind her eyes.

She pushes her fingers into the muscle above his shoulders and pulls him closer. She turns her chin away, and his lips move to her neck. Her fingers fumble with his belt, then his button. There is a nervous, then victorious, search for a condom.

He slides off the last of her clothes, and she takes in the sight of him standing at the foot of the bed.

"Susan," he says, crawling back onto the bed.

"Yes."

"You have no idea how often I've thought of this."

As they kiss, she guides him. Their limbs intertwine. Their breathing keeps a steady rhythm. Susan lays her arms out across the bed and arches her back. Her hands claw into the mattress and the sheets pull taut around her fingertips. Michael is careful to pace himself. He holds her close to him, then relaxes and begins to move his lips down her body: over her neck, between her breasts, to the edge of her pubic hair, and finally her inner thigh. Susan is pleasantly surprised. She feels an energy flowing just beneath her skin. The tips of her fingers are tingling and then, everything is slowing down. Michael's lips make their way back up, more quickly now.

Susan rolls onto her knees and pins Michael beneath her. He grips the curve of her hips. He watches her close her eyes and curve her neck. Her body flows like an ocean, forming to the waves within it. Michael is stunned by how beautiful she is.

The air in the room grows thick. Their skin becomes slippery; their lips taste of salt. They turn, and she wraps her legs around Michael's back and squeezes with her thighs. He slips his hand under her lower back. Their breathing climbs. "Yes," she whispers. Her nerves twist and then snap. Her voice turns to a shriek, "Oh, God!" Their bodies tighten. "Don't stop, just a little more," and then her muscles fall slack in his arms.

Michael collapses beside her, and she places her hand over his. Ripples flow through her body like aftershocks. They both pant to catch their breath.

*   *   *   *   *

The next day they are glowing. Their fingers weave together as they walk through Frick Park. Michael is enchanted by Susan's every gesture and expression. Her soft and simple tone reminds him of how he first fell for her. The path is narrow and empty except for the two of them. Susan surprises herself with how easily she talks about her insecurities.

"It's like there are these shadows that mimic everything I do and I try to ignore them but I just end up staring at them and wondering why they aren't how I want them to be."

They talk about her job at *The Boulevard* and his recent trip to Jamaica. When Michael brings up his deepening connection to Pittsburgh, Susan mentions a desire to leave at some point.

"I mean, I've lived here all my life."

The idea makes Michael nervous, but he tries not to show it. "I think I know what you mean… You should do what you need to do."

Grey clouds encroach on the sky, but they don't notice. Their destination is a grassy hill where the rounded surface of underground rocks form stone blankets that look into the woods. They walk for a while in silence. In a very acute sense, each of them feels rescued by the other. As they arrive at the clearing, Susan feels a drop on her hand.

"Do you feel that?" she asks.

"What?"

"I think it's raining."

They climb onto a patch of stone and lay back. The rain begins to fall more steadily.

"Do you want to go back?" asks Michael.

"Not right now."

The sky cracks with a boom, and the rain starts to pour. The water is warm. Michael pulls Susan closer to him.

"Do you think anyone's around?" she asks. Rain streams over her eyes and lips.

"Only crazy people would come out in this weather." His hair is dripping. They kiss.

"So no one is going to stumble across us," she says. She slips her fingers underneath his shirt and feels his body shiver.

"The rain brings out the light in your eyes."

Year 5
Leah and Susan

Susan wipes off the counter in the kitchen, rests her hands on her hips, and stares at the sink. The drying rack is cluttered with dishes that Leah pledged to clean up before the party. Susan opens the cabinet, and begins to move the dishes back where they belong.

Butter, garlic and onions sizzle in the oven. Vegetables curl and darken. Sweat beads on Susan's forehead. People will be here in an hour, and she's not sure if she'll have time to get ready. Susan regrets agreeing to have this party. She doesn't know anyone who's coming. Leah probably won't know most of them either. Scenes from her morning at work replay in her imagination. She is not interested in the stories she's been working on. She's not proud of the work she's been doing. She grasps for a plate, but it slips from her fingertips and lands with a crash. Shards of ceramic sprinkle her bare feet. Her face tightens and she tries to contain her emotions.

There is a noticeable drop in temperature when she steps into the dining room. The front door squeaks as it swings inward. Leah is home.

"I got wine and cheese," she says enthusiastically. "I'm just so tired of living unpretentiously, you know? It smells *amaz*ing in here. What are you making?"

Susan doesn't answer and Leah moves into the kitchen.

"Oh, you put away the dishes. You didn't have to do that." She doesn't mention the broken plate.

"I know. I just didn't know when you were going to get back," says Susan. Her tone is curt.

Leah emerges from the kitchen with a glass of white wine and begins to howl. Susan looks toward her and raises her eyebrows. *What are you doing?* Leah howls again, pointing her chin toward the ceiling, and Susan cracks a smile.

"See," says Leah. "You just have to get in the mood. A full moon will ruin you if you're not in the mood."

Susan prefers to take her showers hot. The water pressure is strong, and she leans into the sting of the heat as it kneads and loosens her back. The steam is good for her skin. Her eyes are closed, and she breathes deeply through her nose and barely parted lips. She imagines her anxieties seeping out through her pores, flowing with the water down her body over her fingertips and toes. She shaves her legs and decides that she doesn't need to be ready when people start to arrive: it's her house, after all. She stands under the water until it begins to run cold.

Leah lights candles in her bedroom and changes dresses three times. She settles on a black silk dress with lace on the shoulders. She wraps a silver belt around the waist and chooses earrings to match. She hopes that people show up to her party. When she finishes touching up her makeup, she puckers her lips toward the mirror and winks.

The light from the windows turns softer. Leah sets the dining room table with wine, cheese, and crackers. The party is set to begin at sunset.

From her bedroom, Susan can hear people begin to arrive. She tells herself that it will be good to meet new people.

The hours pass without hesitation. Beer clutters the refrigerator, and trays of food are set in the dining room. The kitchen becomes crowded, then sparse, and then crowded again. Smokers take frequent trips outside to form tightly knit circles. Bottles of wine and beer find their way to the recycling bin in waves. Fresh acquaintances ask simple questions with flirtatious tones. Leah entertains, and people approach Susan to introduce themselves and thank her for having them in her home. "Of course," she says, trying to commit their names to memory. By the window, people offer each other pardons for talking too much about their jobs. On the couch, jokes are stretched thin with sarcasm and hyperbole. In the dining room, people speak definitively about politics, religion, and philosophy. Everywhere, stories from wilder days are told with well-polished punch lines. People seem to be enjoying themselves.

Susan surveys the apartment and tells herself she is having a good time. This is the type of life she's always wanted, but the mood feels overly familiar. She gets an image of herself as a potted plant, her roots growing only to curl back on themselves. She pours another glass of wine.

When Leah leads a group of people up to the roof, Susan decides to follow. She steps out from the low-ceilinged stairwell into the open sky and pauses to wonder why they don't come up here more often.

"So," says a voice from behind her, "this is your place."

She turns to see a tall man with a thin beard.

"Yeah," she says and extends her hand, "Susan."

"Russ."

There is an awkward pause. Russ rubs his beard with his palm. Susan excuses herself to go over by Leah.

Leah sits on a bright orange crate, singing along with a drum circle made up of plastic buckets found on the roof. Her voice rises and falls to an improvised melody. Susan sits down on the ground beside her. Wisps of clouds pass over the moon, and a handful of stars shine through the city's lights.

Susan rests her head on Leah's thigh and closes her eyes. She tries to sink into the scene around her. Leah's voice swings with the rhythm, and Susan can feel it pull something inside her. She feels nostalgia for all the other nights she's known like this one and searches her memory for when all of this seemed new, when each night with friends brimmed with possibility, and promises were still in the future. She sets her mind to the thought, but all she finds are forgotten rooftops with forgotten strangers, nondescript dinners drenched in wine, and a sense of certainty that seems more myth than remembrance. There is an overwhelming sense of ambiguity. She tries to clear her mind. She sees Michael touching her hand and asking if they are going to end up together someday. Her chest tightens, and her breaths shorten into hiccups. The air is still. The moon grows smaller as it rises into the sky. Quietly, Susan begins to cry.

Year 3
Leah

Leah's house sits on the slope of a valley in the French Alps where mountain peaks frame the sky. Across the street is a bakery where the owner calls Leah 'ma petite Americane.' A few blocks away, a pair of stoplights makes up the downtown. In the morning the air is moist and cool.

Leah stands before the mirror in her bathroom in a pink silk slip she often wears to bed. She is studying her reflection. Her neck and jaw have grown thick. Her arms are pudgy. Looking into her eyes, she feels distraught. Her nerves are twisted together. She can feel the hairs on her head pull at her scalp. Things are not as they were meant to be.

When Leah moved here after her wedding a year ago, she was ecstatic. She felt that the world had chosen her to live a charmed life. She wrote Susan letters sprinkled with exclamation points. She loved the idea that when they arrived in Pittsburgh, they'd be marked with French stamps. She took long walks into the nearby woods. Her neighbors adored her and were more than generous in helping her with the language. The butcher routinely gave her extra cuts of meat and encouraged her to keep her husband healthy and fat. "Oui, oui. Merci, merci," she'd reply.

Marcel had been good to her. He bought her gifts and told her she was beautiful. They used to sit for hours on the deck, holding hands, reading, and looking into the mountains. When they stood by the railing, he would put his arms around her. She felt safe and at home. She remembers the touch of his lips on the tip of her ear when he whispered, "You, my Leah, are my jewel. My jewel, my Leah."

Now, standing in her bathroom, she wonders if they had been putting on an act. She's overwhelmed by the fear of suffocating beneath a mask. She scratches at the back of her jaw. *This isn't who I was meant to be.*

Leah stares into the mirror and imagines hairline fractures spread across her face. She watches them chip and peel, uncovering the rotten flesh below. Her mind conjures a putrid stench. The blotches of dead cells spread across her cheeks and down her neck. The only trace of her former beauty is the panic in her eyes.

Marcel. She looks away from the mirror. *What did I do wrong?* She's confused by how fragile her happiness proved to be. Thoughts of suicide tempt her with their finality.

"Breathe," she tells herself. "Breathe." She walks out of the bathroom, across a large bedroom, down a long hallway, across a well-furnished living room, and then slides open a glass door that leads to a large wooden deck.

The sun has just begun to rise, and the town is still covered in shadow. A thin fog hangs in the valley, and Leah has the impression she is walking into a cloud. From the mountains, she can feel a great weight pressing down on her. The deck is cold and damp. Her vows echo in her memory, and she admits to herself that she never truly thought that this life would be easy. *Or maybe I did.*

She walks to the wooden railing. Life is long and love is hard. She doesn't want to be the type of person who shuts down when threatened, who closes herself off when things aren't as she wills them to be. Her eyes settle on the outline of the sunrise above the mountains. She remembers the pledge she made when she first moved here: to never take this view for granted.

Maybe I'm being unfair. She thinks of how she's been almost eager to let her frustrations multiply, talking with Marcel as if nothing is wrong, daring him to make the decisive remark to break her open. She blames herself for letting her happiness crumble in her hands.

Marcel is a good man. He has been less affectionate the last couple of months, but isn't that to be expected? When she pictures a life without him, a void opens up inside of her.

She highlights pieces of their life that she finds endearing: the apologetic look he gets when he farts in bed, how he brings her coffee and sets it on her nightstand as she's waking up, and all the nights he's spent with her at home when she didn't feel like going out with his friends because she was too tired to try and think in French.

She mustn't think of her life as if it's already ruined. It's not too late for her to be happy. She can fall back in love with Marcel. She can regain what has been lost. She has no choice. Her conviction is tepid but sincere. "I have been beautiful before," she thinks. *I can be beautiful again.*

Year 3
Michael and Susan

Dinner is being set at their friend Lillian's apartment. Susan stands by the table with her friends and Michael pauses to watch her from across the room. He admires the way her hair cascades over her shoulders and the subtle hourglass of her figure. She fans open her hand as she speaks. Everyone is listening to her. *Love.* The word plays in a loop through his thoughts.

Michael and Susan leave soon after dinner. He rests his right hand on her leg as they drive. At red lights they turn to steal kisses.

"I just can't keep from kissing you," she says.

"We could have worse problems." He flexes his grip on her thigh.

Susan remembers the dinner and the way they told stories in tandem. At times she wonders if it's polite to be so obviously happy around other people.

"I enjoyed showing you off tonight," she says.

"Is that all I am to you?"

"But I'm glad we didn't stay too long. I want to get you home."

When they pull up to Susan's apartment, they kiss once more before getting out of the car. Walking behind her up the stairs, Michael pinches her butt.

"Hey now," she turns with eyebrows raised, "wait til we're inside."

They close the door behind them and Michael leans his back against it. He pulls Susan toward him and kisses her brow.

Here we go.

"Susan." Pause. He can feel his heart pounding. He brushes her cheek. "I love you."

Her eyes widen. Michael is holding his breath. She

wraps her arms around him and grips him tightly. "Oh, Michael. I love you too." She presses her cheek against his chest. She can feel his heartbeat. "Isn't it obvious? Isn't it obvious that I love you?"

He folds his arms over her back, and her muscles uncoil.

She leans her shoulders back and looks Michael in the eye. A suggestive smile plays on her lips.

Year 5
Susan and Leah

The apartment is empty. There are footsteps and then the clack of the deadbolt. The door squeaks open. Susan steps inside and flicks on the lights. Leah follows close behind and drops her purse to the ground as soon as she enters. Susan declares that she is ready for bed. The night has continued longer than expected. Friday happy hour turned to dinner, dinner turned to music, and music turned to dancing. Susan has errands to take care of in the morning, and all week she has been looking forward to waking up on Saturday feeling rested. She is tired, and her feet are sore.

"*So*," begins Leah, "who was that guy you were talking to anyway?"

The question breaks over Susan in a wave of exhaustion. She plops onto the couch, closes her eyes and considers ignoring Leah altogether. The apartment is unkempt. Dishes and newspapers sit on the dining room table, and an array of Leah's shoes circle the couch. A faint odor of yesterday's uneaten casserole wafts toward Susan from the kitchen.

"Russ," she says finally, "I met him at the full moon party a few weeks ago."

"Well, he's cute."

Susan is not interested in this conversation. She considers walking into her bedroom and closing the door but she doesn't want to seem brash. "Maybe," she says.

Leah presses with more questions and Susan explains that Russ is new to town and works as a clerk for a federal judge.

"Well, did you give him your number?" she asks.

"No, but he did give me his card."

"How professional."

"He promised to treat me to an evening if I ever wanted to continue our conversation."

"Well, there we go. Looks like you've found yourself a date." Leah notices a confrontational mood building inside her.

"Leah," says Susan, a warning built into her tone.

"All I'm saying is that some people would be thrilled to have handsome men with no roots in the city promising to *treat them to an evening*."

"Maybe."

Susan can normally deflect Leah's efforts to dredge through her dating life without getting impatient, but it is late, and Susan has watched Leah all night, throwing herself at successive men, practically begging for their adoration. Before her marriage, Leah was always in control of flirtatious situations. She always knew what she wanted. Since the divorce, her technique has become desperate. Men no longer vie for her attention, so she fawns over them. Susan tries to be understanding, but it can be hard.

"I'm just not sure if he's my type," continues Susan. "Besides, you know I'm not trying to get into a relationship right now."

Leah is frustrated. "What do you mean he's not your *type*?" she shakes her hands in the air, making a mockery of the word. "Because he's interested in you?" why is she getting so worked up? "And who said anything about a *relationship*? I don't understand why you seem to be against going on any sort of date."

"I never said I was against it."

"Right," says Leah, thick with sarcasm.

"Look, not everyone needs a man to feel good about themselves. Maybe when we go out I'm more interested in having a good time with my friends than finding someone who's going to sleep with me." Susan already regrets what she's about to say. "Maybe you should focus more on your life than mine," she can see Leah deflating. "Maybe I'd rather not throw myself at every man who's interested in me."

Susan stands, and Leah begins to cry. Susan walks to her room and closes the door behind her.

Leah goes to the kitchen and pours half a glass of vodka over ice before slamming the door to her bedroom. *What's happening to me?* The night was going so well, and now she's crying, and the walls are folding in on her. Susan is right. She's a mess. *Goddamn Marcel.* She sips from her glass. *Be strong.* She shouldn't have pressured Susan so much, but why can't Susan see that she just wants her to be happy. Maybe she shouldn't have come back to Pittsburgh at all. She should have tried to start new somewhere else. *Goddamn Marcel.* The bastard erased over three years of her life. "But I am here now," she tells herself. "I am here now."

Why did I have to go off like that? Susan lies in bed. She is tired but unable to sleep. She should have just come home after dinner. She sits up and considers walking to Leah's room to apologize but isn't sure how Leah would react. Instead her mind turns to Russ. Maybe she shouldn't be so dismissive of him. If she's going to start dating, she'll have to start somewhere. Through the wall she can hear Leah sobbing. Her heart feels heavy in her chest. "I'm sorry," she whispers. She closes her eyes and listens until the sobs grow faint. Part of her envies the fact that Leah can feel so acutely. Susan spends most of her time unraveling feelings so broad they hardly mean anything at all. At least there is clarity in sorrow. Clarity is what she yearns for most of all.

Autumn

Year 1
Michael

Inside the Cathedral of Learning, large wooden desks are spaced generously across the slate floor. Around them, limestone pillars rise fifty feet high before curving into the lines of the vaulted ceiling. Electric lanterns and chandeliers sharpen the lines of shadow that obscure corners and compliment the tower's gothic design. It's mid-afternoon, and the Cathedral is busy with students. The sound of footsteps and conversation carries through the commons room in a muffled echo. Michael searches for his classroom. The atmosphere is invigorating.

Room 327 is one of the Cathedral's Nationality Rooms and metal letters on the door spell out 'India.' The room is designed to represent a courtyard with wooden chairs stacked above and behind each other on both sides of the room. Between them is an ornate wooden podium. Michael takes a seat behind the front row and readies his pen and notebook.

Time passes. Students fidget in awkward silence. Michael stares forward absently. He has been looking forward to this class. Professor Faraday was described to Michael as a 'philosophical juggernaut,' and the idea of developing an intellectual relationship with him has become a recurring daydream for Michael. After twenty minutes the class grows restless. A pair of students stands and walks out.

When Faraday arrives, he is shorter than Michael expected. He is thin with a long face and a gray goatee. When he gets to the podium, he explains how the course will work. They will not use all of the allotted time when they meet, and there will be a short paper due every week. Specific texts will not be discussed or assigned, but thorough references are encouraged in the weekly papers. While he speaks, a female student enters the classroom. She wears thick black hair with red highlights, tall boots, and large earrings. Her leather jacket feigns to hide the curves of her breasts and hips. She sits directly across from Michael but does not look toward him. He notices that she has neither pen nor paper. When Faraday calls roll, Michael makes note that her name is Veronica.

"Our language," Faraday begins, "has different types of words." His voice is soft and measured. "Many words denote objects we can perceive with our physical senses. We can say chair, floor, podium, paper, pen, and we can see and touch the things our words describe. Other words, however, are more conceptual in nature. These words are for the sensations we perceive that cannot be traced back to our five physical senses. These are the words that exist beyond empirical certainty. Words like faith, justice, power, purpose, honor, reason... Truth."

Michael watches Veronica; her gaze is fixated on a point in the floor a few feet from where she sits. Her face is calm, and Michael senses a depth in her eyes. Looking away, Michael picks up his pen and scratches its tip in his notebook.

"Reason and truth. Since the enlightenment, reason and truth have largely been assumed to cohabitate, the one with the other. Where you find reason, there is truth. Where you find truth, there is reason. They have been assumed to depend on each other. And we, in turn, have come to believe in them as a pair. We have credited their relationship with a kind of unassailable bond that should seem most unusual for two words of such an abstract nature. Yes, it's true that the relationship between reason and truth has proven useful. But I will argue that, today, reason does more to limit our understanding of truth than it does to expand it.

"Yes, in the centuries since its transcendence, reason has outgrown its utility. Reason no longer unites us in understanding but divides us. It has acquired a perplexing tendency to mean different things to different people. Reason pollutes our social discourse. It favors argument over analysis. It supplants the particular with the universal."

Faraday's voice is confident but at times descends to almost a whisper. Michael glances at the other students in the room.

"Perhaps the greatest injustice has been the way reason has belittled our aesthetic persuasions. Our aesthetics, those impressions that by definition resist rational explanation, have been slandered as frivolous and untrustworthy."

Veronica smiles. Michael looks toward her, hoping to catch her eye. Her gaze remains fixated on the professor.

"But our ability to create a personal aesthetic is far more central to our humanity than our capacity for rational conjecture. Aesthetics allow us to expand our appreciation of the world as well as our understanding of it. Aesthetics make dialogue unique. They emphasize the subjective nature of shared experience. They rejoice in investigation while distrusting conclusions. They join us together as social beings rather than as stubborn supporters of explainable truths. Aesthetics favor empathy over judgment."

Michael realizes he should be taking more notes. He writes: 'Aesthetics over reason,' and underlines it twice.

"Our philosophical tradition can no longer afford to ignore the aesthetic aspect of our lives. Our aesthetics are who we are. They are the centerpiece of the examined life.

"When we ask how to live a life worth living, it should be obvious that the answer has more to do with beauty than logic. We are *capable* of reason... but we are *aesthetic* beings. The task before us, before each of us, is to create beauty in our world." He lets the statement hang for a moment in the air.

"Now," he smiles, "are there any questions?"

Silence. A phone vibrates on top of a desk.

"Well then, the assignment for next week is three pages

on the limits of reason." Faraday brushes the podium with his palm and walks briskly toward the door.

Veronica stands. Michael watches her follow the professor to the door and then she is gone. The man next to him says "Hey," to get Michael's attention. "What the fuck was that about?"

"Uh. What do you mean?"

"How does he expect us to write about all that shit? Three fucking pages. Jesus Christ."

Year 1
Michael and Susan

Empty cars hug the curve of the one-lane road as it bends around the lake and toward an old barn. A bonfire casts long shadows behind the people who crowd around it. Shadowy figures emerge from the woods with triumphant strides, carrying logs and branches in their slightly numb arms. On the peak of the barn's slanted roof, a row of people are seated with fishing rods, their outlines accentuated by two glowing tips that make their way back and forth down the line. The sound of people gathered late at night hums through the air. The chatter of crickets folds beneath the blare of classic rock music, as people approach the barn.

Derrick refills his plastic cup from a keg by the wall and walks back toward Michael. They stand for a moment side by side. Derrick is shorter than Michael and stands with his shoulders slumped forward. A thick beard makes him look significantly older than his age. Derrick and Michael met shooting pool in the student union during the first week of classes and have gotten together nearly everyday since. Michael's attention is set on an attractive girl with long brown hair standing by the far window. He watches her look down into her cup and then up and out into the room. Her eyes pan from wall to wall. She seems to be taking everything in without judgment. As she looks back to her drink, the right corner of her mouth curls upward, and her head shakes gently from side to side.

Susan regrets coming out here alone. She is frustrated with Leah for cancelling last minute. *Maybe I should just leave. I don't know why I thought I would run into people I know out here.*

"Yeah," says Derrick, "Actually, I think I know her." Michael is intrigued. "Well, not know her. But I think she's in that history of journalism seminar I dropped. Probably wouldn't remember me."

"Well, let's find out."

Derrick starts to protest, but Michael is already walking toward her.

Susan tries to conjure the energy to start a conversation with someone, but the effort is half-hearted. She feels awkward and unnaturally exposed. She told herself that coming here is the type of thing she needs to start doing in order to get over her not-so-ex-boyfriend, Steven, but now she finds herself wishing that he was here beside her.

She is about to toss what's left of her drink and head back to her car when two boys approach her. The shorter one looks familiar.

"Hi," he says. His voice is hesitant. "I'm not sure if you recognize me. We had a class together for a week."

Susan takes a moment to collect her senses. Derrick looks away nervously.

"Right," she's vaguely remembering, "the journalism seminar. Darren?"

"Derrick."

"And I'm Michael." He smiles. "We were just about to head out to the bonfire if you're interested?"

Susan is flattered by the invitation. "Thanks, but I was just about to leave." She tucks a few strands of hair behind her ear.

"Well, feel free to come and find us if you decide to stick around."

Derrick is on the second floor of the barn, searching for a bathroom without a line, when he notices laughter coming through the angled ceiling. Curious, he climbs a wooden ladder and finds a line of guys seated on the peak of the roof with fishing rods in their hands.

"If he asks us what we're doing, should we tell him?"

"Only if he figures it out on his own." Laughter.

Derrick introduces himself and walks closer.

"Have a seat. We're bat fishing."

"You know, fishing for bats. With bugs."

"Does it work?" he asks.

"Not sure. Wanna give it a shot?"

Susan is almost back to her car when she looks back

over her shoulder at the barn. The small lake beside her reflects its light. Michael intrigues her. When he walked away, he left her slightly out of breath, and she wonders why he had such an effect on her. He's more athletic than most boys she's dated, and he seems thoughtful. She considers walking back, and her heart begins to pound in her chest. Her car is directly in front of her. She fingers her keys in her pocket, steps up to the driver side door, smiles broadly and turns around. "Besides," she tells herself, "Leah would kill me."

She finds Michael standing alone by the fire.

"What are you looking at?" she asks as she approaches from behind.

"Hey," he is surprised to see her, "I was just trying to figure out what's going on up there." He gestures to the silhouettes on the roof of the barn.

"Strange."

"I thought you were going home."

"I realized I have a few extra minutes."

Michael looks back to the barn and Susan worries that coming back was a mistake.

"Where's your friend Derrick?"

"He said he was going to find a bathroom."

"I'm surprised he recognized me. I hardly said a word the first week of that class."

"He mentioned that."

"Did he?"

"Yeah. He said that you just kind of stared off toward the windows and that he couldn't figure you out."

Susan laughs lightly. "I don't think I had myself figured out that week either."

Michael looks back toward her, "But now everything's sorted out?" He smiles.

"Yes," she says, returning the expression, "Now I'm all figured out. It's much nicer this way."

"Is it?" he asks.

Susan twists her smile. Michael's fingers fiddle with the bottom of his shirt. He's worried she'll ask what he does, and he doesn't want to let on that he's a freshman. He turns back to the barn. "It doesn't make any sense."

The dark figures suddenly bolt upright and begin to move.

"Something's going on," whispers Susan.

Derrick's eyes pull wide open. Something is running away with his fishing line. *How do I get this thing to stop*?!?! He locks the line and pulls back violently.

"Holy shit, this guy's fucking got one."

The bat has pulled back and is now flying in circles above Derrick, a dark blur against a dark sky. Derrick hollers as he runs across the peak of the roof. The bat turns, and Derrick spins in a circle. His feet clamor to keep their balance. People shout for him to toss the rod and sit down, but before he can register what they're saying, he slips. He catches a glimpse of the bat dipping toward him and shields his face with his arms. His back thuds against the roof. He lets out a loud grunt and then yells as his body starts to roll.

"That sounds like Derrick," says Michael.

Susan's eyes are transfixed.

Derrick's shadow rolls off the side of the barn. A shriek cuts through the air, and he lands with a splash into a large bush.

"It *works!!!*" declares a voice from the roof.

Year 5
Michael

Michael is walking on the Brooklyn Bridge away from Manhattan, when he feels a *Splat!* on the top of his head. He cringes. A wet warmth sinks through his hair to his scalp. A chunky goo drips onto his ear and oozes onto the back of his neck. He is frozen in place. Passersby split around him like water past a rock in a river. Hesitantly he lifts his hand, dabs his fingers into the slime, and brings them to his eyes and nose for inspection. Suspicions confirmed. *Goddamnit. Birdshit. Really?!?!* Several hundred feet from the edge of the bridge, he continues walking. With each step he can feel the offending viscous drip further down his back. He considers trying to halt its progress with his shirt but doesn't want to rub it further into the fabric. Some people, tourists most likely, look back over their shoulders as they pass, apparently to verify that what they saw actually happened. He gets an idea. He walks to the railing to get out of the way of the foot traffic, slips off his left shoe and pulls off his sock. It is damp with sweat. He tries to clean himself up as best he can. When he exhausts the surface area on his left sock, he takes off his right one. *Too much shit to be a pigeon, must have been a hawk or something. Do they have hawks in New*

York City? When he finishes, he stares down at the soiled socks in his hand. He quickly rejects the idea of putting them in his pocket. Leaving them on the bridge seems uncivilized. He chucks them over the side of the bridge toward the water. He hopes no one thinks that he was littering.

Michael has lived in New York City for six months, and he's grown frustrated with the self-aware posturing of people in the city. This is the first time he's made an effort to visit Adam in Brooklyn, and he's looking forward to seeing someone he's known for more than a few months. Michael steps off the elongated ramp that connects the bridge to the borough and spots a street that looks like it should house a coffee shop. His feet stick to the insides of his shoes. Soiled chunks of his shirt cling to his back and shoulders. He hopes Adam has some clothes he can borrow if they go out tonight.

When he steps into the café, he gives a small wave to the man behind the counter and mumbles, "One second," as he makes his way to the bathroom. Once inside, he takes his shirt off and scrubs it in the sink. He takes a handful of paper towels and stretches to wipe between his shoulder blades. He splashes water over his neck and leans forward to rinse his hair in the sink. Before he leaves, he sits down and rubs toilet paper over his feet and inside his shoes.

When he exits the bathroom, he sees the man behind the counter has been replaced by a beautiful twenty-something girl who is swaying her hips to the music and keeping rhythm with her nails against the top of the pastry case.

"Oh, hello!" she says, obviously surprised to see him walking out of the bathroom. He's embarrassed to be caught having spent so much time in there. His hair is still wet and his shirt is stained. He walks hesitantly toward the counter.

"Coming over the bridge, I, uh," he doesn't want to swear, "got *crap*… a bird crapped on my head."

She erupts in laughter.

"Now," he continues, "I just need to kill some time before meeting up with a friend who should be able to help me out."

"Well, we're happy to have you."

Michael orders a chai tea and a brownie. When she serves it to him Michael makes note of her nametag: Ginger.

"I hope your evening is up from here," she says.

"Me too."

Michael walks to a table on the far side of the coffee shop and takes a seat facing the register. He thinks of Adam. It's strange to think that they haven't seen each other in over four years. The last time they talked was right after Adam dropped out of art school. That was over three years ago. He searches for highlights from the past three years of his own life, but his thoughts are depressingly blank. Carefully, he sips his tea. It's still hot.

Michael's attention turns to Ginger behind the counter. He hides his glances at her within slow pans of his eyes across the coffee shop. He feigns interest in the menu above the counter, hoping she'll pass through the bottom of his view. She is distractingly beautiful. She wears torn jeans and a white tank top. Her dusty blonde hair is unwashed and only partially pulled back into a ponytail. Bangs hang down on the right side of her face. As she straightens up the espresso machine and refills a pitcher of water, Michael is taken by the grace of her motions. She seems completely invested in each task she takes on and constantly in motion toward the next one. She disappears into the kitchen. Michael replays their brief interaction in his mind and wonders if she may have been flirting with him. He remembers her laugh and yearns to hear it again. For a moment, he's convinced that if he could find the right words, she would be willing to runaway with him. Together they could tap into a happiness most people only read about. She only has to commit herself completely. Michael is ready.

When she emerges from the back room, he tries to catch her eye, but she doesn't notice. He considers asking her out, but he's sure men must try that all the time. She looks over the room, and he makes eye contact. She smiles then quickly turns her attention back to the register. Another customer swings open the door.

"Hello," she says.

What a charming voice.

Michael tries to reorient himself. He tells himself he should come back here some other time and see if she remembers him. He takes a bite of the brownie. It's dry.

Michael walks over to the door, grabs a copy of one of the free publications, and returns to his seat. Flipping through the pages, his eyes catch headlines and skim paragraphs. He admires some of the photos. His thoughts turn to Pittsburgh, and a soft nostalgia gives way to the idea that there is a lack of intimacy in New York City. He sips his tea. He likes this coffee shop but even the unique parts of New York feel impersonal and strangely promiscuous. His eyes settle on the sidewalk outside. It's quieter than he's become accustomed to. *Maybe I should try and move to Brooklyn.*

Ginger has moved from behind the counter to clean the tables, and Michael can't help but try to catch glimpses of her butt as she leans over them. Wanting to be a gentleman, he forces himself to return to the magazine.

Adam. Craziness. He almost forgot what he's doing in Brooklyn in the first place. He should have tried to get out here when he first moved. He hopes Adam is doing well.

The streets around Adam's apartment building are deserted. He presses the button marked 4D.

"Mikey!"

Michael looks up to see Adam's face jutting out of a window directly above him. His dark hair is curly, drenched with highlights, and overgrown. It flops about his face. A hand pops out the window and begins to wave vigorously.

"Hey Adam."

"Come in! Come in!"

A moment later the door buzzes, and Michael swings it open.

Michael finds Adam standing in his doorway with arms extended.

"It's *so* good to see you," says Adam.

"It's good to be here." The words feel like the first sincere thing he's said in weeks.

Adam's apartment is eclectic. The entrance leads to the

kitchen. An old refrigerator with a TV rested on top buzzes loudly. The linoleum floor is warped. The fixtures on the sink are dated and stained. A small table is pressed up against the wall by the door. From the kitchen extends a long room that is more hallway than apartment. The wooden floors fray and splinter where the finish has worn through. An array of paintings, in various stages of completion, decorate the left wall. Michael recognizes evidence of Adam's previous life sprinkled throughout the room. A lamp from his childhood bedroom sits on a table, a baby doll splattered with paint lies in the near corner, and a small empty birdcage is stapled to the wall amongst the canvases.

"Check this out," says Adam, drawing Michael's attention to what appears to be a large wooden box attached to the right side wall. Stepping toward it, Michael notices a large-scale diorama carved across it in the style of a collage. He brings his eyes closer to the figures and makes out scenes of prayer and dancing, rivers, mountains, letters from a range of alphabets strewn together, and armies of egg-like monsters whose likenesses are shared with the paintings on the opposite wall.

"Cool," says Michael, softly, not looking away to see Adam's reaction.

"And watch." Adam walks to the far side of the box and opens a latch hidden from Michael's view. The top of the box swings away from the wall until it is horizontal with the ground and level with Michael's knees. Inside are a mattress and a pair of pillows wrapped in Spiderman sheets. "This is where I sleep."

Michael smiles and shakes his head, "You're something else, you know that?"

"And back here."

Adam leads Michael to the door at the far side of the room.

"It's kind of messy," says Adam, opening the door, "but this is my work studio."

The room smells of fresh sawdust and metal static. The floor is covered in plywood and paint. A pair of mannequins and a dress form, stand in the corner. A large papier-mâché oak tree takes up the middle of the room. Adam shuts the door before Michael can notice much else.

"So, what is it you do anyway?" asks Michael.

"Let me get you a drink."

They walk back to the kitchen, and Michael notices Legos glued to the ceiling. Adam pours a pair of gin and tonics over ice.

"I can't believe you've been living here for over four years now," says Michael.

"I know, *right*." Adam takes the seat across from Michael at the table by the door.

Michael drags his finger over the rim of his glass. "It's not an easy city to live in. I'm not sure how much longer I'm going to be here."

"But you just got here. What are you doing here anyway?"

"I work as a policy analyst for a research group downtown. Mostly education issues." Pause. Adam is waiting for him to continue. "It's not that interesting."

"I thought you liked politics."

"Technically it's the type of job I've always said I wanted... But the day-to-day is a different story. The whole suit-n'-tie-nine-to-five thing wears on me. And the work is tedious. Not much room for imagination."

Adam's face shows genuine concern.

"I do research and I make reports and presentations and I take them and I toss them into this void. It's annoying... But," Michael continues, "I didn't come down here to complain. What are you up to? You've got a lot to fill me in on. All I know is that you dropped out of art school."

"Hmmm..." Adam stars blankly into the corner of the room.

"Take your time."

"Well, I'm about to start on something really exciting." Adam stands, "But when I got here it was depressing." He begins pacing in small circles around the kitchen. Michael observes how the movement churns his thoughts into words. "Art school was disappointing. Everyone was either crazy or doing things that had been done a thousand times before or stuff that didn't make sense and no one seemed to understand anything I said, like they would get all defensive about stuff, and my teachers would always tell me that my work should be more refined and showed me other peoples' stuff that I didn't like and asked me to do it like they did." Adam's arms flap about his frame. Occasionally he looks toward Michael to make sure he's still listening. "So I did this series of drawings of little monsters using linear perspective and stuff and being like very *very* meticulous the whole time and it was really frustrating and my teachers loved them and told me to do more things like that and that's when I kinda finally figured out that that school was going to ruin me as an artist."

He takes a deep breath.

"And then I started feeling really anxious. I got a job working on sets for different kinds of shows but I was spending most of my time sitting at home and watching TV. Just watching TV. It's like I was chained to it. I would start working on something and as soon as it got frustrating I would switch on the TV. Or I would plan to go out, but, then I would turn on the TV. And months went by and I didn't really know anybody," Michael leans forward in his chair, "and I knew it was all because of the TV and I was thinking about all of this one day while I was watching TV and I jumped up and I grabbed my scissors and I ran at the TV and I grabbed the cord and I cut it and the TV went dark and I shouted 'Ha! *HA!*' and I ran out into the street and I felt free for the first time in months and months. See?" Adam walks over to the TV on top of the refrigerator, pulls its cord out from behind and holds it up for Michael. Its end is cut clean.

"Well, shit."

"I know, right. So a couple more years went by. I dated a few people. I started doing set design and signed on for some mural paintings. I started making friends in the art community. I got a second job as a waiter at this fancy pizza place that I still have but I'm going to quit soon."

"Why?"

"Right. So," Adam sits back down. An open mouthed smile pulls across his face. "The really exciting part. Me and some other people are starting our own business. It's all about a new kind of art. It's about art as experience. Art as a context for dancing and meeting new people."

"Like art parties?"

"Yes! But more than that. For *years*, I've been talking with people about how art should be more experiential, or more aimed at regular people and how it should give people a chance to re-imagine how they see things or just let them escape from the world. Now, people normally say they do this and they organize a gallery crawl, or focus on installation art, or have a Friday night party at the Guggenheim or something, which is cool and fun and everything but it still doesn't feel like it's enough because even though the art is *close* to the experience it still isn't *part* of the experience, you know. The art is still something that you're looking at. You might like the art but you're not part of it. The art just sits there feeling permanent while you and the rest of the party pass over it. It's like art with lipstick." Adam laughs. "Do you know what I mean?"

"I think so."

"So, I had been doing set design and creating these fancy worlds for something fictional to take place in and I started thinking, why not have a set where something real would happen?" Adam's eyes widen. "And I started talking to a friend who does these costume dinner parties in weird locations, like abandoned buildings and stuff, and the idea started to get bigger. We're going to create artistic spaces but the art will be the experiences of the people who come. If we create a world that people can escape into they can begin to re-imagine who they are. That's the type of art I'm interested in.

"The first one is going to be a Shakespeare party called 'A Midwinter Dream,' I'm going to dress as Snow Puck and build an enchanted forest. In the spring we're going to have a Gatsby party. You should definitely come. I can get you in."

"I'd definitely come out for that."

Adam takes a generous sip of his drink.

"So, what have you been up to?"

Michael is embarrassed to follow Adam's story with his own. He doesn't know where to begin. He taps his fingers on the table. "Ummm..." Adam sits back down and looks on patiently. "Not much really. I met a girl awhile ago."

Pause.

"It didn't work out. But a couple years later we started up again."

Adam sips his drink. Michael is surprised at how attentive Adam is being to what he has to say.

"But I fucked up," he continues, "I still think about her though. Probably more than I should. Maybe it's just an instinct I have. I'm not completely happy here so I look back through my past and romanticize things. I say, 'I'm not happy now because I missed my chance to be happy then.'" He smiles. "Probably not the healthiest way to think about things." Michael takes the final gulp of his drink and Adam takes the glasses over to the sink.

"I'm glad you came down tonight."

"Me too."

Watching Adam straighten up the kitchen, Michael feels proud of his friend. He examines Adam's features, noting signs of age. His cheeks have grown thinner and his shoulders more broad. The tornado of hair fits his mannerisms. His face's distinct expressions have become more refined. It's odd to see Adam grown into the body of a young man. They were just kids when they were running around Europe. The memories seem surreal.

"By the way," says Michael, "before we get dinner do you think I could borrow a shirt and some socks?"

Adam tilts his head quizzically.

"A bird shat on me. Thus my shirt and socks."

Adam laughs. "That's delightful."

"What do you mean?"

"I mean, how often does something like that get to happen to you." Adam walks over to his closet.

"Do you have anything?"

He pulls out a pink V neck t-shirt and a leather jacket. Michael shakes his head.

"Okay," says Adam, disappointed. He removes a collared shirt with blue pinstripes and tosses it at Michael. A pair of socks follows.

"Thanks."

Outside, the crispness of the air hints at the coming winter. The wind feels polished by concrete. Michael breathes in deeply through his nose. His nostrils tingle. The sensation is invigorating.

They eat dinner at a Lebanese place around the corner. The food is delicious. They laugh while reminiscing over old times and admit to not keeping in touch with anyone else from high school. Adam goes into detail about his new party scheme and describes an impressive web of contacts, resources and opportunities. They each apologize for not trying to hang out earlier. Brief silences are filled with jokes about the menu and the people around them. They make small talk with the waiter. The mood is light and sincere. Michael's spirits continue to rise. When they ask for the check, a tray of complimentary baklava arrives at the table. It is moist to the touch. Michael takes the first bite, and honey floods his mouth. He closes his eyes as the pastry melts on his tongue.

Michael and Adam split the cab fare and step onto a corner in front of a bar with no sign. The door is painted in alternating blue and yellow tiles. Smokers fan out from the entrance, both solitary and in circles, lending the corner a sense of life on an otherwise darkened block. Half speed electronica from inside mixes with the sound of their voices. The girls outside are dressed in loose fitting pants. Their hair comes in a variety of synthetic colors. This isn't like the bars in Manhattan.

The space is busy but not overcrowded. Adam spots a group of people he knows on a circle of couches at the near corner of the room, and they greet him with outstretched arms. Trying to follow the conversation, Michael makes out that they are a mix of artists, writers and filmmakers. They talk about projects that people they know are working on. Everyone is complimentary. The word "brilliant" is tossed about generously. At first Michael looks for places to insert himself into the conversation, but none come, and he leans back in his seat. He feels far away from the slideshows and spreadsheets that dominated the first half of his day.

He looks toward the bar, and his eyes settle on a girl with familiar hair. When she looks over her shoulder, he realizes it's Ginger from the coffee shop. Without a second thought, he stands and walks toward her.

"Hey," he says, getting her attention, "Ginger, right?"

"Yeah," she answers, not trying to hide her confusion.

"My name's Michael. We met at your coffee shop today. Remember? I had the incident with the bird."

"Oh," her face brightens, "yes. I see you've been able to clean yourself up."

Michael orders a gin and tonic.

"Yeah, my friend helped me out." Michael gestures to Adam and his friends, happy that he can associate himself with them.

"Very kind of him."

Michael doesn't know what to do with the conversation. He knows he needs to say something quickly but he resists the temptation to talk about the bar and the changing weather. He rejects the idea of asking her what she's drinking. Time is running out. At least she hasn't looked away. She must be curious. Fuck it.

"You know," he says, "This afternoon at the coffee shop I kind of fell in love with you a little bit."

"Oh?" She seems intrigued.

"I mean, it's not unusual for me to get crushes on people I see. I think everyone does that..."

"Do they?" She raises her eyebrows.

"But with you it seemed more... elemental or something. You ever feel that just watching somebody move you can get a feel for what type of person they are, that you can feel a kindred soul, or something?" *What am I talking about?*

"You were watching how I move?"

"Maybe," he smiles and she reciprocates. This might be going better than he thought.

"Well, I confess," she briefly looks into his eyes and the gesture catches Michael off guard, "I did think you were kind of cute."

Michael tries to steer the conversation to what she does when she's not making lattes and causing strangers to fall in love with her, but she deflects the questions, and he ends up talking about the details of his policy job. He apologizes, but Ginger insists that it's interesting.

"It's refreshing to meet someone who isn't trying to be the next Jackson Pollack," she says. "You," she pokes him for dramatic effect, "just keep on being you. I'm going to run to the bathroom."

Michael asks if he can buy her another drink. She leans forward and kisses him on the cheek before disappearing into the crowd.

Adam comes over and asks if Michael's interested in moving to another bar. Michael says he's going to stick around for a little while longer. "But you should go with your friends. We'll hang out again soon."

"Good luck," says Adam, "she's cute."

Michael turns and orders two more drinks. Ginger is even more beautiful in the evening. Everything is coming together. He imagines kissing her. Maybe his New York life will turn around after all. His job won't be so bad if he can come out and stay in Brooklyn with Ginger on weekends.

He imagines the smoothness of her hips over his fingertips. She smiled as she said he was cute.

A few minutes pass. Then five. Then ten. Michael's drink is half empty. *I wonder what's holding her up.* He turns in his chair and surveys the room. He picks up both of their drinks and heads over to the bathrooms. There is a two person line for the ladies room but Ginger isn't in it. He investigates the different sets of couches. He sets the drinks on an empty table and steps outside. Groups of smokers but no Ginger. His stomach drops. His eyes feel hollow. *That fucking bitch.* The thought repeats itself and then he mutters it out loud as he grinds his heel into the ground.

The G train takes forever to arrive. When it does, Michael is one of the only people in his car. His mind is quiet. After his second subway transfer, his thoughts grow actively bitter. He thinks of Ginger's kiss as a gesture of condescension. She could have at least said goodbye. He remembers his summer coffee date with Veronica, when she just stood and walked out of his life. A steeping anger boils inside of him. He's glad that he's done with her.

The train rumbles through its underground tunnels, and Michael wishes it would stall and lose power. Without its lights, the darkness would be complete. He would be trapped away from the world. He could embrace his seclusion.

He thinks about the polite formality that defines his relationships in New York and doubts if he'll ever find someone who can understand him. He fears his next relationship will be a matter of convenience. The train rattles as it turns, and the lights flicker. Metal screeches against metal.

Susan. Her name rises from the clatter around him, and he holds onto the thought of her face. He plays with different memories from when they were together, and each is flooded with light. He imagines bringing her to New York for Adam's Shakespeare party. She'll dress as a fairy, and they'll dance together. *Did we ever dance together?* It all seems so far away. Susan. He wonders if she's seeing someone, and the thought terrifies him. He feels a decisive need to reach out to her. He checks the time. It's just past 3 AM.

Michael climbs out of the subway on the Upper East Side and is soon inside his apartment. He pours a tall glass of water and spends the next two hours typing and revising the e-mail he's going to send. At dawn, his energy crumbles, but he doesn't want to send an e-mail dated for 5:30 in the morning on a Saturday. He eats some ice cream and paces, led footed and weary eyed, through his apartment. At 7:15 he decides it's time. He reads the message over once more and clicks 'Send':

Susan,

I'm going to be in town next week. I was wondering if you'd like to get together. It would be nice to see you.

- Michael

Year 1
Susan and Michael

Susan slides a pile of crumbs from the kitchen counter into the trashcan and drops the paper towel in behind them. She checks her phone and finds a message from Michael: "Some independent shorts on Melville St. tonight. 8 PM. Interested?"

The line excites her. Over the past week, her regular routines have often been derailed by thoughts of Michael. Her mind will stitch together fragments from their half-dozen conversations into a stream of emotions. She replays images of the night they met. She sees him silhouetted by the bonfire and remembers his look of playful alarm when they heard his friend yell from the roof of the barn. She surprised herself by running alongside him when he bolted to check on Derrick. Susan was a runner in high school, but she hadn't moved that fast in years. Derrick sat up when they arrived and clutched his shoulder. He smiled toward Susan while she panted to catch her breath.

The day before yesterday, she spoke on the phone with Michael for almost two hours. He asked questions about her opinions and told stories that made her laugh. When they hung up she stared blankly forward. A sense of guilt pierced her thoughts. *Should I have said something about Steven?*

Susan sits down and spins her phone on the table. She wants to see Michael but she feels dishonest. She wonders what Steven is doing tonight. The last time she spoke with him, he said that he had been thinking about her constantly and promised he would call her again soon, but that was almost a week ago. She leans back in her chair and dwells on his promise to call. *Everything he says is empty.* She tucks a few strands of hair behind her ear, spins her phone once more, and picks it up. She reads Michael's text twice more and decides to call Leah.

Leah is lying facedown in her blue bikini on a yellow beach towel spread out on the roof of her house in Highland Park. Her eyes are closed.

Her phone vibrates beside her, and she reaches for it lazily.

"Susan. Can you believe the weather? It's gorgeous." Leah rolls over and slips on an oversized pair of sunglasses.

Susan replies with a description of Michael's invite and adds that she has reservations because of Steven.

"Well," Leah's voice is animated, "you know how I feel about *St*even… I know I've never met him. And I don't want to meet him. I'd probably punch him in the nose and then I'd have to find ice for my hand, that's what happens when you punch men in the face. Look, there's no debate here, OK, if you think there's a chance of something with Michael you need to go out with him."

Susan explains that she's not comfortable having more than one love interest at a time.

"Then get rid of the one that's a *douche*bag. Look, this isn't about Steven. This is about you." Leah pauses to light a cigarette. "*You* think that there's something wrong with you and you want Steven to tell you what it is so you can fix it and be suddenly magically happy with him," she takes a drag, "but that's not going to happen. If there's something you don't like about yourself you need to find it on your own. And you can start with how hung up you are on this self-centered sadistic asshole. He started messing around 'cause he's a douchebag, you shouldn't be waiting around for him."

"You're one to talk. I've never heard of anyone who spent more time thinking about how she appears to men."

"Yes, men in general, not any particular man."

"More like every particular man."

"Susie. You know I love you and you know you're beautiful but you're not ready for my kind of lifestyle. I'm operating at a very high level of femininity here."

Susan is frustrated with how flippant Leah is toward her feelings for Steven, but she doesn't hold it against her. Leah gave her the advice she was looking for.

Susan puts on a pot of water for tea. She wishes Michael would have given her more notice but the idea of being next to him in just a few hours is exciting. *I'll need to take a shower. Should I wear a dress? No. Not tonight.* She grabs her phone, types, "I'll meet you there," and then hesitates before adding, "Can't wait ☺."

Michael has trouble finding the theater, but he finally discovers that it's at the end of a dark and nearly abandoned street, shifted half a block from where he thought it should be. He's nervous, and he's going to be late. He hopes the films are good.

The theater is accented by blue neon lights. A small

crowd of people mingles in the lobby. Most are young, and many seem to know each other. Unbuttered popcorn is sold from a folding table for two dollars a box. Susan finds Michael standing by a water fountain surveying the room with a wide-eyed look on his face. She realizes that this is probably one of the first events like this he's been to.

"I got our tickets," he says.

"Thanks, you didn't have to do that."

"I know." He smirks.

"So, you know anything about these films?"

"No, just sounded cool," his eyes light up, "I think the director of one of them is over there," he gestures to a circle of people around a gray haired man dressed in black.

Susan considers warning Michael that the shorts will probably be terrible, but she doesn't want to come off as cynical. Besides, he seems to be having a good time.

"Have you ever been out here before?" he asks.

"It's been a while."

"I like it, at first I was kinda spooked, but it's nice, like a little bed of culture around all these abandoned warehouses."

She smiles. His enthusiasm is adorable. Steven is always condescending about places like this. She notices a sign advertising the films and reads the titles out loud, "Situational Reality; Morning Commute."

"Could be interesting."

"We should probably get to our seats."

"By the way," he says, "You look very nice tonight."

"Thanks," she says, "I'm glad you invited me out."

Inside the theater, Michael takes out his phone to put it

on silent and finds a text from Kelsey, "Is everything ok? Call me."

True to Susan's suspicions, the films are awful. The first is a parody of reality television, and the second one follows a middle-aged man through his morning routine and ends with him placing a gun in his mouth. When the second film is over, the lights go up, and the white haired man from the lobby begins taking questions about what he was trying to get across and how he found the courage to do a short film without dialogue. Michael leans over to ask Susan if she wants to stick around, and she shakes her head.

As they step into the street, she turns to him, "You didn't want," she laughs, "to stick around for the Q&A?"

"Just because you *can* have a conversation about that thing doesn't mean that you *should*. Ugh. That was really disappointing."

"Yeah, I like the venue but it doesn't always pull the best talent."

When Michael mentions walking to the bus stop Susan offers to drive him home. She's surprised to learn that he's not living in a dorm. On the drive over, the mood is comfortable. Susan talks about the scarf she started knitting and how she enjoys the process. Michael calls the hobby 'enterprising,' and she laughs. He says he's thinking about joining a flag football league and talks about some philosophy books he wants to read to help him with Faraday's class.

Michael is unlike other boys she's dated. Susan is used to dating thin and quiet boys. Michael is tall and somewhat muscular. When he talks about philosophy, it comes off with genuine curiosity and not the mixture of pretension and intellectual intimidation that she's used to hearing. She's amazed at how at ease she feels. She wonders if he'll try and kiss her goodnight.

When they arrive at Michael's place, he invites her up for something to drink, and he's surprised when she says yes. Michael lives in a small attic apartment in South Oakland, and when he walks to the kitchen area to boil the water, he needs to bend his knees and tilt his head with the slant of the ceiling. He apologizes for the mess as he clears her a space to sit at a small round table in the center of the room. The only other pieces of furniture are the bed, a small bookshelf, and a second chair facing her. While Michael stands by the teapot, she glances over the titles on the bookshelf.

She reminds herself of her decision to tell Michael about Steven. When Michael sets the tea in front of her, she takes a short breath.

"Michael," she says, "There's something I should probably tell you," she looks away and pulls her hair over her shoulder. "You're a great guy and I enjoy spending time with you but… you should probably know that I kind of have a boyfriend. His name is Steven." She can hardly believe she's put herself in a position where she needs to say this. The glow in Michael's expression is washed away. He takes a seat on the edge of the bed.

"Well, this is awkward," he says rubbing his palms into his knees. "And, I guess you're a better person than I am 'cause… I kind of have a girlfriend."

"*What?*" The tone is more surprised than accusatory. Michael smirks and they both begin to laugh.

Susan tells Michael about her semi-open relationship with Steven and Michael admits that he likes Susan and has been unfair to Kelsey. He explains that he doesn't want to hurt her.

"A month ago," he continues, "it would have seemed impossible that I'd be trying to forget about her. At home she practically defined my life. But…"

"But you don't feel that way anymore."

"I don't know what happened."

"I know what you mean."

"Like you and Steven?"

It's strange to hear Michael say Steven's name. "I guess so." She sips her tea. "My best friend thinks I'm just sticking around for some sort of validation."

"But you don't think so?"

"I don't know what to think. I know I hate feeling like I'm being taken advantage of."

"I guess I don't know what to say except that you should do what you think will make you happy."

She smiles. "You're sweet."

"I prefer to think of myself as chivalrous."

Susan laughs.

"Well," says Susan, "I don't think there's much to talk about after those little confessions of ours. We both have some thinking to do." She takes a slow breath, "I'm glad we were able to talk about this though."

Susan stands and steps toward the door. She's tempted to say that they probably shouldn't see each other again, but she can't voice the words. She realizes that she doesn't want to leave.

Michael stands and catches her eyes.

"I had a really good time tonight," he says.

She opens the door and looks back at him. His hair nearly brushes the ceiling. She steps toward him, and he wraps his arms around her lower back. She rises on her toes, closes her eyes, and as they kiss he pulls her body gently against his. Their lips break, and Susan steps back. She finds him overwhelmingly attractive.

"Michael, I think I might like to see you again."

"I'd like that."

She considers leaning in for another kiss but resists the impulse.

When she leaves, Michael sits in the frame of the door and listens to her footsteps grow fainter as she descends the stairwell. Looking back at his apartment, he gets the feeling that it has been blessed. *There's where she sat. This is where we told our secrets. Here is where we kissed for the first time. Here is where I sat to listen to her footsteps. Tonight is when I began to fall in love.*

Year 3
Derrick

The pizza shop is on North Craig Street, just outside of campus. A large aluminum hose carries the smell of pizza from the oven to the green awning above the storefront. Prices are written on paper plates that are taped to the window.

Derrick arrives exactly on time, and Tony greets him from behind the counter. Frank, the owner, looks up at Derrick and then returns to rolling out the dough in front of him. Frank is a short and heavy older man with bushy eyebrows and wisps of gray hair above his ears. His clothes are worn and caked in flour. Derrick glances on top of the oven to see if there are any pizzas ready for delivery, but the space is empty. He slips on a red apron and asks if there's anything he should do.

"No," says Tony, "Freddy's in back doing some prep. You can go back and help him if you want." Tony's voice is flat, but Derrick knows he's kidding.

"That's alright."

The front of the shop is small with just a few stools and a window that faces the gas station across the street. Derrick picks up a broom and begins to sweep. He listens to the fluorescent lights buzz and feels relieved that soon he'll be done working here. At some point tonight, he'll have to tell Tony.

Frank brushes past Derrick and mumbles something but doesn't wait for a reply. He pushes open the door, and Derrick watches him walk across the street and climb into his car, which faces a brick wall at the edge of the gas station parking lot.

"Forty-two," says Tony.

"You sure?"

"Yeah. I'm sure. Been counting since last month." Tony slides the pizza Frank prepped into the oven.

"Damn."

The count is the number of days Frank has worn the

same clothes to work. At different points in the last year, it has broken thirty, but this is the first time Derrick remembers it being this high. Derrick sweeps the crumbs and dirt he's collected into a dustpan and empties it into the garbage. He looks back out the window. Frank is still sitting in his car.

According to Tony, Frank arrived from Italy about twenty years ago. He took a job washing dishes for a buffet restaurant and slept in a trailer behind the building. He was paid in cash and didn't spend any money for over ten years. When he bought the pizza shop, he paid for it with cardboard boxes filled with yellowing ten and twenty dollar bills. "The man can't live," said Tony. "Just once I'd like to see him sit down and drink a glass of wine. But he won't do it. I told him that once, and he didn't even look at me."

Derrick slides a slice of cheese into the oven. When it's warm, he puts it on the same paper plate he used for lunch yesterday. Frank once scolded him for throwing away a paper plate after just one use. Frank also tries to save the scotch tape they use to hang up order slips. Derrick often wonders what kind of childhood Frank must have had, growing up in Italy after the war. He finishes his slice and throws away the plate.

"So, are you going out this weekend?" asks Tony.

"No. I don't think so."

Tony shakes his head, disappointed. "And. Still no women?"

"No. Still no women."

Again, Tony shakes his head. "You're young Derrick. Sometimes I don't think you understand what it means to be young."

Tony often tells Derrick stories about when he was in his twenties. He is originally from Argentina but he lived in Spain for a long time. He had money and friends there and a large house on the coast. There were always women, he said. Beautiful women. "If you have enough cocaine," he once told Derrick, "you can have anything you want."

But that was all thirty years ago, and now he's working for Frank at a pizza shop in Pittsburgh. He talks about getting out of this place and starting his own shop. He'll sell gourmet pizzas in some rich neighborhood. "It's all about the ingredients. People will pay if you have quality ingredients. Not like the shit here." When Derrick first heard him talk like this, he believed it might happen, but that was almost a year ago and nothing seems to have changed.

It's been over an hour, and Frank is still in his car facing the brick wall. He does this a few times a week. Tony and Freddy joke that he's at the drive-in. Derrick has a recurring fear that one day Frank won't come back in, and he'll have to go check on him, and he'll tap on the window and Frank will be dead. Derrick will be queasy, but he won't tell anyone. He'll take the keys and look to see where Frank lives and go to his house. Under Frank's bed, he'll find boxes of money. He'll carry them to his car and lock the door behind him. No one will know the difference. He'll be free.

The bell above the door jangles, and two attractive brunette girls enter. They smile at Derrick, and each orders a slice of cheese. While Derrick heats up the slices, they talk and laugh and text the people they're on their way to meet. Derrick tries not to listen. They eat on the stools facing the window. When they leave, one of them turns over her shoulder to catch a glance at Derrick.

"She was looking at you," says Tony.

"I don't think so."

"I'm telling you. There's plenty of pussy out there. You just need to learn how to take it."

It makes Derrick uncomfortable when Tony talks this way about girls. Derrick has no interest in blindly hooking up with someone. He'd like a girlfriend, but he can never bring himself to try and flirt. It feels phony. Besides, he needs to keep his life on track.

Next month Derrick will start an internship at a local architecture firm. The application process was competitive, and he wasn't confident he'd be offered the position, but yesterday he found out he got it.

Tony pulls a pizza out of the oven, slices it, and says he's going to go back and prep the sauce for tomorrow. He won't let Freddy prep the sauce. He thinks Freddy is on drugs. "Look at the way his hands shake," he said last week. "And the twitch in his face." Tony scrunched his face forward and clacked his front teeth together by way of impression. "Like a fucking rat."

Derrick laughed. Freddy does look kind of like a rat.

While Tony is in the back, one of the regulars, Mick, comes in. Mick is old and frail, and even in summer he's weighed down by a heavy gray overcoat. Last winter Tony said something to him about the cold, and Mick said, "This isn't cold. I was in the Ardennes during the war. The Battle of the Bulge. This isn't cold… You know I can still tell the people who were there. Even the guys who were in the Pacific. People who saw what I saw. I can see it in their eyes… Not many of us around anymore. But every once and awhile I see it." Derrick thinks about this exchange whenever Mick comes in now. He thinks about his own eyes. It makes him feel sheltered.

"Hey, Mick's here," Derrick calls into the back. Mick always gets the same thing.

A few minutes later, Freddy strides up front with a white paper bag and hands it off. Mick thanks him and shuffles over to the register. Like most of the homeless customers, he pays with change.

Freddy lingers up front and tells Derrick about what the weather has been like in Seattle the past week. Freddy is always talking about Seattle. He says the rain is different there. It's more of a mist, and it keeps you cool. When the phone rings, Tony comes up front to answer it. It's an order for delivery. In the next five minutes, there are two more.

Derrick waits until the pizzas are almost done, "I should probably tell you guys," he says, "starting next month I'm not going to be able to work here anymore. I got an internship."

The news seems to put Tony in a good mood. "That's great. *Really* great. Being around here isn't doing you any good. I'm jealous, you know. You're a smart kid. You deserve to do something with yourself."

Freddy walks up to Derrick and grabs his hand between both of his own and pumps it up and down, "Congratulations. You're a good kid. I've worked with a lot

83

of different people and I can't say that about all of them," Freddy nods sincerely, "if there's anything I can do for you, you just let me know, wherever I am, I'll do whatever I can to help you out."

Derrick thanks them both and retrieves his hand. He boxes the pizzas and slides them into their delivery bags.

The first delivery is to a large house with a horseshoe driveway. A mother answers the door. Two small children stand behind her, their large eyes fixated on the pizza. She uses her leg to keep a shaggy brown dog from running outside. She thanks Derrick for being so quick with the delivery.

"Of course," he says.

Driving to the next house, Derrick thinks about his time at the pizza shop. He remembers the day a few months ago when he showed up to find a woman named Tina working in the back. Tony explained that Frank was doing her a favor, by letting her get a few hours. She made an ashtray out of aluminum foil and smoked cigarettes while she made sandwiches. Derrick asked how she knew Frank, and she said Frank was like family to her. He had given her money and was always there for her. Tony said that Tina came in once asking Frank for money and offered to pay him with sex, but Frank just gave her the money. Derrick isn't sure if he believes the story. He's never sure what to believe at the pizza shop.

Derrick is in Bloomfield. He walks up a pair of concrete steps, stands under an aluminum awning, and knocks on the door. He hears a woman yell something from deep in the house, and an aggravated male voice yells back at her. The door opens, and a thin man in a white shirt and tattoos across his neck answers the door.

"Daddy!" calls a little girl from the other room.

The man looks back, "Shut the fuck up," he says, "I'm talking with somebody."

Derrick gives the man his change and accepts his tip. It's more than he got from the woman at the last house.

The final delivery is to a stoner house in South Oakland. His arrival is celebrated. He's invited in for a slice, but he declines. "I need to get back to work," he says.

When he returns Frank is sitting at the window eating a slice. His paper plate is crinkled and stained with grease.

"Hey," calls Tony, "we got two more for you."

He hands the boxes to Derrick over the register, and Derrick heads back into the street.

When Derrick gets home he peels off his shoes and looks for his new Mississippi John Hurt album. He slides the record from its sleeve and sets it on the record player. It's a mid-60s console-style record player that he bought at an antique store last summer. He sits down on his couch and counts through his tips. He'll be taking a decent pay cut when he starts the internship next month. When the record player clicks off, Derrick opens his guitar case. He strums through a few chords and picks out some scales. He plays a blues progression and then starts to play "Mr. Tambourine Man." He closes his eyes and sings the lyrics under his breath. He can see himself in the song. He stares into a city of lights and commotion and watches as it turns to sand and crumbles. He feels pulled toward a distant shadow. There is a pulse of futility and also the need to push on, and suddenly, he's dancing, suspended above the midnight sea, *with one hand waving free, feeling memory and fate, sink deep beneath the waves,* and not thinking about anything at all.

The final chord hangs in the air and then falls silent. Derrick starts into another song.

Year 5
Susan

Susan is lying awake in bed. The dry and earthy scent of a young autumn seeps into her room through cracked window frames. She wears white boxers with blue stripes and a gray t-shirt. Her right leg is straight, resting on top of her light blue sheets. Her left leg is bent and covered up to her knee. Her fingers gently twirl the hair on the back of her scalp. The light from the windows is bright and the crossbar casts a shadow across her waist. She takes a deep breath and convinces herself that she's poised to have a good day. She has already shopped for the week and a new book she's looking forward to reading rests on the nightstand. She tells herself that she is giving herself what she needs to feel stable. Tonight, she has a date with Russ. She's looking forward to it. A date with Russ is just the sort of evening she can keep under control.

Maybe I'll wear my new blue dress. Leah says it's flattering to her hips. Susan sits up and swings her legs over the edge of the bed. She bounces gently onto her blue and white rug and stretches her arms into the air.

Leah is seated at the dining room table eating the second half of a grapefruit and reading the *Post-Gazette*. When she hears the door to Susan's room creak open, she looks up.

"Happy Saturday!" she says. "You ready for your big night?" Leah has taken great joy in convincing Susan to finally reach out to Russ.

Susan walks into the kitchen shaking her left hand through her hair.

"I have plenty to think about other than my silly dinner tonight, Leah. You talk like I've never been on a date before."

"When *was* the last time you were on a date?"

"What's it matter?"

Susan opens the refrigerator and grabs the orange juice. The carton weighs less than she anticipated, and she shoots Leah an accusatory look.

"What? Orange juice is healthy. You don't want me to be healthy?"

"What I want is for you not to eat my food, or at least tell me when you do, so I can adjust my expectations." The words come off more sternly than Susan intended. "I'm sorry, I didn't mean to sound like that." She pours out the final third of a glass of orange juice.

"It's OK," says Leah, "next time I'll let you know." It's a promise she's made before.

Susan leans lightly against the counter and sips the orange juice. "Do you know what you're doing tonight?" she asks.

"I am going to take a long bath and read and put on my

new pajamas and watch a movie in bed."

"Sounds relaxing."

"That's the idea. *Finally*, the world is ready to give Leah some Leah time."

Susan laughs and starts to walk back toward her room. She shakes her fingers on the top of Leah's head as she walks by, "Oh, *Leah*," she says.

Leah calls after her, "The blue dress, your new blue dress, you should wear it tonight."

"I'll wear whatever I feel like wearing," she replies and disappears back into her bedroom.

Susan sits down at her computer. She brings up her e-mail. At the top there's a new message. *Michael?* She turns abruptly away from her computer. She looks back to the screen and hesitates briefly before opening it. She hasn't heard from him in almost two years. Again she looks away from the screen and then back again. She reads slowly, careful to not misunderstand anything and then reads the message again. He's going to be in town next week. He wants to see her. Of course she'll see him. The clarity is startling.

Year 3
Veronica

Veronica wakes at 7:30 in the morning. Professor Faraday is still asleep beside her. A feeling of nausea builds in her chest. The room is eerily quiet.

Veronica hadn't heard from Faraday in months when he called two days ago to say that his family would be out of town. She knew she shouldn't see him, but she also knew that she would. Now she's naked in his bed, and her unzipped gym bag lies at the foot of his wife's dresser. A familiar filth crawls beneath her skin.

When she climbs out of bed, Faraday opens his eyes and watches her walk across the room. He stares possessively at her body. The curtains over the window glow with the light of the morning sun, and Veronica says that she needs to get to work. Faraday knows that she has several hours before her shift starts, but he doesn't protest. He says that he'll call her later, and Veronica takes her bag into the bathroom without looking back. She puts on a pair of black pants and a green t-shirt with a picture of a slice of pizza next to a glass of beer. She stares at her reflection, presses her fingers into her cheek, and then drags them to her chin. *What the fuck am I doing here?*

The bathroom is unusually cold, and the skin on her arms is slightly numb. She digs her hand into her bag and pulls out her phone. There are a dozen missed calls from her boyfriend Chris going up until four in the morning. She chooses not to listen to any of the voicemails. Chris has a jealous temper, and she's not sure what she'll say when she sees him. She feels a rush of anger that quickly disappears. Her nausea sinks deeper into her stomach.

Veronica suspends herself above the actions around her. She feels like a tightrope walker fighting the urge to look down. She walks across plush carpet as she collects her things. Her thoughts are blank as she stuffs a half empty bottle of whiskey into her bag and leaves through the back door. As she walks the two blocks to her car, there is a pain in her back, and a sheet of clouds covers the sun. Men in suits drive past her on their morning commute.

She tosses her bag onto the passenger seat and settles behind the steering wheel. She feels a compulsion to drink and stares with ironic appreciation at the One Way sign at the corner in front of her. A middle-aged woman in flannel pants walks her golden retriever on the other side of the street, and Veronica watches her, feeling invisible. She reaches for her bag, pulls out the whiskey and drinks two longs swigs. The liquor burns and raises the hair on the back of her scalp. She takes another swig and tries to ignore the feeling of consequence that surrounds her.

Veronica shows up twenty minutes early to work, and her manager, Gene, comments how kind it is for her to show up less than ten minutes late. When she's behind the bar, Benny, the other bartender, says that she looks like shit.

"Well, you're quite the gentleman today aren't you?"

"Is everything all right?"

"Yeah. Everything's fine."

"I hope so. Steelers game is on in an hour. This place should get kinda crazy today."

"Oh, fuck, the game."

Within thirty minutes the tables are full and only a handful of seats remain at the horseshoe-shaped bar. The radio switches to the pre-game show, and the customers look intently toward the TVs. Veronica loses herself in the motions of her job. She lets a customer buy her a shot, and a regular named Stanley asks her about the grad program that she applied to.

"No, I still haven't heard anything."

"What are you trying to study again?"

Veronica hesitates but decides to tell the truth, "Math. I'm going to study math."

"Why the hell would you want to study math?"

"Well, when I'm doing math I don't need to worry about being hit on by assholes like you." She flashes her bartender smile, and Stanley laughs.

"I just didn't know you were all smart and shit."

She glances around to see if anyone else is waiting for service.

An unfamiliar face stands behind the row of stools and orders an Iron City. Behind him, she sees her boyfriend Chris enter the bar. She takes a half step back and catches his eyes as he moves toward her. He's wearing torn jeans and a tight white undershirt. Homemade tattoos cover his arms. From across the room, Veronica can tell that he's coked up. He stares at her like she's being hunted.

"Where the fuck were you last night?"

"Go home Chris. I'm working."

He begins to walk to the open end of the bar.

"You were fucking that old guy weren't you? What, you think you're too good to return my fucking phone calls?" Customers stare with amused curiosity.

"*Chris!*" she says sharply, "What are you doing?"

"You fucking slut."

Chris rounds the open end of the bar. Someone yells for him to calm down, and he storms toward Veronica. She reaches for a wine glass behind the bar and swings with her

91

whole body. The glass shatters against his face, and he recoils.

"You fucking bitch!" Chris lunges toward her, but Gene grabs him from behind and drags him to the other side of the bar. Chris presses his hands to his face, and blood streams between his fingers.

"I'll fuckin' kill you," he screams as he walks backward toward the door.

Veronica's body shudders as she tries to contain the wave of fear inside her.

Gene places his hand on her back and she jumps forward.

"Are you OK?"

She takes a moment to calm her breathing, "Yeah... That bastard better hope I don't cut off his balls tonight."

The pre-game show returns from commercial, and the customers return their attention to the screens. Gene takes a step to the side and surveys the room for other signs of trouble. Veronica grabs a pint glass from the rack and looks back to the unfamiliar face still standing beside the bar.

"Iron City, right?"

Year 5
Derrick

A small restaurant with a tin roof and no walls sits at the intersection of two long dirt roads. A small counter separates the kitchen from four plastic tables. An old woman with a large hat and tattered skirt sits, fanning herself, while a trio of children with dirty faces laugh and chase each other around and under the tables. At the edge of the shade, a group of men are speaking and gesturing toward the land around them.

A ball of dust appears in the distance along the road that comes from Managua.

"Viene el bus," calls out the old woman.

The children stop chasing each other and dart into the kitchen. Moments later they emerge with bottles of icy cold water. They stare toward the bus, and when it slows, they run into the dust and jump up and down waving the bottles of water at the windows.

"Agua!" they shout, "Agua! Diez cordobas! Agua!"

Derrick is amused by the children out the window. When the bus doors fold open, he stands and grabs his backpack. As he walks down the aisle, he takes a subtle pride in the handful of confused looks he pulls from the other passengers. "Gracias," he says as he descends the stairs.

The children swarm on Derrick, thrusting their bottles of water toward him, still shouting at the same volume.

"No, I'm sorry," he says, shaking his head, "I don't need any water. No agua."

The children persist, but he remains firm. They turn and run back to the restaurant.

Derrick looks around on all sides. The sun hangs high above him. He can feel sweat begin to spread across his back. *I'm almost there.*

"Der-eek!" comes a voice from across the intersection. A pair of men stands next to a large tractor. Behind them, a lush, green mountain range stretches along the horizon.

They wave at Derrick.

"Der-eek!" Yells the other man, "Ven aca!"

When Derrick was told he would be picked up at the base of the mountain, he didn't expect it to be by a tractor. He had imagined pulling up to the village in a dark SUV, but as he sets his bag in the wooden flatbed attached to the back, the fantasy seems suddenly ridiculous. This is much more appropriate.

The men introduce themselves as Ramon and Alfonso. Derrick answers in Spanish, "Mucho Gusto." The men smile, and Derrick wonders if they're amused by the thickness of his accent. He climbs into the wooden bed. The engine coughs and spits, and they begin to move.

Derrick watches the intersection disappear behind them. So far, everything feels perfectly natural. The road becomes less descript as it melts into the forest, and Derrick braces himself to keep from being jostled by the steep slopes and uneven road. There is a sense of fulfillment. *I'm here.*

The doubts that clouded his last few months in Pittsburgh seem very far away. He ducks beneath an oncoming branch, and congratulates himself on the decision to come work in Nicaragua. He stares into the forest and watches the trees pass by at speeds relative to their distance.

"Four more hours," says Alfonso.

As they move deeper into the forest, the road narrows and then widens again. At times the surface is so uneven that Derrick fears he'll fall over the side. Occasionally the tree cover opens up, and they find themselves in a village. People climb in and out of the tractor bed. None of them says anything to Derrick.

After a couple of hours, a light rain begins to fall. Ramon turns to Derrick and smiles. "Rain," says Ramon. "It's raining?" Derrick realizes he's trying to test his English.

"Yes," he answers, "It's raining." He feels the rain soak his hair and run down his back between his shoulder blades.

Derrick imagines pulling into the village. Children will run up to the tractor to meet their new English teacher. Women will offer to cook for the visitor. Men will shake his hand with firm grips and thank him for coming. He imagines the rain as a kind of baptism.

It's dusk when they arrive, and Derrick is the only passenger left. The road has come to an end at the top of the mountain. The clearing is deserted.

When Derrick stands, he realizes that his butt has grown numb. Ramon leads him into a barn. In the back corner is a small room with a cot. Derrick drops his bag, and Ramon shows him to another door. He pushes it open and points to a small outhouse at the end of a path of mud and rocks.

"Toilet," he says, and places his hand on Derrick's shoulder, "Bienvenido." Ramon smiles broadly and walks away.

Back in his room, Derrick considers unpacking his bag and decides against it. He lays back in his cot and stares toward the ceiling. Moonlight brings a faint glow to the room. Here he is. For miles around in the large towns and small cities of central Nicaragua, people are staring toward this mountaintop, not knowing they are looking directly toward him. He turns his head to the side, and his eyes snap open. A scorpion is perched on a beam less than a foot from his face. He is suddenly wide-awake. He rolls off the cot, slowly, away from the scorpion and keeps watch on it out of the corner of his eye as he looks around for something to kill it. He finds a thin wooden rod. The scorpion claws its way down the beam closer to where Derrick's head used to be. Derrick approaches, aims his thrust, and jams the wood into the scorpion's back. The tail snaps into the wood. There is a sharp crunching sound as Derrick twists the rod back and forth to make sure the bug is dead. Derrick lies back down. He takes pleasure in the idea that most people wouldn't be able to handle this kind of trip.

After a while there is a knock at the door. The sound startles him.

"Yes?"

"Hey," the voice is American. The door cracks open, "Can I come in?"

"Uh, sure." Derrick is confused.

A short blonde girl steps into his room wearing a headlamp. She is holding a plate of bread and a glass of water.

"Hi," her voice is perky, "I thought you might want something to eat." She sets the bread down on the floor next to the cot and then sits down next to it. She hands Derrick the water and turns off her headlamp.

"Um, thanks," says Derrick sitting up.

"I'm Amanda, the girl you're taking over for."

"Oh." He feels stupid for not realizing that, of course, there would have been an English teacher before him. "I didn't realize you were still here."

"I thought about taking the tractor down today but I

figured it would be better for the classes if I was here to introduce you, you know? I mean, I didn't want for them to be like, 'Who's *this* guy?'" she throws her hands in the air and tilts her head, "'What happened to Amanda?' I mean, they know I'm leaving, but still, I wanted to stick around and meet you, and stuff. It's strange that this is my last night."

Derrick is flustered by this girl. The bubbly cadence of her voice seems horribly out of place.

"Oh," she continues, "you're going to have such an amazing time. The people are incredible but try to use the bathroom before it gets dark, it can get kind of spooky," she twists her lips to the side of her face, arches her eyebrows and laughs.

"I'm sure I'll be alright."

"Yeah, I mean it's probably different for us girls. But you're going to love the classes. The kids are wonderful. They take education very seriously." Pride rises in her voice, "Some of the other villages make the children work collecting coffee beans in the forest but here they have to go to school. It's like, I love this, the *only* building in the village with electricity is the school. Isn't that incredible? If we have time in the morning we can talk about the lessons I've been doing. How's your Spanish?"

"Pretty awful."

She laughs, "Well, that's good for the children; it's better for them to just get English, but you'll have a hard time talking with anyone else beyond the basics. I've tried to teach Ramon and a few others, but the adults are slower to commit themselves, you know, God, it's good to be able to speak English, like, normally and know that I'm being understood. It's good to have you here, I'm sure you're going to do great."

The conversation is wearing on Derrick. He wishes that she would leave.

"I'm sorry. Thank you for the bread, but I'm really exhausted and I need to get some sleep for tomorrow."

"Oh, of course, of course. I'll see you at breakfast. It was good meeting you."

When she's gone, Derrick eats the bread in small pieces. For the first time, it dawns on him that he's going to have to teach classes of students tomorrow. He's glad that Amanda will be around to introduce him. He's confident that he can be a better English teacher than she's been. He hopes he'll be able to learn all of his student's names.

He finishes the water and realizes he needs to go to the outhouse. He walks out of his room and swings open the door. The forest rustles, snaps, and whispers. He sees the darkened outhouse and remembers the scorpion from his room. The ground is soft beneath his feet. He tries not to admit that he is terrified.

The next morning, Derrick finds a patio on the other side of the barn. It faces away from the mountain, and beneath it the earth drops straight down so there are no trees to obscure the view. The Nicaraguan landscape unravels toward the horizon. In the distance, the mountains crest above the clouds, their outlines blurred by a smoky haze. Far below, the valley's fog rolls back into itself like steam in a covered pot. The orange hues of sunrise linger between the clouds, and Derrick is struck by the layers of color that bleed through the sky.

"Hey," Amanda's voice calls from behind. Derrick turns. "I've got something for you." She holds her headlamp toward Derrick. "I saw you tip-toeing to the bathroom last night and I figured you probably didn't have one of these and I don't need it anymore."

"Thanks."

"So, are you *ready*?"

"Ready for what?"

"Class. School starts in like 15 minutes."

"What?"

"Shoot, I should have known no one would tell you. Everyone around here is kind of used to people taking care of themselves. Don't worry, today will be easy, just have everyone write you descriptions of who they are and what they like to do and don't like to do, and stuff. I mean, you need to get to know them, right? Just make sure after today you take your lessons seriously. I mean, the parents expect their children to be able to speak English, they have very high hopes, so just remember, we're not here for us, we're here for them." Derrick is staring blankly toward Amanda. "Ugh! I'm sorry, listen to me going on like a lecture, I'm just nervous about leaving my classes, you know, anyway I'm sure you, like, know all of this stuff. I'll meet you over at the school. Oh, and if you ever need any help try and find Rosa, she's amazing. "

"Hey," Derrick yells after her, "thanks for the headlamp."

When Derrick arrives at the school, Amanda is standing

in front of the class saying goodbye. A pair of students has latched onto her on either side, wrapping their arms around her waist and pressing their faces into her ribs. Amanda wipes the tears from her eyes.

"You have a new instructor now," she says, gesturing toward Derrick. The lack of enthusiasm is palpable. "He is very smart and he is going to teach you even better English."

She peels the student's arms from her waist and walks over to Derrick.

"They're all yours," she says, "I need to get to the tractor before they leave. Good luck."

Amanda disappears out the door, and the children sulk back to their seats. Derrick takes his place at the front of the room. All of their eyes are trained on him. He wipes his palms on his shirt.

"Hello," he says, "my name is Derrick"

"Hel-*lo* Dar-eek," answers the class.

Year 1
Susan and Michael

The well-kept yard gives way to the beginning of a forest, and Michael stands barefoot at the border observing the wide paths between the poplar trees. Leaves fall between their branches and sprinkle the forest's floor. The air is chill. His feet are cold.

Susan awakes alone in the bedroom. The blankets where Michael slept are twisted and curled at the lip. She feels cleansed. Rays of light accent the air by the window. This is just what she wanted.

Michael sees Gus walking through the woods, and they raise their arms to each other in greeting. Gus walks slowly while his dog sprints around him. Gus and his wife run this house. Last night they made dinner for Michael and Susan. "It's so nice to have a young couple out here," said his wife Helen. Gus cupped his hand over hers, "Yes, we're happy to have some young faces about. When you get to be our age, young love can be quite refreshing."

The words ring in Michael's ears. He likes being called part of a 'young couple.' *Love.* Just hearing the word Michael felt closer to Susan. He wonders what Susan and Helen talked about after he went to bed.

From the window Susan can see Michael standing outside. He looks handsome. He is not wearing any shoes. She wonders what Helen and Gus are up to. Helen is a very pleasant woman to be around. The morning light warms Susan's face. She decides to take a shower.

Michael is walking up the stairs. Yesterday, as they were leaving a rest stop, he caught sight of Susan standing outside in the sun, her face turned away. For a moment, she seemed like a beautiful stranger. "She is mine," he thought, "she is waiting for me." When he stepped outside, he almost ran toward her. "What are you so happy about?" she asked.

Susan hears the door to their room open. The sound of

Michael's footsteps are muffled by the sound of her shower. There is a soft knock at the bathroom door.

"Yes?"

"Mind if I come in?" asks Michael.

"Be my guest."

Michael slips off his pants and shirt and steps into the shower. Susan's skin is slippery to the touch. He reaches to pull her close, but Susan takes his hand between her thumb and forefinger and moves it back to his side. She picks up the soap and lathers her hands. She paints his body with her fingers. She turns him around and massages the shampoo into his hair. He submits to the pleasure of her fingers against his scalp.

When she's arched his neck and rinsed his hair, she whispers into his ear, "Now, both of us are clean." She takes his hand and places its palm just below her bellybutton.

They lay side by side, and their hair dampens the sheets. Susan rolls toward Michael and sets her cheek against his skin. She wishes she could pull even closer to him. She wishes she could curl up inside his chest.

The narrow trail opens like a river to the sea. Michael and Susan step out onto a large rock that juts out from the mountain. When they are a few feet from the rock's edge, they stop and set down their picnic basket. The view is divided by forest and sky. Only at the crest of faraway hills does the blanket of trees disappear.

"This is incredible," says Michael.

"I love it here."

Susan first found this place in high school the day Leah got her driver's license. They drove east and pledged to find places they had never heard of before. Susan remembers being overwhelmed by the wave of new emotions that accented their drive away from the city and into the foothills of the Appalachians. Leah sang along to the radio. They rolled down all the windows. Near the top of a mountain, they turned onto a dirt road which then turned to gravel. They parked in a clearing and started down a trail. When they found the rock, it was like the world had fulfilled a promise to them. "I think," said Susan, whispering for theatrical effect, "We're the only people here."

Michael wanders toward the edge to take in the view, and Susan takes the lid off the picnic basket.

"I thought you said you packed the sandwiches."

"Everything's in there," he says and turns back toward her, "Isn't it?"

She smiles. "Next time let's remember to *make the sandwiches* before we leave."

"Do you want me to make yours? What kind do you want?"

"That's all right." She pulls the plastic clasp from the loaf of bread. "It'll be fun to make sandwiches out here."

Michael walks to a solitary tree growing out of a crack in the rock. He reaches up and pulls down on a branch, testing it for support. He jumps and pulls himself up, walking his feet up the trunk. When Susan looks up from the basket, he is hanging under the branch by his hands and ankles. She watches as he turns himself upward so that he's seated and looking toward her. He slips and catches himself, but Susan panics.

"Michael," she says, her voice straining to be calm.

He grins.

"I don't want you to kill yourself. Please."

He slides toward the trunk and drops back down to the rock.

"Sorry," he says, walking back over, "But it does look pretty cool up there."

She smiles and pushes the bread across the blanket. "Don't forget to make your sandwich."

He sits beside her. Susan slides toward him, and he rests his hand on her thigh. She kisses him on the cheek, and when she looks into his eyes, he slips his fingers between hers. She feels close to him. Closer than she anticipated.

"You know," he says, "you really should forget about Steven. Then we could be together like this all of the time. I've already decided to break up with Kelsey."

She pulls her hand away. "Don't talk about them like that. It's cruel." She slides away and reaches for a drink of water.

Thoughts of Steven have been rolling through her mind since they got out of the car. As they walked along the trail, she remembered the camping trip when she first met him. He had a nice backpack and a scruffy beard, and he listened to her questions with care and thoughtfulness. He taught her about the birds that they heard calling in the forest. He talked about landscapes in geologic terms and explained the seismic histories of the mountains beneath them. He told stories about hunting with his father. When the group broke for lunch, they sat together on a fallen tree and shared their meals with each other. He struck her as sweet and honest and calm. He asked if she wanted to meet up in the city sometime and she said "Of course." It's been a long year since then.

Michael is afraid he's ruined everything. A minute ago he was fantasizing about making love on the side of this mountain, and now Susan seems to have pulled into herself. *I shouldn't have said anything about Steven. Christ. That seems like a pretty basic thing, 'Don't mention the other guys name.' I'm an idiot.*

Susan wonders if Helen will be around when they get back. It was nice being able to talk with her last night. Michael went to bed, and Susan knew he expected her to follow soon after, but Helen offered to make her some tea instead. Susan watched her make the tea, and the unhurried calm in Helen's gestures made her feel safe and relaxed.

"How long have you and Gus been married?" she asked

"Oh, almost thirty-five years."

Susan shakes her head. "I couldn't imagine being with someone that long."

"And we still have a while to go."

Susan laughs, "Yes, I guess you do."

Helen sips her tea.

"And what about you and your Michael, how long have you two been together?"

Susan hesitates, "Oh, about a year."

"You don't sound very enthusiastic."

"Well," she feels uneasy, "Sometimes, I worry that we're not as close as we used to be."

Helen reaches across the table and takes Susan's hand.

"I am truly sorry to hear that." Her voice is smooth and gentle. Susan realizes that she probably has these sorts of conversations all the time.

"It's just... we're—" Michael and Steven are getting twisted in her mind.

"Listen darling, I don't know much about you and Michael but I'll tell you what I do know." Susan picks up her cup and feels its heat in her hands. "People change while they're in love. When I was young I thought love was a kind of thing that froze the people around it. But now I know that staying in love comes down to luck more than anything. At the end of the day you're you and he's him and there's no telling how much somebody is going to change in thirty-five years."

"Do you think that you and Gus have grown apart?"

"Oh, I guess you could say we've grown together as we've grown apart. But we've been lucky."

Susan sets down her tea. "I hope I'll turn out to be lucky."

Helen's cheeks widen into a warm smile. "Listen dear, you gotta work hard to have good luck."

"I know," she returns the smile then looks down at her cup, "Everyone always says that love is work, but how do you know when you're working too hard?"

"Oh darling," she laughs. Helen stands and grabs Susan's glass by the rim, "we're always working too hard." The cups clink against each other as she sets them in the sink. She rests her hand on her hip. "Which is one of the reasons I think I need to head off to bed. Feel free to stay out here as long as you like though."

"Thank you. Thanks for staying up and talking with me. This was nice."

"Please, don't take anything I said too seriously. I mean you've met my Gus and we both know, he isn't the wisest owl in the woods," she laughs.

"But he's yours," says Susan, standing, "at least you have that."

"Yes. Yes he's mine alright."

Susan breaks the silence, "I'm sorry I got angry." She takes a breath, "We do need to talk about them, I know that, it's just that he was the furthest thing from my mind, and you brought him up when I was feeling this, well, you know, with you, and it just threw me off."

Michael is relieved, "I'm sorry, it was horrible timing."

"The truth is, I still don't know what I want to do."

"Well, I'm glad we came out here. "

She reaches for Michael's hand, "Me too," she says. "I've always wanted to share this place with someone."

"It's pretty incredible. You found this place with Leah?"

Helen takes Susan in her embrace and holds her for an extended hug goodbye. Susan understands it's meant as a gift of strength. Michael shakes hands with Gus and pats his dog on the head. They load their bags into the car and drive back toward Pittsburgh.

A few miles, out Susan's phone picks up reception for

the first time since they arrived. The phone beeps and shakes to inform her there are missed calls and messages. Her heart skips: three voicemails from Steven. She wants to listen to them, but she can't bring herself to do it while Michael is sitting right next to her. He seems so innocent. She feels badly for dragging him through all of this. It's not fair to him; she knows that.

Her feelings for Michael have dug deeper than she expected. He flatters her, and she doesn't feel pressured to be anything but herself when she's with him. But it's strange to be the older one in a relationship. She knows that he'll admire her no matter how she acts.

Michael cracks the window and takes a deep breath. He is trying to muzzle his anxieties. Thinking back on the weekend, he feels very mature, very adult, very much in love. Susan is growing more obviously fond of him. He can tell she feels relaxed around him. He knows he can make her happy, and he's almost surprised at how much he enjoys doing so. He reminds himself to be patient. It's only a matter of time. Soon they'll be together for real.

The messages are burning at the edge of her thoughts, making it hard to concentrate. She's tempted to listen quietly, but the thought of Michael asking her what she's doing terrifies her.

"You know," she says, "The Appalachians are older than the Rockies. They used to be just as big but they've been worn down by the elements over the years." It's a fact she first learned from Steven.

"Whoa," says Michael.

"In time the Rockies will get worn down too." It feels

oddly appropriate reliving this conversation with Michael. Like it's the only thing she can do.

"That's kind of crazy."

"Isn't it?" Pause. "You know, it's too bad the leaves have only just started to change. A few weeks from now the hills will be full of color."

"We should come back out here then," he says, nervous about his projection of their relationship into the future, curious to see how she'll react. She looks out the window.

"I'd like that."

Year 5
Michael and Susan

"I heard you come in late last night," says Leah.

Susan is by the sink, pouring a glass of water.

"What are you insinuating?" she asks.

"I'm insinuating that I heard someone else come in with you. It looks like patience paid off for our friend Russ, didn't it?"

Susan takes some ice cubes from the freezer and drops them into her glass.

"I can't believe how hung over I am. I never drink like that," she says evasively.

"Well, *I* for one am glad that my Susie is getting a little loving. I hope Russ understands what a lucky man he is."

"Leah, *shhh*… It's not Russ in there."

Leah's eyes jump open, "*What?*"

"I didn't tell you because I didn't know how to bring it up. But," she pauses, "Michael came into town yesterday and we met up for some drinks."

"*Michael*, like *Mi*chael, Michael?"

"Yeah," she touches her forehead, "We had a really good time."

"Apparently."

*   *   *   *   *

The night begins casually. They meet in a bar with dim lighting and diner-style booths. Michael is there first, and when Susan arrives, they both order martinis. The conversation flows without effort. They talk about their jobs and about how their lives have changed as they've gotten older.

"It's harder to meet people," says Michael, "It's harder to make friends."

"I meet plenty of people, but none of them ever want to talk about anything. They act like being polite is the only point of conversation."

They order another pair of martinis. When the drinks arrive, they raise them in the air. The gin tingles on their lips.

"Michael, I should probably mention," Susan's voice is more detached, "I've kind of started dating someone recently."

Michael tries to mute his reaction, "Is it serious?"

"No, not really. But maybe. We've been on a couple of dates and they were both kind of awkward. But... I guess it's always awkward when you start dating someone you don't really know. I mean, he could be worse."

"It sounds like you're trying to talk yourself into liking him."

"Why would I do something like that?"

*   *   *   *   *

Michael gets dressed and listens to Susan talking with Leah in the kitchen. He hoped they could get out of here before Leah woke up, but it looks like that's not going to happen. He walks into the bathroom in the back corner of Susan's room and splashes water on his face. There is a steady thump in his right temple, and his pores feel clogged with oil.

Michael tries to distance himself from the fantasies that brought him here. He is not sure what to expect. He hopes she's still up for going out to get breakfast. Scenes from last night seem clouded in a haze.

*   *   *   *   *

"Susan, I have a confession to make." His tone is deliberate but light. They are halfway through their second martini, and her cheeks feel warm. "I didn't really have a reason to come to Pittsburgh this weekend. I came hoping to see you. If you said you didn't want to see me, I wouldn't be here."

Susan is tempted to ask why he would do that but catches herself. There is a mood that's building, and she doesn't want to rattle it.

"I'm glad you're here," she says. "It's weird, I've been

thinking about you kind of a lot recently. Even before you sent me that e-mail."

"Because of this guy you're seeing?"

"I guess so. I keep telling myself it's not fair to compare him to you."

Michael plays with an arrogant grin, "Of course not."

"Oh, shut up," says Susan and she feels a flash of something between them.

Michael moves his hand across the edge of the table in front of him, "I probably shouldn't say this but if I don't, it'll feel like I'm keeping something back," Michael pauses, "Sometimes I think about you and the thoughts crowd out everything else I'm thinking, and I get taken up by this idea that, we're soul mates or something." He shakes his head, "I'm sorry, that must sound pretty intense."

"No, it's OK." She takes his hand.

He finishes his drink and pushes it away, "Do you want to take a walk someplace else?"

*   *   *   *   *

For breakfast they decide to get crepes in Shadyside. The restaurant is long and thin with room for a single row of tables along the right wall. Michael and Susan descend the stairs, and Michael holds the door open as they enter. Susan walks toward the coffee station and wonders if Michael has changed the way he likes his coffee.

Their breakfast is quiet. They split a newspaper between them, and they each refill their coffee. Michael questions the selection of stories for the front page, and Susan mocks the tone of one of the opinion pieces.

"You know what," says Michael, as they're walking to the door.

"What?" asks Susan, playing along.

"I really do enjoy your company." He opens the door.

"Well, thank you. You're not so bad yourself." They laugh together and lean into a brief embrace on the stairs before stepping back onto the street.

*   *   *   *   *

They arrive at the next bar and slide into a corner booth. They sit with their thighs touching together. They each drink another martini while musicians set up equipment across the room.

"You know," says Michael, "You should really come to New York." His words are slightly slurred together.

"Oh!" exclaims Susan, "I would *love* to go to New York! You know I've never been. I've always wanted to go to New York. I've always wanted to *live* in New York."

"Well, a friend of mine is throwing this fancy party in a few months. You could come up for it." The band takes their places. "You could stay with me."

"I'd like that. I'd like that a lot." She rests her head on his shoulder.

*   *   *   *   *

Susan and Michael walk down the sidewalk and the wind sweeps around them. Michael puts his hands in the pockets of his jacket and he realizes that last night may be the last time he is ever alone with Susan. He is nervous.

"Last night," he begins, "were you serious about potentially coming to New York?"

"Well, that's a big question isn't it?" They walk for a while before she continues, "Obviously, I hadn't really considered it before last night. But, I don't know. Maybe." They're almost back to Susan's house.

"You don't sound too enthusiastic."

"I don't know. I think it could fun. It's just a lot all of a sudden. First you need to tell me when this party is."

"I think I can figure that out."

"And Michael," she says softly, slowing down in front of her house, "I'm glad we were able to spend some time together. I really needed this."

"I had a nice time too." Michael looks at the door and back to Susan. "But I guess this is it."

Susan steps forward, rises on her toes and kisses Michael on the cheek, "I'll call you."

Year 3
Leah

Leah is making choices. She dismisses the two couches to her left and walks toward the blue one on her right. It is broad and full. She presses the center cushion with her hand and watches as it molds to her touch and then slowly returns to its resting shape. It seems like a very high quality couch. She tries to imagine it at the foot of the Persian rug she has back at the house, but the image is elusive.

Something about the color feels off. She wonders if the right curtains could bring it together.

There is a darkening at the edge of her thoughts, and Leah looks away from the couch. She is working hard to keep her mind occupied. The idea is to immerse herself as long as possible in complete distraction.

Decorating a house is more difficult than she expected. When she first elected to take on the task herself, Marcel was skeptical, but she persisted. She persuaded him that it was important to her to have a hand in their new house. He said that he understood, but since then, he's been more skeptical. Now there's an incredible pressure for her to produce something special. She wants the house to have a personal flare but also feel dignified. It should be simple but not austere. Modern but not pretentious. She needs to create a home.

Leah feels a quiver behind her eyes. She's having trouble balancing the ideas in her head. Something feels off. She can feel her heart thumping in her chest. *What the fuck do I know about decorating a house?*

Leah paces the wide aisles of the furniture store. Her head begins to ache. Life has been good since Marcel's business began to take off, but recently, Leah has been overwhelmed by the feeling that she is in constant competition with his success. She's confused by her passive role in his life, and she's tired of feigning an unbothered tone every time he comes home from a weekend away without seeming to care that she has been waiting for him. She wants him to remember that she's just as smart as he is. She wants him to remember that she's the most important part of his life. She tells herself that he has nothing to hide.

After a few hours in the store, a vision of a living room is beginning to come together. She's found a new rug that will better anchor the room. Plants will hang in the corners. A pair of mahogany end tables can bring the couch a sense of depth and respectability.

She is passing an aisle of scented candles when her mood deflates again. She is exhausted. Her fingers scratch at her palms. *An affair...* There's an otherness to the phrase that obscures it. Still, she can feel its talons pierce her thoughts. She is creating a home for her husband to share with another woman. Leah feels lightheaded. She leans against a chair to keep her balance. No one in the store seems to notice.

Last night he took her to the symphony in the city. Annelies. His colleague. *Annelies.* What a stupid European name. She's probably shameless. *Gold digging slut.*

"You don't want to go," he said to Leah, "It's going to be horribly boring. It's really more for networking and I know you can't stand those types of people. It really does make more sense for me to go with Annelies, don't you think?"

She agreed. It wasn't the time to make a scene.

Focus. She is trying to stare at an array of lampshades. *I'm jumping to conclusions.* When she reaches for a lampshade on the lowest shelf, her dizziness returns, and this time it's accompanied by a dense weight in her chest. *Have I eaten today?* She straightens up and presses her fingers to her temple. *Maybe Marcel is innocent. I know that he loves me.* She steps out of the aisle and makes her way to a large leather armchair.

I wonder what he would do if I asked him? She takes a moment to visualize the exchange and the fantasy excites her. *I'll have to pick a moment when he's unguarded, when I'll be sure to catch his authentic reaction. 'Marcel, are you having an affair with Annelies?' I'll look him straight in the eye.*

She settles into the armchair and a feeling of relaxation seeps into her shoulders and thighs. "Tomorrow," she tells herself, "Tomorrow I'll ask him." *There's nothing else I can do.*

Year 1
Michael

Faraday's class rarely starts on time, but Michael makes a point not to be late. He takes out his notebook and begins looking over his notes from last class. This is the only course he's taking where he keeps notes. A few minutes later, Veronica walks in and he looks up from his desk. She is wearing a hooded sweatshirt and loose fitting jeans. She walks straight for her seat, sits down and closes her eyes. Michael, as always, is taken by the effortlessness of her sexuality. When Faraday enters, he steps to the podium, coughs, pushes his glasses back with his forefinger and begins.

"Faith. Faith is a difficult concept to discuss. The word is plagued by religious associations." At times, Faraday sounds like he's thinking out loud to himself. "In this era of mortal significance people prefer to pretend that they have outgrown the concept of faith, that they have left it behind in a more barbaric intellectual age. They dismiss it as a childish form of argument. And, in doing so, they fail to appreciate its fundamental place in our human potential. They fail to realize that faith is the experience which inspires religion, and not the other way around."

Michael has come to admire Faraday.

"Faith is belief that cannot be verified by reason. Faith is the function of our values. Faith is a vehicle of truth. Faith is the foundation of creativity."

Even in her sweatshirt and without makeup, Veronica is undeniably the most beautiful girl in the room. He wonders if she'll speak today. He remembers each of the three questions she has asked throughout the semester. Her voice was calm and direct.

"Faith is the foundation of art; the belief that something can exist which has never existed before. As human beings we are pulled toward the act of creation. In creation we find balance. Balance between ourselves and the shared reality of our generation. Balance between what is and what can be. In creation there is both fulfillment and communication. We create art. We create the lives that we live. You see, our potential as people is directly linked to our capacity to create what has not been created before. When we understand this, we can understand that creation is the root of meaning, is the root of purpose in life. But first, we must understand that every act of creation is, first, an act of faith."

Michael writes 'Faith ←→ Creation' in a blue pen. He wonders what Susan is doing and if she's happy. Since their vacation to the bed and breakfast, she has seemed more distant, and he suspects that she's been talking with Steven. Michael's feelings toward Steven have devolved from calm respect to jealous anger. He can't imagine Steven without also seeing himself punch him in the face.

"When we accept that faith is just as important to our lives as reason it is as if we are free to use both of our legs for the first time. We are free to run and jump and dance. And while we may always be surrounded and outnumbered, by those who hobble about, who glorify only reason, it is plain to see that they are the misguided ones. To look at the scope of human experience is to see clearly that, it is reason, and not faith, that limits humanity."

He takes a breath. The lectures always end the same way.

"The assignment is," he begins, and Michael readies his pen. "Three pages on the history of faith and human experience."

The class begins to pack up. Michael wants to talk with Faraday more about the lecture, but he notices that Veronica is already talking to him. The thought of standing next to her is almost too much for his nerves to bear. He turns and joins the train of students leaving the classroom.

It's not unusual for class to let out an hour early, but when Michael steps out of the Cathedral, he finds that it's nearly dark outside. The Cathedral's shadow has dissolved back into the night around it. He looks up at the graying sky. An aimless urgency ricochets inside of him. He's always surprised when the days begin to shorten.

Year 3
Michael and Susan

Michael rolls out of bed, careful not to wake Susan. Her body is wrapped tightly in the covers. Her head rests gently on her light blue pillow and her cheek is soft and warm in the morning light. Dust swims in the rays of sun that pass above her. He tiptoes away toward the kitchen.

Michael pours his first cup of coffee and sets up the cutting board. He slices mushrooms and chops spinach. He can hear Susan rustling in the bedroom.

"I'm making breakfast," he says.

A few moments later, Susan walks, heavy-footed, into the kitchen wearing one of Michael's t-shirts. It hangs down to the middle of her thighs.

"Morn'ing," she yawns.

"Good morning, love," he answers, whisking milk into a bowl of eggs.

Michael enjoys making omelets. He pours oil into the pan and begins to cook the vegetables. Susan pours milk into her coffee and kisses Michael on the cheek while he stirs the pan with a wooden spoon. They enjoy these mornings together. There's a sense of ease infused with sensuality, a balance between possibility and fulfillment.

"What time do you think we should leave?" asks Susan.

He pours the eggs into the pan and listens to them sizzle.

"In probably about thirty minutes or so. We want to get there early."

"Are you sure it's not going to be cold?"

"No," he laughs. "But if we don't go this weekend we'll have to wait for spring."

Susan walks over to the window and notices the cloudless sky. "I guess the weather is pretty ideal."

They carry their raft from the wooden rental shop down a slope and over a narrow path to the banks of the river. Michael carries a backpack with lunch, a pair of towels and a change of clothes for each of them. When they reach the river, Susan kicks off her flip-flops, touches her toe to the surface, and then jumps back while pulling her arms to her chest.

"Cold! The water is *cold*."

Michael walks past her and steps into the water up to his shins. He grabs the raft and pulls it into the water. A large grin is carved across his face. "Come on. I'll hold it while you climb in."

After the first bend in the river, the sky opens wide. They lift their oars from the water, and a breeze licks its way across the water. The shores are lush with color. Michael remembers the first time they took a trip together in autumn. The forest hadn't had time to change. It's as if a promise is finally fulfilled. Susan looks down the river and then back over her shoulder behind Michael.

"I think we're the only people out here," she says.

"I know."

"It's gorgeous."

They listen to the sound of the water. As they drift toward the next bend, they can hear the percussive growl of the upcoming rapids.

"Scared?" he asks.

"Not if you promise to save me." She picks up her oar, and Michael steers them into the turn.

They spot a large boulder at the edge of the water and steer to the eddy around it for lunch. Their clothes are specked with water. Susan has enjoyed the way the rapids make her work with Michael as a team. She unwraps her sandwich and watches an array of orange and yellow leaves flutter in the wind and land on the river. A turtle walks along the bank, and Michael reaches out to tickle Susan's knee.

When they pull back into the center of the river, Susan looks back at Michael.

"You know," she says, "we're really good at life."

"Yeah, I think so too."

Again, the echo of the rapids reaches them before it comes into view. Susan notices a wider range of depth in its sound. When they turn the bend, she sees that it's twice the size of the other rapids they've seen. From bank to bank, the water is chopped and churned into swaths of white foam. The current crashes into walls of stone and then folds back on itself. Susan's eyes are alert as they enter the whitewater. "Rock!" she shouts. Michael thrusts his oar into the water, and the raft spins sideways. They hit a drop, and Susan lets out a shriek. They pick up speed as the water sweeps them toward a large boulder. *"LEAN!"* shouts Michael, but they move too late. The rock side of the raft lifts into the air. They are weightless, then submerged in the water. Their lungs tighten. Susan bats her arms and stretches her neck for a gasp of air. She feels Michael's arm wrap around her. He holds her as they float toward a second drop. Again, weightlessness and disorientation. They are both coughing and spitting when their lifejackets buoy them back up for air. Susan reaches out to a passing rock, and her fingers slide across its slippery surface. The next rock has a sharper edge, and she catches a grip. They pull themselves on top of it. Their wet clothes cling to their skin. When the raft floats toward them, Michael grabs it by the rope around its side and flips it over.

When they open the backpack, they find it's not that bad. One of the towels is thoroughly soaked, but the other one isn't as bad, and the clothes are largely unharmed. They climb back into the raft, and Michael's teeth chatter. Susan checks to make sure that they're still alone. They undress, dry off, slip into their dry clothes and hold each other close to stay warm. The raft floats slowly in the center of the river. The slopes of the mountains burst with shades of red, orange, yellow, and violet. Each tree contains its own palette. Up ahead an abandoned railway bridge accents the scene. Fallen leaves pass them by in the current.

"I do admit," Susan whispers, "That was kind of fun."

*   *   *   *   *

Several hours later, they're with Jane and her new boyfriend Josh at a bar in Polish Hill. The front of the bar is painted black. The back room is better lit with large booths, a pool table, and a currently empty stage. Regulars talk to each other with manufactured enthusiasm. Over half the crowd wears unkempt hair and worn out boots. Michael gives himself the last few drops of their pitcher of beer. Susan has just finished recounting their story from the morning, and Jane is expressing her jealousy. Susan notices a distinct sense of awkwardness between her and Josh. She feels a tinge of pity for Jane's unambitious approach to dating.

Michael sees Josh's attention drift to the pool table and asks if he wants to play.

"Sure," says Josh.

"Let's do it," says Michael. He stands and sticks his hands in his pockets to search for quarters.

"Don't worry about it," says Josh, "I got it."

When they reach the table, he sets down two quarters to announce their challenge to the winners of the game being played.

"Susan," says Jane, "there's something I need to tell you." She sets her palms on the table and looks Susan in the eye, "I may be leaving the paper soon."

Susan is shocked. They've always complained about the paper, but she didn't realize Jane was actually looking for other jobs.

Jane continues, "There's a magazine in Columbus that's going to hire me as a feature writer."

"Columbus? Who would want to live in Columbus?"

Jane laughs, "Oh, Susan, don't make fun."

"Why didn't you talk to me about this?"

"I don't know. I guess I didn't really believe it was going

to happen."

"Well," she hesitates, "I'm going to miss you."

"I know sweetie. I'll miss you too." Pause. "You'll find a way out sooner or later."

Across the bar, Josh and Michael are still waiting for the game to finish up. They are talking about Steelers football when Josh changes the subject, "So, you and Susan are pretty serious, huh?"

"Yeah, I guess so." Michael is slightly uncomfortable with the question. "What about you and Jane? What's going on with you two?"

"We have a lot of fun but I think we both know that's all we're looking for."

A shot on the 8-ball is lined up and missed.

"By the way, you any good at this game? Think we can take these guys?" asks Michael.

"Shouldn't be a problem."

Michael turns to inspect the pool cues. *'Pretty serious.'* He turns the phrase over in his mind. *I'm in a serious relationship.* The thought sits with him differently than the idea of being madly in love.

Michael and Susan head back to the apartment early. Their bodies ache from their morning on the river.

"We're home," announces Susan, as she swings open the door.

Michael plops on the couch while Susan picks up the mail and walks to the bedroom. It's almost midnight and Michael is exhausted. He kicks off his shoes and pushes off his socks with his toes. His feet feel liberated.

Susan calls from the bedroom, "You didn't tell me I got a letter from Leah."

"I didn't notice. I just set the mail in the basket." It strains him to raise his voice.

"Are you coming to bed?"

"In a minute," he says.

By the time Michael gets to bed, Susan has read over Leah's letter three times.

Leah is not doing well. She is not happy. She says she knows for sure that Marcel has been cheating on her and doesn't know what to do. Susan is devastated by the news. She feels an urge to fly to France and rescue her. How could Marcel turn out to be such a scumbag?

Susan turns to Michael and watches him read quietly on his side of the bed. She is lucky to have Michael. She is lucky to be with someone that she trusts. More than once she has imagined her and Michael visiting Leah and Marcel. More than once she has imagined her and Michael getting married. She will have to call Leah tomorrow and find out what is really going on. It pains her to think what Leah may have gone through since she sent this letter.

"Honey," Michael looks away from his book. "I think I may invite Leah to come visit sometime soon." Susan's voice sounds anxious.

"Is everything all right?"

"I just think she could take a break from being over there. It's hard being surrounded by people you hardly know."

"Well. If she comes she can always stay at my place."

"That's sweet hon. But she'd probably stay here, and *you*

could stay at your place."

When Michael is finished reading, he turns off his lamp, and the room goes dark. Susan is curled up next to him but not yet asleep. Leah's letter has stirred something inside her, and she's now remembering her conversation with Jane. Susan used to imagine that once she got both feet in the world of journalism she would leap from one success to another. Instead, she has become mired in triviality. She feels a need to do something big, to anchor herself to something she can be proud of. The digits on the bedside clock flick forward.

"Honey," she says, "are you awake?"

Michael grunts.

"I think I'm going to write a book."

"I think that's an excellent idea." His voice is groggy, "Do you know what about?"

"Something nonfiction maybe. Something interesting. Something where I could do some reporting. Or maybe something that weaves in poetry too."

"That's a lot of somethings."

"Will you read it as I go and tell me if it's any good?"

He stretches his arm around her, and she rolls next to him. "I would love that. I would love to read your book."

*   *   *   *   *

Michael is on his bike. On weekdays, while Susan is at work, he has most of the day to himself. Usually he studies and goes to class for a couple hours. He spends time

127

walking along Liberty Avenue and reading at Crazy Mocha. He normally tries to have dinner started by the time Susan gets home. Sometimes, like today, he meets her in the park for lunch.

Good at life. Michael likes the idea of being good at life. It reminds him that he can be proud of his own happiness. He's almost outside her office. She'll be happy to see him.

They walk from her office to a bench in front of the Allegheny River. She is more light-hearted about her day at work than usual. A cold wind blows up from the water. Above them, flocks of birds pass by on their way to warmer weather. At their feet, a group of smaller birds are daring to inch closer toward them. Susan asks why they don't wish to fly south and drops a piece of bread by her foot. The crumb is snatched away, and the remaining birds inch closer. Michael takes a larger chunk of bread and holds it just above the ground. The birds step closer, waiting for the crumb to drop. Then, one of them flies up to his hand and grabs the bread in its beak. Michael feels a gentle tug and lets go. The bird flies away, followed by several others.

"Well done," says Susan.

"Why, thank you."

"By the way," excitement creeping into her voice, "I've come up with a title for my book."

"Yeah? What are you going to call it?"

"*Love in America.*"

"What's it about?

"It's going to be stories of people in love."

Year 5
Susan

Susan is on her fourth date with Russ. They are at a restaurant, and their table is covered in a white tablecloth. The lighting is low, and the surrounding tables are full of people. The last time she was here was four years ago with Michael. They sat in the corner booth by the window.

Susan wanted to postpone this date, but Leah argued strongly against it. "You are not going to redefine your life because Michael swooped into it for one night," she said. Susan thought it was a good point.

Nevertheless, she regrets being here.

Russ is friendly and upbeat. He talks about a vacation he is looking forward to, and she feigns enthusiasm for the stories that she's working on at the paper. She is trying to appear warm and composed. It is important to her to come off as a nice person.

After their drinks arrive, Susan excuses herself to the bathroom. Walking between the tables, she fears that her knees will buckle, and she'll tumble to the ground. She doesn't want to have to explain herself.

Alone in the bathroom, she allows her shoulders to sag. She stands in front of the mirror, arches her eyebrows, and looks into the eyes of her reflection, "What are you doing here?" she whispers.

She has yet to regain her balance since Michael's visit. Last week she was telling herself that she didn't want to be in a serious relationship, and now she is fantasizing about moving to New York City.

She wonders what Russ could be thinking. He must think that things are progressing smoothly. She has been nothing but pleasant toward him. At first she thought this was the polite thing to do, but now she fears that there's an element of cruelty in it. *He probably hopes to have sex tonight.* The thought triggers a sigh of laughter and she rolls her eyes. She realizes at some point she'll have to be honest with him. There is a knock on the door.

Russ welcomes her return to the table with a grin. He asks if she's been to this restaurant before and she says no. He begins to talk through his analysis of certain items on the menu. He explains that he is in the mood for something light and recollects a time when he got the Mediterranean salad here. It was delicious.

"Russ," she says. "I'm sorry."

Russ takes a moment, "For what?" he sounds confused.

"I'm not being entirely honest with you."

"What do you mean?" his confusion turns to concern.

"The other night I went out with an ex of mine and we had a really good time."

He waits for her to continue.

"And I'm basically all mixed up right now and," she hadn't planned to say this, "I don't know if this is the best time for us to be getting to know each other."

"What exactly are you saying?" he asks.

"I'm sorry, I hate to do this like this. I think I'm going to go."

She stands.

"Can I call you?" he asks.

Susan is horrified that other people are eavesdropping

on their conversation.

"Maybe," she says, "but not right away." She moves toward the door, and again, she fears her knees will buckle beneath her.

Standing by her car, a half block from the restaurant, she pauses to take a deep breath. She expects to feel a wave of relief, but instead, her nerves are tighter than before.

Year 3
Camping

Leah listens to the forest as it dances with the wind. She's surrounded by a deep sense of relief. When the breeze passes, she leans forward to pick up a handful of metal rods. She and Susan are setting up her tent. Without Susan, she feels like she would dissolve in the wind. *It's good to be home.*

On the other side of the flattened tent, Jane is raking leaves and twigs to the borders of the campsite. Leah would like to get to know Jane better. She regrets feeling jealous when Susan first introduced them. It's not Susan's fault she hasn't been able to make new friends in France.

In the woods, Derrick is carrying branches that he has broken down to fit across his arms. He reminds himself that when he goes camping, he always needs more firewood than he expected. He comes to a fallen tree across the path and steps onto the trunk to get over to the other side. His foot slips, the branches fall, and his shin smashes against the trunk. When he regains his balance, he sets his foot against the tree and wipes the dirt from his leg. The skin is scraped, and a red drop emerges just below his knee. He takes a slow breath and decides to walk on for a while longer.

Leah watches Susan. The shadow of a maple leaf quivers across her face, and she looks toward the sky. Visions from Leah's confrontation with Marcel flicker in her mind like shadows around a fire. *Susan is the lucky one.*

When dusk begins to fall, the six of them gather around the fire pit where Michael has arranged sticks and logs into a teepee above a pile of leaves and pinecones. Josh passes out beers while Susan and Leah unpack dinner. Derrick takes out his guitar and begins to tune it. He is still not completely comfortable being on this trip. Being single never bothered him until Michael started spending most of his time with Susan. Now he seems constantly bombarded by displays of affection. When the guitar is tuned, he starts playing a delta blues song he's been working on. Derrick enjoys being able to disappear behind his music. It allows him to contribute without having to speak.

Michael and Josh keep a close eye on the fledgling fire. Susan, Leah, and Jane watch while they eat pasta from plastic containers. Michael kneels down and blows into the flames. Leah swats a mosquito from her foot.

"I don't know why we don't do this more often," says Jane.

"I know," says Susan.

"It's good to get out of the city," adds Josh.

Leah inhales the fresh air with an exaggerated breath. "I'm just happy I made it here to visit before it got too cold for us to do something like this."

"So, you're living in France, is that right?" asks Josh.

"For the time being. We'll see."

"Well," says Jane, "I would simply love to hear all about what life is like over there. I've always imagined living in some European hamlet stuck up in the mountains."

"Leah," interjects Susan. She regrets not warning Jane about Leah's situation. "May not want to talk about home while she's on vacation."

Jane looks confused.

"What she means," says Leah, "is that I'm here because my husband is intent on proving himself as a douchebag." Awkward silence. "More on that," she adds in a theatrical tone, "after a few drinks."

The line gets some laughter and Josh changes the subject, "When I was a kid I used to dream about living on a mountain."

Jane says she would never choose a mountain over a city. Before long, the group is comparing trails to bars and balancing tranquility against culture. There is debate about which setting is more appropriate for children. Speaking while he plays, Derrick joins the conversation.

"I don't know. I think it's easier to listen to yourself when you're in the mountains. I mean you can be alone when you're surrounded by people, but there's a special awareness that comes with the isolation you can find in the mountains."

"Well," says Leah, "I live between some mountains right now, and I find nothing soothing about it. The awareness that you're talking about can be terrifying." The words sound coarser than she intended. Derrick misses a note in the melody he's playing and the sound scrapes at his nerves. He sets down the guitar.

Leah fears that she has disrupted the mood of the conversation. She is not used to fumbling in social situations. Everyone is looking in her direction.

"Well," she says. "I guess I may as well talk about what happened. As you know, I've been married and living with my husband in France."

She lowers her knees from her chest and crosses them in front of her, freeing her hands to help guide the story. She opens her palms.

"I have recently discovered that my husband Marcel is having an affair with a slut named Annelies. I know this because I asked him," she twists her wrist, "Marcel," her eyes go wide, "Are you having an affair with... now, he begins to sweat... and I say, *Annelies*. God I hate that woman's name. And he lies, of course he lies, but after that he also stopped trying so hard to hide it and now it's clear enough to both of us what's going on."

Leah takes a breath, and her voice turns more introspective, "And so I've been alone and unhappy for a while now, and I'm confused about whether or not I should try and save my marriage or just run away and try to pretend the past two years don't exist." Tears begin to rise. She wipes them away and realizes she needs to rescue the scene that she's making. "But..." she collects herself, "For now, I'm home and I'm looking forward to having a really amazing weekend with all of you."

She raises her beer to the circle.

"To Leah," declares Josh.

The toast is repeated as a chorus, and Leah begins to blush. Derrick picks up his guitar and starts to play *Walk On* by Brownie Mcghee.

Leah is glad that she unburdened herself. She feels much more relaxed. "It's amazing how easy it is to be honest," she thinks, "when you're with people who care what you think."

She tosses a stick into the fire.

As dusk expires, the light flashes more vibrantly from the fire. Faces are cast in dark shadows and reddish hues. They feel a chill against their backs and a strong heat on their hands.

Derrick is watching Leah. She has been quiet. He wonders if she remembers when they first met. It's crazy to think that it was his first month in Pittsburgh. Derrick has often thought about that night, and Leah in particular. Her defining characteristic was that she was fantastically beyond his reach.

Leah is thankful for Derrick's guitar playing. It creates an ambiance that allows her to sit and watch the fire. As she listens to the conversation around her, Leah is struck by how young everyone sounds. She feels detached from them. She feels aged beyond her years. The idea alarms her. There is a slight tightening in her chest. Her wedding ring feels heavy on her finger.

Susan pulls herself closer to Michael, and he slides his arm across her shoulders.

"Are you getting tired?" he asks.

When she touches her ear to his chest she can feel the

beat of his heart. He brushes the hair from her face.

"Maybe."

Derrick stares into the fire. He watches as tongues of flame contort themselves and leap from the logs. They seem to vanish and reappear. At the fire's base, embers glow with a dynamic intensity. The air around them melts into waves. He can hear the wood sizzle in its heat. Derrick has always found fires to be mesmerizing. His guitar playing is becoming repetitive.

Michael and Susan announce that they are going to bed. Jane and Josh follow soon after. Derrick sets down his guitar and moves to get up.

"You can keep playing if you want to," says Leah, "I mean, I'd like to stay up and listen a little while longer if that's alright."

Susan is surprised by how dark it is inside their tent. She searches for the zippers on their sleeping bags while Michael looks for a rootless patch of ground. He lays his sleeping bag flat on the ground and spreads Susan's as a blanket on top of it. They lie down and listen to Derrick's guitar through the tent.

"I've been thinking about *Love in America*," she says.

"Are you getting any ideas?"

"I think it'll be a mix of interviews about how people fall in love. I'll need to find people willing to talk. That'll be the difficult part. There'll probably be a personal component too, and that's where I think I can weave in some poetry."

"I'm sure it'll be brilliant."

Susan closes her eyes and rests her head in the curve of his chest. She listens to his breathing while Michael runs his hand from her shoulder to waist and back again. She savors the touch of his fingers on her skin. Michael wonders if he and Susan will be together forever. He can't imagine being without her, but he's rattled by the idea of never being with anyone else. He wonders if it's possible to regret falling in love.

"Michael," Susan whispers, "I love you."

"I know," he rests his palm on her cheek and kisses her brow, "I love you too."

"Derrick," says Leah, "do you remember the first time we met?"

The line startles him, "I'm not sure."

"I do," her voice is just above a whisper, "it was on Flagstaff. Michael and Susan had just met, and the four of us decided to meet there to watch the sunset. I asked you about your life and you said everything was going according to plan."

The still red embers crackle between them.

"I'm pretty sure I was joking when I said that."

"So you *do* remember." Leah stands and walks over to Derrick's side of the fire. She sits next to him, and he sets down his guitar.

"Yeah. I remember."

"Tell me," she says, "am I much different than I was back then?"

Derrick insists that he hardly knew her then, or now, so it's difficult to say, but Leah is persistent. She wants to know what he thought of her when they first met.

"You must have thought something," she says.

"Well, the truth is," he pauses, "I thought you were very sexy and smart and not like anyone I'd ever met."

Leah's smile shifts the shadows on her face.

"And, now," she asks, "what would you think of me if tonight was the first night we met?"

Derrick is nervous. "I'd think," he begins, "that you have been less lucky than you deserve to be, and that you are a strong woman in the process of rearranging her life."

"I suppose that's fair."

Derrick pushes one of the embers with a stick.

"Tell me," says Leah, "do you think I'm still beautiful?"

Derrick is silent. He can tell that she's searching for something. Without thinking, he touches her chin and leans toward her. She closes her eyes and readies her lips. They kiss. Leah sets her hand on Derrick's knee. Her lips, he thinks, feel like they are full of tears.

"I'm sorry," he says.

"No. Don't be. It was nice."

"What I meant, I guess," he smiles, "is that, yes, I think that you're still very beautiful."

She wraps her arms around his torso.

"Will you stay up with me?" she asks. "I'm not very tired. You seem like a good person and I think I'd just like to talk for a while."

Derrick feels like he is lost in the surreal.

"Of course," he says, "I'd like that."

The next morning everyone hikes to a waterfall where

the stream flows over a large boulder and then drops twenty feet into a pool of water. The girls climb around the falls and set up a blanket by the bank of the pool below. Michael, Derrick, and Josh decide to walk onto the boulder so that they can slide off and dive into the water.

When they are directly above the falls, they stop and sit down. The water is cold, and the rock is slippery.

Jane yells from below, "Be careful!"

Leah continues, "Please, boys, please don't die!"

"Don't worry about us!" answers Josh.

He stands up to show them he has everything under control. For dramatics, he raises his arms and flexes. The water runs over his feet.

"Now," he yells, "Behold!" Josh slowly raises his right leg, "I am—" His left foot disappears from underneath him and his buttocks crash against the rock. A deep thud echoes through the trees. His body twists as he slides over the lip of the rock, falls, and splashes into the pool. He lets out a scream when he surfaces and swims toward Jane.

"Are you ok?" she shouts.

"I'm cold," he says, "I'm fucking cold."

"Don't worry," says Jane, "I'm not going to tell you 'I told you so.'"

On the falls, Derrick looks over to Michael. "It's too bad we won't be able to do anything like this again until after winter," says Derrick.

"True. I'm glad this worked out though. Susan wanted to do something special since Leah is visiting."

"We had a good talk last night."

"You and Leah?"

"Yeah."

They sit quietly.

"Sometimes," says Michael, "I forget how beautiful it is out here."

"I like it when the seasons change."

Susan panics when she sees Michael stand up. He takes a step back, pauses, then, steps and leaps forward. He lets out a long howl as his body arcs through the air, just missing the lip of the rock. When he lands in the water, his feet are still running beneath him.

Year 7
Love in America

A lover's song,
of longing drawn,
around the places
we have been.

Kelsey's voice is trembling, "I don't understand."

Don't forget and don't explain.

"I just can't do this anymore," he says.

Let your hopes and worries rain.

Michael is stunned by his absence of remorse.

Down on you and down on me.
The horizon we both see.

"But *why*? What have I done wrong?"

Always far, out by the sun.

"I'm sorry Kelsey. Goodbye."

Dreams of love when we were young,

-

Sometimes,

Love,

Leah,

Is the cause of love,

prays to a God she imagines to be her own.

Love,

She whispers, "Let him accept my heart,"

Is the mirror of the soul.

"And he will hear the love I'll feel for him."

Love me more than light can shine. More than water flows.

Tonight she will see Marcel. In his arms she will surrender her purity.

Love like yours and mine will make the mountains grow.

He is the one she's been waiting for.

Love.

"Marcel, my angel, I will make you mine."

Is this love?

-

Michael looks up from the pool table.

Lust prevails

Veronica. He recognizes her instantly.

over silent storms.

She says that she's been watching him.

Temptation's promise.

"Would you like to buy me a drink?" she asks.

Pleasures born.

He is grateful that he came here alone.

-

All we are is how we love.

-

"Michael," says Susan.

We have faith in the spring of love.

"I don't think I can come to New York."

We embrace the renewal of beauty.

He is silent.

I climbed the mountain.

"It's not a good idea."

The truth I saw,

Glass shatters inside his heart

that love is the language

"I'm sorry Michael,

man has called God.

part of me will always love you."

-

In learning how to love we come to know ourselves.

Through learning how to love we come to know ourselves.

Year 7
Michael

Spanish Town is the oldest neighborhood in Baton Rouge, and the houses are close together. It sits in the corner of downtown and on the edge of the parks that surround the Capitol building. Its streets are lined with broken sidewalks and shaded by trees whose branches bend from one side to the other. When Michael moved here four months ago, Derrick gave him a tour and pointed out how the houses dated from different periods of architecture. Weathered shacks stood near large plantation style homes. The streets were quiet. On each block Michael counted the cats reclining in the grass and on the pavement. They cast him weary glances as he passed. On seventh street, they paused to pick figs from a tree. Michael mentioned that life seemed to move slower here. "I know," said Derrick, "you can feel it in the air."

Michael hadn't thought long about the decision to move here from New York City. Derrick said that if he enrolled in a teacher certification program, he could probably get a job at the middle school where Derrick worked. Two weeks later, Michael loaded everything he owned into his car and drove south toward Louisiana.

Soon after Michael arrived, people started to talk about the hurricane. Each day there were reports that it was growing larger and aiming more stubbornly toward Louisiana. People started to get nervous. Michael and Derrick did their best to prepare. They bought bags of canned food and boxes of bottled water. They bought batteries, flashlights, and a charcoal grill. Their block became crowded with friends and family evacuating from New Orleans. They looked up satellite images of the storm. Its clouds filled the gap between Florida and Mexico.

On the morning of the hurricane, Michael went to stand in the street. He lifted his arms from his sides. The wind was brisk and the air felt lighter than usual. Drops of rain pelted his face and palms.

When the storm arrived the house began to shudder. Michael and Derrick looked out from a pair of large windows. They watched the roof tiles of a house across the street be peeled away by the wind. A large branch flew through the street. There was a loud blast, and the lights went dark. They decided to move away from the windows and open some beers. It was going to be a long storm.

They sat on the floor and talked about Louisiana. They played chess. They read books in the light of their headlamps. They stacked their empty beer cans on the windowsill. Michael watched a tree snap and twist in the wind as it fell. He felt hypnotized by the thundering of the wind. He imagined the storm as an extension of his own destruction and rebirth. Everything until now, he thought, has been before the storm.

After eight hours of trembling, the house fell quiet, and they stepped outside. The world was transformed. Nearly every inch of ground was covered in small green leaves. The rain glistened in the sun. The streets were empty. They walked to the corner and looked down Spanish Town Road. Fallen trees and telephone poles divided the street into sections. Power lines lay coiled on the sidewalk. In the distance, by the capitol building, they heard the ring of a large iron bell.

"What was that?" asked Michael.

"I guess we're not the only ones out here," said Derrick.

By the capitol, they found a group of people trying to recruit for a game of football. The guy carrying the ball tossed it at Michael. "I'm Jason," he said, "we're all scientists." The other four people, two guys and two girls, waved and began to walk toward the field.

"I'm Michael."

"Derrick."

Jason smiled, "Good to meet you."

The grass was tall and swampy. It splashed when they ran. Less than ten minutes into the game, both Michael and Derrick were both winded. At the end of a multi-play drive, Michael dove for a pass from Jason and extended his arms. The ball landed in his palms, and he gripped it tightly. His body splashed into a pool of water, and he slid more than the length of his body before he felt the shoulder of one of the scientists crash into his side. He was beginning to enjoy himself.

At the lawn in front of the capitol building they found a giant oak tree that had been uprooted. The long trunk like branches, which normally bowed to kiss the ground, were angled into the sky. The wall of earth that clung to its roots hung several feet above their heads.

"Rumor has it," said one of the scientists, "this tree was planted by Andrew Jackson."

"Well, *shit*," said Derrick.

That night there was a party at one of the scientist's houses in Spanish Town. Two charcoal grills cooked chicken and hamburgers while people talked in candlelight. The weather radio reported that over half the state was without power. People from New Orleans celebrated that the levees had held up. Derrick found a guitar and took it to the porch, and Michael met a girl named Laura. She laughed at his jokes and told him about her work. She was doing graduate research in coastal restoration. Her father was a fisherman. Michael felt nervous and awkward. It had been a long time since he flirted with a girl at a party.

For the next thirty-six hours, Michael and Derrick reveled in the novelty of living in the wake of a hurricane. They warmed water for coffee on the grill and positioned candles around the house. Michael met Laura for a walk through the park, and they went to another party at Shane the scientist's house. But after two days the heat started to get to them. It coated their skin and sunk into their pores. At night the only way they could sleep was to open all the windows. When they woke, mosquito bites covered their legs. It was four days before the air conditioning came back on.

Less than a week later Michael found himself in an empty classroom. There were no desks and no chairs. There was no whiteboard on any of the walls. The floors had just been waxed. In three days he would be a teacher. He wondered if his students would think he was cool. He was excited about having an opportunity to do something worthwhile.

*   *   *   *   *

In recent weeks the heat has let up, and Michael looks forward to a winter without freezing temperatures. He sits in his rocking chair on the porch while he waits for Derrick. They've decided to walk to the farmer's market downtown. The stroll to the market has become a familiar routine. The market itself is only a block long, but Michael enjoys comparing it to the one in Union Square and telling himself that he prefers the intimacy of Louisiana.

When they arrive at the market, they each buy a dollar cup of coffee and then split up. Michael makes conversation with the woman selling goat cheese and buys a small brick along with a pint of milk. Derrick buys a basket of squash and zucchini. At the end of the block is a tent selling flowers, and beside it a husband and wife in their mid-sixties play folk songs on fiddle and guitar.

When they return to the house, they empty their bags onto the counter. Derrick puts the milk in the fridge. When he closes the door, the magnetic calendar catches Michael's eye.

"I can't believe we're only three months into the school year."

"I know," says Derrick, "It's gonna be a helluva year..."

Winter

Year 1
Susan and Michael

Twilight seeps toward the horizon. The sound of leaves scraping over sidewalks can be heard from blocks away. Susan's hands are growing numb. Plastic bags filled with bottled liquor sag from the joints of her fingers and add to a sharp pain around her knuckles. Tonight Leah is going to introduce her to Marcel. She takes a deep breath. The air tingles her nose and moisture rises over her eyes. She is expecting a call from Steven. Her teeth begin to chatter and she clenches her jaw. *I need a new scarf.*

Upstairs, she puts on water for tea and stands by the window. At the edge of the neighborhood's light, large snowflakes begin to accent the sky. She watches them rock gently, side to side, through layers of air and then disappear into the still unfrozen ground. "The first snow," she whispers to herself. The sight stirs a spirit of celebration. For a moment, she senses a spell of tranquility. The kettle begins to rattle against its burner. Her phone lights up as it vibrates against the kitchen table.

Susan is taken aback by the vulnerability of Steven's tone. "I'm sorry, I know I've been a jackass through all of this but…" Susan sits in the nook of her large bay window. She holds her hand next to the glass and can feel the cold emanating from its surface. "I'm not going to see her anymore. I want to be with you…" She watches the snowflakes cling to the windowpane and melt into streaks of water. "More than anything I want us to be together." Silence. Steven's voice takes on notes of desperation, "Remember, *this*, and I know I've been a jackass, but remember, *this was the idea*, the whole idea was to give each other a chance to see other people but we always said we'd come back together."

"Whose idea was it Steven?" She can feel him trying to compose himself. Her emotions seem suspended above her. A sense of empowerment plays counterpoint to her bitterness. The snow outside is growing thicker.

"Yes, things got more complicated than I expected, and I know that you've been seeing someone else too. It's just that, look Susan, I miss you and…"

"Yes?"

"You know that I love you."

The words take her by surprise. "Steven, you can't just

blurt things out like that." Her instinct is to curse at him. She wants to punish him for the ways he's made her feel, but she's afraid. She thinks of Michael and feels a sting of pity.

"It's true," he continues, "for a while I thought I didn't, but I do."

"Steven," her voice is harsh, "just because things didn't work out with your other little girlfriend doesn't mean we can just start up like nothing has changed."

He answers immediately. "No, that's not what I meant, I know things have happened, but what I mean, what I'm trying to say, is that we can have something even better than before because… we won't have any *doubts*. The only thing I've learned from the past few months is that I want to be with you."

She rests her head against the window. Snow is beginning to build on the branches of barren trees. She slides the palm of her free hand across her thigh. She wonders what Michael would want her to say. Anxiety builds on the back of her neck. She remembers standing at dusk during a first snow as a child. She held her mother's hand and laughed when the flakes melted on her face. She fears her distance from the beauty around her.

"Steven."

"Yeah?"

"You know it's snowing? I've always loved the snow."

Steven is slow to answer.

"I remember. We were together last year for the first snow of the season."

"We made angels in front of the Cathedral." The

memory is still vivid.

Steven is relieved to be talking about something other than the last few months, "When we were laying there, you said something. We were in the imprints of our angels and we were watching the snow appear in the light of the Cathedral and float down to us, and you said something, what did you say it was like?"

Susan remembers the feeling of the snow melting underneath her body and seeping through her jeans and how she didn't care about the cold. "I said the flakes were like ashes from heaven."

Michael is seated facing the slanted wall of his attic apartment with a seaweed green blanket draped on his shoulders and wrapped over his feet. He is trying to start on his paper for Faraday's class, but he's distracted. His mind feels giddy at the thought of Susan's party tonight. Ever since breaking up with Kelsey, he has sensed the components of his life aligning. He is destined to be happy in love.

Last night, he dreamed of being together with Susan. Their touch brought light to the corners of they sky. They found themselves suspended above a field of even snow. "I," she whispered, "love *you* Michael."

Susan regrets inviting Steven to her party for Leah and Marcel. She stands at the door of her kitchen and blankly surveys the apartment. Sections of the morning's paper lay scattered on the coffee table. Dried teabags sit on stained paper towels. A pair of coffee mugs sits on the floor by the couch. She sees an image of Michael and Steven standing side by side. In the kitchen, dishes pile above the rim of the sink. *This is going to be a disaster.* Two strong knocks at the door shake her from her daze. The door swings open, and her friend Lillian steps into the apartment.

"Susan!" she says and thrusts out her arms. A bottle of wine hangs from each hand. Drops of melting snow fall from her arms. Susan takes the bottles, and Lillian braces herself against the wall to pull of her shoes. Her socks are grey and wool. "Can you believe the snow out there?" she asks.

Lillian has dark skin, large eyes, and a heart shaped face. She has been friends with Susan and Leah since freshmen year, but since then she has spent as much time out of the country as she's spent in Pittsburgh. Susan has always envied her sense of adventure and wondered at her ability to make people feel comfortable the moment she meets them. When Lillian's around, it seems the whole city reaches out to see her, but she always makes time with Susan a priority.

"I know," says Susan. Her voice sounds detached.

"Susan, what's wrong? You sound like someone just strangled a kitten."

Leah's energy is bursting. When Marcel opens her door, she springs from her seat to the sidewalk and jumps into his arms. Marcel pulls her against his chest and spins. Her toes carve waves into the sheets of falling snow. Leah feels transcendent. She can't wait to introduce Marcel to Susan and Lillian. Marcel's arm drapes around her shoulders and he pulls her close as they walk.

"Are you looking forward to meeting my friends?"

"Of course," he says, "I want to know everything about you."

"How did I get so lucky?" She tickles Marcel through his jacket.

"I thought it was because you were the most beautiful person in the world."

"That's right. And don't you forget it."

She presses her cheek into Marcel's jacket. *Susan will be happy for me.*

Michael takes the bus from Oakland to Squirrel Hill. Looking out the window, he sees his reflection projected onto the bright storefronts and newly white hills that pass by. A group of girls across from him are on their way to a frat party and are laughing loudly. Two of them have elaborately curled hair and heavier eye makeup than the rest. They talk about liquors they're going to stay away from. The scene strikes Michael as vulgar. He's happy to not be jockeying with frat brothers for the attention of girls like these. He remembers waking up with Susan at their bed and breakfast. Her cheek glowed in the morning light. Tonight he will debut as her boyfriend.

Leah has trouble processing the somber mood she finds when her and Marcel bound into Susan's apartment. Lillian sits with her hand on top of Susan's, and they both turn, long-faced, toward the door. Marcel is beaming. He tracks snow across the floor as he strides toward them with an extended hand.

"Susan...Lillian," her tone trying to stir a spirit of celebration, "this is the *Marcel* I've been telling you about!"

Susan takes his hand and smiles. "Oh, Marcel, I'm so glad to finally meet you. I'm sorry about the mess." She turns abruptly and begins to clear the coffee table. "I completely lost track of time."

Lillian gestures to her opened bottle of wine and a bottle of vodka. "Who wants some drinks?"

The bus stop is a few blocks from Susan's apartment. Michael exits along with three other people. One of them, a shorter man with a slender frame, crosses the street in front of him. Cars slow their pace to a crawl, and the snow fractures the light from their headlights. Michael becomes nervous. The slender man from the bus turns onto Susan's street a few steps in front of Michael. Michael pulls his hat down over his ears, and wipes his nose with his coat. The two of them end up standing together in front of Susan's building. When the door buzzes, they step inside.

"Are you a friend of Leah's?" asks Michael.

"Yeah, and Susan too," he replies. There is nothing friendly in his tone.

Their two pairs of boots approach but never quite reach a steady rhythm as they thud against the stairs up to the third floor. They are shoulder to shoulder when they knock at the door.

Susan refills her glass of wine. She watches Leah stare adoringly at Marcel. He is friendly and handsome, but Susan fears that Leah is giving too much of herself to this stranger.

Maybe she's just jealous. Susan doesn't like to admit that there has always been a competitive streak between her and Leah. Again, there is a knock at the door.

Susan stares dumbstruck. Her gaze seems to halt just before the plane of their faces. They stare back, innocent and impatient in snow-dusted jackets. Michael holds his hat in his hand.

"Um… Steven. Michael. I guess you two have met." They turn their necks toward each other, just enough to see the other in the corner of their eye. "Come in. Come in. We have drinks."

Michael and Steven offer Susan wobbly one-legged bows as they bend to pull off their boots. Neither one seems eager to talk first. She feels disoriented. Suddenly Marcel is in front of her holding his phone between both hands.

"Some friends of mine from France," he says, "they're at a bar around the corner and I was wondering if I could invite them over here."

Her response seems to come from a voice standing behind her. "Of course. Of course."

Leah is frustrated with Susan. *Doesn't she realize how important tonight is to me? All I wanted was for her to take time to get to know Marcel. Instead she has to go and make herself the center of attention.*

She needs a drink. Steven is already by the liquor topping off his glass of vodka with a splash of Sprite.

"You know," says Leah, "you have a lot of nerve coming out here tonight."

"Susan invited me."

"Well, I wish she wouldn't have."

"Cheers." He taps his glass against hers and walks toward Susan and Lillian.

Michael is lost in a haze. People arrive in a steady stream while, across the room, Susan talks with Steven. Michael tries not to stare, but he can't seem to look away from them for more than a few moments before his eyes settle back to their corner of the room. Steven is smaller than he imagined, even slightly shorter than Susan. He is tempted to be angry, but he tells himself he just needs to be patient. At the end of the night, he will be alone with Susan.

Over an hour passes without any contact. He watches her finish with Steven and disappear into the bathroom with Leah. Marcel's friends arrive with more bottles of wine. At one point, Lillian appears beside him to assure him that Susan is "horribly torn up about all this," and "she knows it's unfair to put you and Steven through this," and "it's really her fault for not knowing what she wants."

"So she invites both of us to the same party and tries to keep from looking at me?"

"Michael. I know she cares about you."

Michael realizes he has hardly moved since he arrived. He watches Steven pour another drink and throw a half-drunken glare in his direction. Leah emerges from the bathroom and whispers, "You're my favorite," before she passes by and leaps toward Marcel. Everyone seems to be speaking French. They laugh at words he can't understand. The snow forms a perfect curve as it piles on the windowsill. Susan is still nowhere to be seen.

Susan stands before the bathroom mirror unable to look her reflection in the eye. She feels guilty, yet oddly detached from the responsibility of souring the mood of her party. The tension has a sense of forced inevitability. It's been hell trying to untangle her feelings for Steven and Michael, searching for names to put to her doubts and desires. She knows tonight will be decisive, but for now, she is paralyzed. She clings to the comfort of her indecision. She presses her fingers into her forehead and worries that Steven is getting drunk. Michael must hate her. Maybe Leah is right: maybe she is doing all of this just to steal attention for herself. *What is wrong with me? Do I even deserve to be happy?*

"I'm sorry love," says Leah, "I was hoping tonight would be different."

"It's OK," replies Marcel, pouring her another glass of wine, "I'm still having a good time."

"Because *I'm* here?"

"Yes, because I'm with the most beautiful girl in the world."

"From now on, to be happy, all we'll need is each other."

Marcel sets one hand on Leah's hip and raises his glass in a toast.

"To us," he says.

Michael has decided to leave. He puts on his shoes and grabs his coat from the closet. He hopes no one will notice him. When he closes the closet door, Susan's voice startles him from behind.

"I was just about to ask if you'd like to go for a walk."

"I thought you'd disappeared."

"I'm sorry. But. If you can wait a minute I'd like to take a walk with you outside."

"I'll meet you downstairs."

She tries not to react to the coarseness in his tone. "I'll be down in a minute."

Susan moves quickly from the front door to the curb where Michael is standing and takes his arm. The streets are empty and thick with snow. Cars hidden by a blanket of powder offer a feeling of desertion. The trees glisten in the streetlight.

"I love this," says Susan. "It's so wonderful when the first snow can be a real snow."

"It's good to hear your voice."

They begin to walk. There is a block behind them before either of them speak again.

"I broke up with Kelsey."

"You didn't have to do that."

"No, I did, it wasn't right."

"No I guess it wasn't."

Michael looks at his feet and then back to Susan.

"I was hoping that you and I…"

"I know… Me too."

They turn away from the street and toward Schenely Park. Their footprints mark their path in the snow.

"So, what's going on with you and Steven?"

"I'm not sure."

"Well, I think he may be passed out in your bedroom."

Susan laughs. "Don't worry, I'm not going to let him spend the night." Then, worrying he's misunderstood, "I think I just need to be alone tonight."

"Oh." He sounds hurt.

"I'm sorry Michael."

The light from a distant road marks the edge of the park. Michael wonders if Susan will want to turn back soon. He can feel the conversation weighing on her.

Without ever having decided, Susan is suddenly aware of what is about to happen.

"So, I guess this is it," says Michael, hoping that Susan will protest.

She rests her head against his shoulder. He feels stable and strong. "Michael, you're one of the greatest people I've ever known." Her voice is somber.

"But."

"But I'm not sure I'm ready for…"

"You're not ready for us to be together."

"I'm sorry."

"But you're ready to get back together with Steven?"

Susan stops walking and lets go of Michael's arm.

"Maybe, I don't know. I can't get away from this feeling that things between me and Steven aren't finished yet. Like we owe it to each other to try and make it work."

"I understand." His voice is bitter.

"Michael, remember, we never made any promises to each other. I never asked you to break up with Kelsey. You've always known that Steven is an important part of my life."

Hearing Steven's name is like salt in his eyes. "I guess I never really expected this to work out," he says, wondering if it's true.

They catch each other's eyes.

"We've had something special."

"I know."

"I should probably head back now. Do you want to come?"

"No I think I'll stay out here for awhile."

Susan steps forward, kisses Michael gently on the cheek, and then turns away without looking back.

Michael walks on, taking notice of the blurred borders between snow and shadow. The freshness of the landscape borders on fantasy. As he walks, his mind sews a thread of inevitability through his memories of Susan. *I guess love can never be true for very long.* When he reaches the light from the road, he turns and looks back at his tracks. The trail makes a gentle crescent. He traces it back until he finds the place where he continued on alone.

Year 5
Derrick

Derrick sits at a small table next to his cot. His travel journal is open to a blank page in front of him. He twirls his pen around his thumb and looks absently toward the corner of the room. In an hour he'll walk to Rosa's house to have dinner with her and her mother. It's the only dinner invitation he's received since he arrived and he's nervous about what to expect. He turns back to the blank journal and dates the corner of the page. He begins to write:

It's been just over a month since I arrived in Nicaragua. I've wanted to write more often but I spend most of my time working on lessons for school and grading assignments.

Life is good here. In the mornings I wake up just after dawn, boil some coffee in a pot and fix myself an egg with rice for breakfast. Sometimes I take a walk through the trails in the woods but normally I sit on the deck by my room and just try to think through my lessons for the day and remember what I need to talk about with different children. Most of the families are up at dawn but people move quietly in the morning and my room is removed from the other houses so I mostly just hear the sounds of the forest. Sometimes Ramon asks me to help him load the tractor.

The school is a short downhill walk from here, and I normally arrive half an hour early to get things ready for the day. The time just before the children arrive is nice. I feel calm. There's a unique kind of optimism that comes with teaching and I enjoy it.

He moves his hand to start a new paragraph, but instead he turns the pen upside down and taps its dull side twice against the page. He leans back in his chair. Derrick first met Rosa after his first day at the school. She came to pick up her cousins and made a point to introduce herself in English. Derrick admired her straight black hair and earth brown eyes. She seemed shy. Derrick imagined her cousins talking about how they played games all day and felt embarrassed that he hadn't taught them more. He told her the children had a lot of energy and she laughed. Rosa walked away and her cousins darted in circles around her as they played. Derrick thought of her as a shepherd and warned himself against becoming attracted to her. *That's the last thing I need.* Derrick hears a songbird outside his window. He leans forward and touches his pen to the page.

Everyone has been kind to me. The parents send me food and a couple times a week Ramon will come by and offer me a beer. Ramon is interesting. He doesn't talk much. At first I thought the silences were awkward but now I realize he's somewhat of a loner. I think I'm the only person he feels like he can just sit with to drink a beer. I enjoy the company.

Sometimes on weekends I help him plant new coffee trees. The soil comes from compost the whole community contributes to. When we're done he'll slap my shoulder and tell me that I'm becoming a real Nicaraguan. It's good to feel useful.

Derrick's thoughts return to dinner with Rosa and her mother. Soon he'll have to walk over. He replays the conversation from yesterday when Rosa invited him. She seemed both hesitant and eager, and the memory makes him smile. He dismisses the idea that she was flirting with him. *But maybe…* The idea seems ridiculous. He's sure that the rest of the village would disapprove. Besides, he's not here for romance. *She's probably just being friendly.* He reminds himself that her mother is ill and feels guilty for the flirtatious edge to his thoughts. He's never met Rosa's mother. He hopes that she's feeling better but doubts that she is. The village has been supportive to her and Rosa. They send over food, and the children help with their chores. Derrick can't always understand what people say about them, but he's noticed how they always seem high-spirited when Rosa is around, and then speak with a kind of resigned sympathy when she leaves. He wonders if anyone has an accurate idea of her condition. He knows that everyone is praying for them.

It's strange, I came here looking for something in myself that could bring me some sort of balance. I never imagined that the change would come from what I've found in other people. Something about this community has worked to show me that everything is OK. Beneath everything back home that annoys me there's a human spirit and I can't let myself forget that.

Anyway... Today is my birthday. I haven't told anyone but it's been a good birthday and I've been invited to a dinner at Rosa's house with her mother. It's the first time I'll eat in one of the family's homes. I hope I'll be able to hold a conversation in Spanish.

That's all for now. I want to try and write more often.

Derrick closes the journal and ties it shut. He stands, brushes his fingers over his hair and rubs his beard with his knuckles. He's in good spirits. Rosa is looking forward to seeing him. As he walks toward her house, he finds himself imagining where each of them was six months ago and what they were doing. He sees an image of her carrying water down this path, back to her mother, and of him bent over textbooks in the university library, and he relishes in the improbability that their lives are now intertwined. Some children pass in the distance and wave toward him. He knows that he's an outsider, but for the first time in several years, he feels that he's somewhere he wants to be.

Year 3
Michael and Derrick

The snow from earlier in the week has broken down and mixed with the dirt in the sidewalk. A light rain falls on turned up collars and downcast faces. The sky is layered in shades of gray. Michael steps between the piles of slush and listens to the escalating patter of rain against pavement. His thoughts fold back against themselves. *I should have told Veronica about Susan.* He remembers the steadiness in her voice when she told him to call her *sometime soon* and wrote out her number on a cocktail napkin. She looked at him like he had been chosen. She smiled when he touched his hand to her knee.

A sharp breeze splashes his face with rain. A city bus lets out a mechanical groan as it slows to a stop across the street. Veronica's gaze pierces his thoughts. On the next block there is a flower shop. He decides to buy Susan a dozen white roses. He'll have them delivered. Slush soaks into his shoes.

Derrick arrives at the venue before Michael and takes a seat by the small stage. The table is small, round, and wooden. Derrick is surprised more people aren't here. Glasses clink from behind the bar. He checks the time: twenty minutes until Dahntae is scheduled to start his set. He leans back and notices that his chair is uneven.

Each time the door opens, a flash of cold air barrels

toward him. He considers putting on his jacket but decides against it. A waitress comes for his drink order and he asks for a Yuengling. Tomorrow he has exams. His internship at the architecture firm is growing tedious. For the moment, he feels good. He has been looking forward to this show for weeks.

Michael takes his seat, unties his scarf, and inquires about "this Dahntae character."

"I found some of his stuff on the internet a few months ago. He's pretty cool."

"Is he local?"

"I think he tours around the east coast. He was in New York last month."

"What's the drink situation?"

"Somebody's coming around."

Dahntae is a tall and slender black man with rich brown eyes framed by thick-rimmed glasses. He wears dark denim jeans that are frayed around the knees and pockets, and he holds his acoustic guitar by the neck as he walks onto the stage. Michael watches Derrick lean forward and focus his attention.

The room settles and Dahntae's guitar makes a clean sound. Michael's feet are beginning to warm up. He slides his hand into his pocket and fingers the napkin with Veronica's number. *Maybe I have to call her.* Dahntae's voice has a soothing tone. Michael conjures pairs of incompatible certainties: *I can't be dishonest to Susan. I can't ignore Veronica's invitation. I'm too young to settle. I'm already in love.*

He collects himself and tries to focus on the music. Dahntae is finishing up an arrangement of "Lonesome Valley". A light applause dusts across the room. Dahntae says that the next song is an original composition.

Derrick is drawn in by the guitar line. It is intricate yet crisp. Dahntae closes his eyes. Derrick can feel the room grow more attentive. He narrows his attention to Dahntae's right hand. His fingers flutter across the strings. The baseline asserts itself and then softens behind the melody. There is a narrative feel to the progression. As Derrick watches he becomes aware, slowly at first, of a steady resonance pouring out from the body of the guitar, a unifying purr sliding toward him, like a razor over glass. Dahntae opens his eyes, and leans toward the microphone.

You'll have to stop thinking, he sings.
If you hope to understand,
that you are you, his voice rings with informal certainty,
and I am who I am,

While nothing, may be,
what it means to be.
I know, alright,
how it seems to me.

People can't be purchased,
nor plot their plans to come.
Nothing false will flower
and much is left undone.

Though nothing, may be,
what it seems to be.
I know, alright,
what it means to me.

Dahntae transitions directly into the next song. The chords scrape against each other, creating a pattern of dissonance without resolution. Derrick's mind wanders to the monotony of his week. He is not proud of the work he's done for the architecture firm, but he has been consistently praised for it. He feels contempt for the naked enthusiasm of the other interns. An impatient foreboding churns in his thoughts. He feels a need to disappear. The chair wobbles beneath him. *How much of life is sacrifice?*

Derrick closes his eyes and returns his attention to Dahntae's guitar. He imagines the music entering his flesh and lifting him from his seat. He watches himself float through the roof of the café and over the hills of the Southside. Moonlight shimmers in the Monongahela and his body begins to glow: pillars of light jump from his skin, the city is watching, there is a flash of light, the stars shine in a golden sky and suddenly, he is gone.

Michael says goodnight to Derrick but decides not to go straight home to Susan's. He drinks a beer at the bar and fingers the napkin in his pocket. He drives out of the Southside and crosses the bridge toward Oakland. He parks a few blocks from the Cathedral of Learning and decides to walk there and back. The rumble of house parties carries through the empty streets to his right. He walks with his hands in his pockets and crumbles the napkin into a ball. He tries to clear his mind.

The scene behind the Cathedral gets his attention. Rain has frozen on top of the snow, and the lawn has the look of a frozen sea. Trees cast shadows into the waves around them. Barren branches stab into the night. Michael decides to walk across the ice toward the trees. He focuses on keeping his balance and for a moment feels very much alone. Michael looks right and notices the silhouette of a man sitting beside a bench. He turns to walk by and is surprised to realize that the man is Dahntae.

Dahntae doesn't notice Michael until he's just a few yards away. He looks up, recognizes Michael from the show, and then returns to the paper between his hands. Michael notices a pair of lifelike paper trees sitting on the bench beside him and hesitates before walking on. Dahntae gestures for him to sit down.

"Origami?" asks Michael.

Dahntae nods, "Most art," he says, "is a process of addition or subtraction. We add paint to canvas, we connect pieces of iron, we chisel marble to reveal a form, we place words on a page; we cut, sand, and polish wood, but origami..." He pauses and presses his forefinger into a fold. "In origami, there's no addition or subtraction, there is simply a re-imagining, a manipulation of a single sheet. Infinite possibilities within the most severe limitations." He twists the paper and places a small paper bench between the trees beside him. "I like to think of art as having less to do with breaking boundaries and more to do with reimagining within our limitations."

"I'm guessing you're not just talking about writing songs."

"No," Dahntae smiles wide, "*life man*, I'm always talking about life." His tone mocks his choice of words.

"Well, the limits of a sheet of paper are easier to see than the limits of ourselves," says Michael.

"Yes," he jokes, "that's the trouble with metaphors. They're always breaking down."

Dahntae picks up another sheet of paper and folds while he talks, "All I mean is that we don't have to try and construct meaning through only addition and subtraction. Meaning, more than anything, is woven with passion and *passion* can only come from within..." At the word 'passion' Michael's mind instantly skips to Veronica. "At least, that's how I like to think about it."

Dahntae lifts his hand from the flattened sheet, and a paper crane takes form. He stands, hands the crane to Michael, tells him to keep it, and walks away. Heading back to his car, Michael bends the wings of the crane at their crease and mimics the sound of a bird under his breath. The paper is thinner than he imagined. He unfolds the crane back into a square sheet and tries to recreate the bird as he walks. It doesn't take long for Michael to become frustrated. He makes a paper airplane instead and then unfolds it again before crumpling the paper into a ball. He drops it into a trashcan on the street. He tells himself to try and learn origami but then lets the thought float away, out of reach.

When Michael returns to his car, the cold is heavy in his limbs. He takes out his phone and finds a text from Susan, "The flowers are beautiful. Thank you my love." He sets the phone on his knee, pulls Veronica's napkin from his pocket, and straightens it on the steering wheel. He looks at the number and then back to his phone. He begins to dial.

Year 7
Susan

Susan stands motionless in front of the sliding doors of the Tampa airport under a sign that reads "Baggage Claim." The air is wet, and sunlight gleams on the hoods of the cars that peter by. She hopes that she will recognize her aunt Barb when she arrives to pick her up. It's been ten years since her last visit.

Groups of people Susan recognizes from her plane gather together in front of large concrete pillars. They hold cell phones to their ears and wave toward cars that pull to the curb beside them. Middle-aged women wearing airline uniforms smoke cigarettes by the door. A young couple reunites a few yards to her right, and their stomachs press together as they kiss. Susan is surprised when she notices rings on their fingers.

When Aunt Barb pulls up, Susan is the last person from her flight still waiting.

"The traffic," she begins, "was *aw*ful," Barb cuts the wheel and hits the gas to speed in front of a large white truck. Her hands are a mess with nervous energy and her head repetitively jerks to look back over her shoulder, "I'll tell you what, driving down here sometimes you gotta fight for yourself, you'd think they were trying to keep me pulled up on the curb back there." She takes a dramatic breath and assumes a more matter-of-fact tone, "Anyway, the traffic, as I said, was awful, although it shouldn't be so bad going back, and you know I had the worst time getting away from your mother and grandma to get down here, your mother, bless her, sometimes just can't make up her mind what she wants," Barb jerks the wheel and the cab of the car sways above its chassis. "And I tried to tell her this wasn't the best time for you to fly in but it is was it is, you know, it's what God means it to be, and unlike some other people I try not to let the little things get to me too much. Goodness, your aunt Tracy has been a wreck since all of this started, just snapping at everyone, trying to bite the head off of anyone who tries to do something nice for her. But," she smacks the wheel with her palm, "I'm glad to see you Susan. It's a good thing you came down here for your grandmother."

"Thanks for coming to pick me up."

"Oh, of course darling, of course. You're family."

Susan dressed in Pittsburgh this morning and still has two shirts on under her sweater. She scratches at her shoulder and looks out the window. The land extends around the highway in a single sheet and is marked mostly by palm trees and parking lots. The steady hum of the road rings in her ears. Susan is already looking forward to going back to Pittsburgh, but she's glad that she's here now. She cracks her window.

"So," says Barb, "your mother tells me you've been seeing someone."

"Is that what she says?"

"Is it serious?"

"I guess you could say that. His name is James."

"What do you mean, you *could* say that? He's not just stringing you along is he? God, that would break your mother's heart."

"No, it's nothing like that. It's just that we've only been together about a year and a half."

"That's *long* enough, I'd say."

"Well," she hesitates but then continues, "not to disrespect family tradition or anything, but before I make a commitment, I'd kind of like to be sure that it's actually going to work out."

Barb snorts in a fit of laughter, "Good luck with *that* one sweetheart." Barb slaps her knee and then lays on the horn as a light blue sedan cuts in front of her. "Would it *kill* people around here to learn how to drive? *Would it?*"

When they arrive, Susan feels a pang of guilt for being more concerned with when she'll be able to call James than with the purpose of her visit. She hopes her mother is coping all right. She wonders in what condition she'll find Grandma. The door is unlocked. She knocks twice and then pushes it open.

"Mom?"

Her mother's voice: "Oh, Susan, we're in here."

She passes through a dining room and a small kitchen and then finds her mother and grandmother seated in front of a large newly unpackaged television.

"Susan, I'm so glad to see you," she smiles, "Mom. Mother. You remember Susan don't you? Your granddaughter."

Susan's grandmother fidgets awkwardly and sinks

further into the wheel chair that rises above her on all sides. Susan remembers her mother saying that Grandma weighs seventy-three pounds.

"I want to go home." Grandma's voice is weak but demanding. The phrase rattles Susan.

"You *are* home Mother."

"I want to go home."

"Where is home?" Susan's mother takes her hand, "Is heaven home?"

The question makes Susan uneasy.

"No, no, no. I want to go home. *Home*."

Susan hears Aunt Barb walking up behind her.

Her voice cuts into the air, "I see how you were raised. Leave your elders to haul in your luggage from the car." Theatrically, she swings the suitcase and plants it beside Susan.

"Barb!" scolds Susan's mother. Barb laughs.

"Oh lighten up," she turns to Susan, "I'm just joking with you girl; you know that."

Susan retreats to the guest bedroom and changes her clothes. Stacked in her suitcase are four dresses that she's made over the past several months. She takes out each dress and lays them out on the neatly made bed. Looking at the dresses calms her nerves. From left to right, she can see her improvement as a seamstress. Each dress reminds her of a collection of challenges she had to overcome. When she's sewing, the hours pass far beneath her. When she's finished, she feels satisfied. She credits James with centering her enough to be able to focus on sewing. She asks herself if she has time to give him a call.

"Susan," it's her mother, "What are you doing in there?"

"Nothing Mom, just changing."

"Aunt Tracy said she was preparing some soup for grandma. Do you think you could walk over to her place and pick it up for us? She's just around the corner."

Aunt Tracy is smoking a cigarette while sitting on a wicker chair by her front door. When she sees Susan approaching, she smiles broadly and stands.

"Oh my goodness, *Susan*, look at you," her voice is hoarse, "it's good to see you, come in, come in." Tracy opens her arms for an embrace and then leads Susan into her house, her cigarette still burning.

"Susan, you look great. And such a beautiful dress. Where did you get it?"

Susan tries not to sound boastful, "Oh, I made it. I made it from a vintage pattern I found online."

Tracy congratulates her on being so useful with her talents and again calls her beautiful before walking to the stove and turning off the top right burner. The room smells of cigarettes and chicken soup.

"How long are you going to be staying?" she pours the soup into a plastic container.

"Just 'til the day after tomorrow."

"Oh," she sounds disappointed, "well, it's good that you're here. I'm glad you and your mother can watch Grandma for at least a little while. Lord knows I can use a break." She sighs to emphasize her exhaustion. "I swear, I don't think I've slept two solid hours since the stroke."

"How is Grandma doing?" Susan asks, fearing the

worst.

"Oh, she's coming along, it's not going too well though. Lord knows she can't do much on her own, keeps yapping about how she wants to go home. Keeps looking confused when her children come over. 'Home,' she says. 'I want to go home.'" Tracy presses down the lid of the container with her palm and hands it to Susan. "You should probably get along now with grandma's lunch. Lord knows your mother will get to worrying if she thinks you're spending too much time over here." Tracy stubs out her cigarette in the ashtray on the table and reaches for another one.

"Thank you," says Susan.

"Oh," calls Tracy, "before you go, I told Brittany you'd be coming down. I know she's looking forward to seeing you. You know Sophie is almost five now, and your cousin Brit, she's still a beauty. Gonna be a lucky man that gets those two."

"It'll be nice to see them," she says. Susan tries to remember if she's spoken with her cousin at all since Sophie was born.

After they eat, Susan's mother decides to take Grandma on a tour of some of her old houses. "It may help her realize that this is her home now," she says.

Susan helps her grandmother into the passenger seat of the van. She cringes at the squish of her grandma's flesh around her fingers. Susan takes the seat behind her, and the van jostles them both as her mother backs out of the driveway. Flat, familiar looking houses pass by the window. Susan feels naïve for expecting this to be a very different type of visit. A thread of regret stitches its way through Susan's blunted emotions. On the plane, she rehearsed questions to ask her grandmother. Questions about her relationship with Grandpa and what her mother was like growing up. She was never close with her grandmother, and now she realizes she never will be. The failure stretches around her like clouds across the sky.

As they drive, Grandma looks at the dashboard. When they arrive at one of her old houses, she fixes her eyes on the curb outside her window.

"Is this home, Mom?"

Grandma shakes her head. "No," she says emphatically.

Susan's mother looks back over her shoulder and laughs through an awkward smile. The gesture is meant to bring lightness to the situation, but it just makes Susan uneasy. "Please Mom," she says, "don't laugh at her."

When they return to the house, Grandma protests, "No, not here. I don't want to go *here*." But Susan and her mother ignore her complaints and lift her back into her wheelchair.

Once inside, Susan walks straight to the guest bedroom. She takes a deep breath, tucks her hair behind her ear, and calls James. He answers on the second ring and asks how she's getting along with her grandmother.

"It's complicated," she says, " I miss you."

"My apartment seems colder when you're not here."

The sound of his voice helps her relax. "It's good to hear your voice. Without you I think I might just fall to pieces out here."

"Well, when you're not here I feel like I'm beached on the shore. You're my rising tide. You lift all my boats."

181

Susan laughs.

There is a knock at her door. "Susan, can you come out here? I want your help getting Grandma into bed."

"I have to go," she whispers to James.

"Tell your mom I say hello."

"Susan?" comes the call again, her mother's voice balancing between impatience and concern.

"OK," she says to James, and then louder, "I'm coming Mom." She whispers her goodbye and then opens the door. Her mother is standing with her arms crossed. A few feet behind her, Grandma is sitting quietly.

"Susan, I love you and I'm glad you're here but you could have at least helped me get Grandma inside. We're here to help her you know." She sounds hurt and exhausted.

"I'm sorry Mom."

The next day, Susan sleeps in. When she wakes up, she lies in bed and listens to her mother clear the table and wash dishes. She thinks about the pages from *Love in America* she brought with her and wonders if she'll have time to work on them. She thinks about James and wishes he were here. The room is cluttered with wooden furniture and metal picture frames. Drawings of angels hang on the walls. She hopes that Grandma has a better day today.

Barb and Tracey stop by in the morning, and by noon their frustrations have turned to hostility. Susan watches on with growing discomfort.

"Look Tracy," says Barb, "we can't keep going on like this."

"No one is going to tell me that I shouldn't be taking

care of my own mother."

"She needs *professional* care Tracy."

"The only thing places like that want to care for is her money. Just because you don't want to help out around here doesn't mean we should cast her away."

"*Help out?* All I do is help out around here."

"Right Barb. And when was the last time you stayed overnight?"

"Tracy, you're not certified for this type of thing and I hate to say it but I don't trust that mother is getting the best care that she can get."

Tracy's eyes grow wide, "I see, you'd rather she was with a bunch of strangers in white coats than with—"

"Please," interjects Susan's mother, "this is not the way that family should talk."

Barb and Tracy look away from each other.

"Aunt Tracy," says Susan, "Did you say that Brittany and Sophie were coming by?"

"Yes," she says, her tone softening as if to prove that she would much rather be civil, "I'm so glad you reminded me. They should be here soon."

The mood continues to fray. Susan wishes someone would acknowledge that it's normal for this to be hard on everyone.

Grandma's voice crackles over the baby monitor, "Someone come help me pack. It's time I have to go home."

"Mother," yells Barb, "You are home. This is your home. You're home right now."

Brittany, Sophie, and Susan have set up on the patio furniture in the backyard.

"A couple months ago I was offered the job of Lifestyle editor. It's a promotion. I like it," answers Susan.

"How long have you been at the paper now?" asks Brittany.

"About six years now."

"It's really been forever since we've seen each other hasn't it?"

"I guess it has."

Sophie's attention has been hooked by a squirrel playing at the base of a nearby tree. She slides from her chair and begins to approach it. When she's halfway there, she turns toward her mother and offers a full-toothed grin. Her thin blonde hair waves in front of her eyes.

"She's adorable," says Susan.

"Everyday she's more and more her own person. She wears me out, but I love her more than anything."

"It must be hard."

Brittany hesitates, "Well, it'd be harder if her father was still around. Then I'd have two people to take care of."

Susan isn't sure why she fell out of contact with her cousin. When they were children, they would always celebrate the time they spent together. They could be inseparable for days on end. Since going to college ten years ago, they've hardly spoken at all.

"That bad?"

"Well, he gave me Sophie. I like to say he was the best mistake I ever made."

Brittany leans back and watches Sophie running

recklessly around the tree with her eyes fixed upward into the branches. She lets out a long, soft sigh. The gesture betrays her state of perpetual exhaustion. "I hope she doesn't trip and hurt herself," she says.

"She seems to be having a good time."

Brittany calls to Sophie, "Sophie, come back here and visit with your cousin Susan." Sophie looks disappointed but begins to walk back quietly.

"So," says Susan, "tell me about your life. How have you been the last ten years or so?" They smile at the absurdity of the question. Sophie stops in front of her chair, "The squirrel's name is Eli. He told me he thinks you two is very pretty."

Brittany pulls Sophie into her arms, "He sounds like a very nice squirrel."

"He is. He is."

The breeze picks up, and Susan enjoys its warmth. *It's good to be in Florida again.* She watches Brittany kiss Sophie on the forehead and envies the connection she sees between them. A breeze brushes her hair against her face. Susan is taken by the sense that something has shifted inside her over the past twenty-four hours. Her daily life seems cloistered and far away from here. There is a feeling like she has just stepped out of an ice cold bath.

As the conversation continues, Susan is surprised by how much time she devotes to talking about her and Michael, and how insecure she sounds when describing the other phases of her life. Brittany listens intently and asks a number of questions about James. Susan explains that he's a chef and is working on opening a second restaurant. She is tempted to describe their relationship as bound for marriage, but decides against it.

"We're happy," she says, "and we're in love. But the future is always difficult and I wouldn't say we're absolutely perfect for each other."

"Wow. Perfection. That's quite the bar you're setting."

"Stop. You know what I mean,"

"Hey, I'm going to run inside for a minute. Can you watch Sophie?"

"I'd love to."

When Brittany is inside Sophie turns to Susan. It's clear that she has an idea.

"Do you want to play imagination?" she asks.

"Of course I do. How do you play?"

"You don't know how to play imagination!" Sophie is clearly excited to explain, "First *I* say part of a story and then *you* say part of the story and we make a story with our imagination."

"OK. I think I got it."

"I'll start," says Sophie emphatically, "Once there was a little girl and a fairy came to the girl and said she could fly… Now you go!"

"OK… But at first the little girl didn't believe her and she said, 'but Fairy, I am not a fairy, I can't fly'…"

"'No.' said the fairy. 'you *can* fly.' And she touched the girl's hand and they both flew off the ground and flew over a tree and the girl went 'Wheeeeeee. I can fly.'"

"And they flew through clouds and over mountains and under bridges and all around the world."

"But when the girl got home, her mother was angry

'cause she missed dinner."

"*But,* when the girl explained what she was doing, the mother forgave her and said that she was proud of her and said that she was the luckiest mother in the whole world."

"That's right," Sophie spots Brittany coming back from the house and raises her voice, "she's the luckiest mother in the whole world!"

In the evening the house is quiet. Grandma has fallen asleep, and Susan and her mother are straightening up the kitchen. Susan remembers that, in the morning, she'll be flying back to Pittsburgh. James will meet her at the airport. Their stomachs will press together as they kiss. By afternoon she will be back at her desk at work. Maybe over the weekend she'll try to sew a jacket, she's never done that before. She returns the final stack of plates to their place in the cupboard and turns to her mother.

"Mom, I brought some dresses I wanted to show you. You want to see?"

In the bedroom she places the dresses across the comforter.

"Oh my," says her mother, "the things you do. I never dreamed I'd have such a talented daughter. You know your great-aunt Bessie used to make her own clothes. These are wonderful."

"Thanks. I really enjoy it. I've been getting better too." Susan takes a seat on the edge of the bed, and her mother sits next to her.

"Mom," she says, "Is Grandma going to get better?"

Her mother looks to the ground and fingers the edge of

the bed. "No. I don't think so. She could be like this for a long time. But I don't think she's going to get better."

"I'm sorry."

Her mother looks away, and Susan thinks she'll cry, but she just dabs the corners of her eyes with a tissue and turns back toward Susan. Susan has always admired her mother's ability to ration her emotions.

"It's certainly not easy being here. I hope to God you never have to see me like this." Susan takes her mother's hand, and her mother grips it firmly. "You know, you should tell that young man of yours, James, that I'm looking forward to the next time I get to see him. I like this one a lot."

"Thank you Mom. I will."

"Have you two started thinking about… well… have you talked at all about the future?"

Susan has known that this question would come up, "We have. But I seem to have trouble thinking about it too much. It's like… Well, for somewhat obvious reasons, I'm kind of terrified of marriage. Or at least I'm terrified of divorce."

"Oh honey, your father…" She collects herself, "Your father and I, we were both very selfish and insecure when we had you. We didn't know how to love each other and we didn't know what we wanted from each other." She pauses, "It was very rough for me, and I know it was rough for you too, when your father left, but sometimes we're not meant to understand God's plan for us. And your father was a very selfish man and I don't think I realized that until after we were married. I always thought it was something wrong with me, that I wasn't giving him enough." She stands and brushes her palms on her jeans, "I don't think James is like that and I think you have more self-esteem than I did back then. I think that if you're in love you two will be just fine."

Susan reaches out her arms and pulls her mother toward her. Her mother holds her close and then relaxes.

"Thank you Mom. We don't talk like this often enough."

"You have no idea how grateful I am that you came here to be with me. Between your grandmother and your aunts I don't think I could have taken it here without you."

"Why is it that you sisters fight so much anyway?"

"Oh honey, that's how grandma raised us."

The next morning Susan steps out of the shower and looks at her figure in the mirror. She watches the steam waft between herself and her reflection, and she begins to question, in a relaxed way, the type of life she wants for herself. She inhales deeply through her nose and enjoys the way the hot air makes her feel. Slowly, a sense of certainty seems to encroach. A thought begins to form in front of her like a drop upon the mirror. Her hands are drawn to her stomach. *I need to be a mother.*

By the time she is drying her hair, a sense of urgency has built up around the idea. She thinks of James and wonders what he'd think if she told him. There is a sense of promise. When she turns off the hair dryer, her mother's voice calls through the door.

"Come on hon, we don't want you to miss your flight."

Year 7
Michael

Michael stands still in his classroom and listens to the distant rumbling of students at dismissal. Torn paper and broken pencils litter the floor of his classroom. The desks are either crooked or entirely out of place, and most chairs are at least two feet from the desks they are paired with. A few are knocked over with their backs to the floor. Michael begins to work his way around the room, straightening desks and pushing in chairs. Sometimes this end of day ritual frustrates him, but sometimes, on days like this, he finds it soothing. He surveys the walls of his classroom and feels embarrassed by how bare they are. He should have math theorems and student work and class rules on display, but instead the only thing hanging is a sheet of chart paper with "I Don't Get It" written inside a circle with a line crossed through it. He looks at the pile of yesterday's unit tests stacked on his desk and hopes his students did well.

When he sits down to start grading, Takeya and Farhea walk into the room. Farhea is tall for an 8th grader and rail thin. Her hair is pulled back tightly over her scalp, and she has an energetic smile that she often displays in place of a 'Hello.' Takeya is slightly shorter and pudgier than Farhea. Her natural hair sticks out in different directions. She holds her lips pressed tightly together, and she averts her eyes as she normally does when she approaches Michael. He is happy to see them. Farhea speaks up and asks for help with their homework.

"Of course," says Michael. He gestures to a group of

desks in the middle of the room.

Takeya and Farhea are two of Michael's most motivated students in his sixth hour class. They can always be counted on to listen attentively to the day's lesson and try to stay focused on their classwork. Unfortunately, most of their classmates tend to treat math class more like an indoor recess where they are occasionally forced to hold pencils. Still, day after day, Takeya and Farhea do their best to block out the noise and focus on their work while Michael spends his time trying to diffuse the misbehavior that boils up around them. Today Deiby took the classroom broom and chased a pair of students around the room and into the hallway screaming, but Takeya and Farhea held one hand to the side of their faces and never set down their pencils. Michael knows it can't be easy for them. He often feels guilty for not being able to offer them the education they deserve.

The three of them sit together, and Michael goes back over the class notes they took today. The new unit they've started involves graphing lines in the coordinate plane, and Michael soon realizes that introducing the concept of a function as well as vocabulary for y, m, x and b was probably too much for the first lesson. The girls scrunch their eyebrows as he tries to describe why 'b' will always tell us where the line crosses the y-axis. Takeya chews on her eraser. Michael leans back in his chair. He should have limited the lesson to plotting points.

The girls stay with him for close to an hour, and by the end, they are able to draw lines when given an equation in the form of $y = mx + b$. As they're packing up, Takeya asks if he knows what she got on yesterday's test.

"I'm about to grade them right now," he says.

When they reach the door, Farhea extends her arm in an exaggerated wave goodbye, "Thank you Mr. M," she says.

The door shuts, and Michael slouches in his chair. His feet are sore. If he hadn't just told Takeya he would have her test for tomorrow, he would probably push off grading them until the weekend. *At least tomorrow is Friday.*

He is almost finished grading when he hears two knocks on his door and looks up to see Sasha walk in. Sasha is small and athletic with short blonde hair. She is only two years older than Michael, but this is her fifth year teaching. When Michael passes her classroom, he is always impressed by how efficiently the students are working. He is most impressed by the fact that she never seems worn down. During his last evaluation with his assistant principal, Michael was encouraged to observe her teaching, but he hasn't gotten around to it. Watching her enter his own classroom, Michael is acutely aware of how disorganized it must appear.

"Hey, I don't mean to barge in but I was just heading home. I noticed your light and thought I'd stop in. I heard you gave a unit test yesterday. How'd it go?"

Michael looks down at the tests in front of him and back up again, "Not great. More Fs than Bs. A few As. Mostly Cs and Ds," he says, sounding more exasperated than he intended.

Sasha takes a seat on one of the student's desks, "Do you know what the problem is?"

"Well, I kind of expected this from 4th and 6th hour. There are a few students in each of those classes who are committed to making it nearly impossible for anyone to get any work done. But 1st hour is a pretty quiet group and I really thought they were going to do alright, but their scores are as bad as the rest of them."

"So, you're doubting yourself."

"It's kind of hard not to."

She smiles. "I know how you feel. A lot of this job comes down to faith more than anything."

"I just hate feeling like I don't know what I'm doing."

"Well, do you enjoy doing it?" she asks. "I mean are you glad that you decided to become a teacher?" Sasha's tone is sincere, and the question takes Michael by surprise.

"I am. I feel like I have a very clear purpose. And I'd rather be doing something challenging than boring. And I love the kids. Well. Most of them." Sasha laughs. "It's just that sometimes I feel like nothing I'm doing is making any difference."

She slides off the desk, "Well, at least you think you're supposed to be making a difference. Some teachers are content to just talk at the kids. If you keep trying to get better, it'll get easier. I'll let you get back to grading, but trust me: it would be weird if you were good at this right away."

"Thanks. It's good to hear something positive from time to time."

She pauses by the door, "If you ever want to plan together, let me know. I'd be happy to help you out. And also, you should decorate your room a little. At least get a

Word Wall up or something. It says a lot to the students, the type of environment they're in."

"I know. I need to do that."

She steps into the hall and then leans her head back into the room, "And get some rest," she adds before closing the door behind her.

The last two tests Michael grades are both As, and they lift his spirits slightly. He packs up his things and takes a deep breath. When he switches off the lights to his classroom, he feels satisfied with a good day's work. As he walks down the empty hallway, he remembers that he still hasn't put together a lesson plan for tomorrow. *I need to get better about planning ahead.*

Year 3
Michael and Susan

Susan cups her hands together and breathes warm air into her palms. She turns up the heat in the car. Michael asks if she's cold, and she says that she's freezing. Michael laughs and rubs his hand on her knee.

"You know it's going to be a lot colder in the mountains," he says.

"I know, I know. I'm allowed to be cold though."

"Yes. Yes you are."

She leans over and kisses Michael on the cheek.

"You're the best boyfriend, you know that?"

He offers an awkward smile. "Well," he says, "I try."

"Are you going to miss me?"

Two weeks ago, Susan decided to visit Leah in France. Michael said it was a good idea, but since then she's noticed a peculiar distance in his behavior toward her. She wonders if he's angry she decided to go away without talking to him about it first.

"Of course I'll miss you." There is a pang of guilt. He squeezes her thigh and returns his hand to the steering wheel.

"You know I wouldn't be going if Leah didn't need me."

"I know. But you don't need to apologize about taking the chance to spend a week in the French Alps."

"It'll be fun to go skiing. I haven't been skiing in years."

A green sign with white letters announces that the airport is under two miles away. He wonders what Veronica is doing.

"Susan," he glances toward her and then back to the road, "I hope you have a really good time."

"Me too. I'll call you when I get there."

Back in his apartment, Michael's guilt disappears beneath a swell of anticipation. Susan is on her way across the ocean, and tonight he will be alone with Veronica. His mind won't focus on anything else. He tries to read, but the words don't form a larger meaning. He turns on the television, but he forgets what he is watching during the commercial breaks. He begins to clean but ends up standing above a sink half-full of dishes and staring blankly toward the cabinets. Every few minutes, he checks the time.

Susan is seated by a window toward the rear of the plane. Her eyes are fixed on the line of clouds that stretch out beneath her. When she catches a glimpse of the ocean, she feels drawn to its depth. She wishes that Michael were here beside her. She wants to rest her head on his shoulder and feel him take her hand. She closes her eyes and pictures his face. She feels safe.

Heinz Memorial Chapel dominates the lawn behind the Cathedral of Learning. Large stone arches frame an elaborate array of stained glass windows. The chapel is one hundred feet tall at the nave and its steeple extends another fifty feet into the air. Ironwork weaves across the large red doors. Above the entrance an image of Jesus is carved next to symbols of Christian virtue. Michael approaches the chapel and listens to the wind brush against the stone.

The large door creaks as he pulls it toward him. Veronica is waiting for him in the entranceway. She smiles when she sees him enter.

"I'm glad you made it," she says and slips her arm into his. "My friend Jay is about to start playing."

A few dozen people are scattered in pews throughout the chapel. Veronica leads Michael to an empty pew near the rear, and a small grey-haired woman steps up to the lectern. Her speech is measured and sophisticated.

"We thank you all for attending this evening of music in Heinz Chapel. Tonight, local pianist Joseph Gattoni will be performing a series of fugues for organ composed by Johann Sebastian Bach. During the opening, piece we will light the stained glass windows. Again, we are happy that you have joined us on this wintry evening, and we hope that you enjoy the program."

A thin man with short hair and a trimmed beard stands from the first pew and approaches the organ. With the first chord, music pours down from the ceiling. Veronica slides next to Michael, and her knee rubs against his thigh.

"Look," she whispers and points to the windows that surround them. According to the program, there are twenty-three windows made up of over 250,000 pieces of stained glass. The tallest windows on either side are over seventy feet tall. When Michael arrived, the images in the glass were dull and cloaked in shadow. The music increases in intensity, and the light begins to bleed through the windows. Each piece of glass glows in its own hue, and Michael watches as they grow more brilliant by the moment. Veronica takes his hand, and he lets her fingers weave between his own. The notes of the organ seem to speak to each other as a pair of melodies intertwines. The lanterns above grow dim, and the altar becomes bathed in colored light.

Michael turns toward Veronica. She is wearing tall black leather boots, dark jeans, and a knee-length leather jacket. Her breasts swell beneath a tightly fitted white sweater. She flexes her grip on his hand, and then lies back on the pew and closes her eyes. Her body sways gently with the music. He remembers the first time he saw her walk into Faraday's class. Even now, he feels like he is watching her from afar.

Before the program is over, Veronica suggests they find someplace else to go. Her voice is smooth and assertive, and Michael is happy to follow her lead. At a bar around the corner, they order two beers and two shots of whiskey. She tells him about the first time she heard Bach as a child.

"There was something beautifully ordered about it. That's how I first got interested in math. It got me thinking about the beauty in structure. Sometimes when I solve theorems it's like I can *hear* them. Do you know what I mean?" Michael shakes his head. Veronica orders another pair of shots.

"You hear them?"

"I mean I can sense what's coming, I anticipate the rhythm." She glances at their reflection in the mirror behind the bar. "It's not the type of thing you can explain."

Michael feels out of his depth. "Pythagoras invented the modern harmonic scale didn't he?"

Veronica smiles suggestively. "Yes. He did."

Veronica's apartment is a single rectangular room. A mattress and box spring are centered on the wall opposite the front door. An oven and sink are built into the left wall and separated from the rest of the room by a few feet of tile-patterned linoleum. On the opposite side of the room, a small, faded blue couch faces toward a pair of windows overlooking Frick Park. Beneath the windows and on both sides of the bed are stacks of books and unpacked boxes. Michael steps inside and focuses on maintaining his balance. They've been drinking for over three hours. Veronica drags her fingers across Michael's waistline as she passes and leads him toward the couch. She asks if he wants to smoke some pot and picks up a plastic bag and a small glass bowl. He says yes and begins to scan the titles of the books stacked around him. Most are contemporary fiction. There is a stack of essay collections ranging from Cicero to Robinson. Beside them is a taller stack of math textbooks and battered composition notebooks. Ibn al'Arabi's "Bezels of Wisdom," is opened on the floor. Beside it is a copy of "Sein und Zeit."

"You read Heidegger in German?" he asks.

She hands him the bowl and a black lighter. "I like German," she says, widening her eyes as she smiles. Michael feels the need to kiss her but hesitates.

He takes a hit and passes the bowl back to Veronica. He feels caught up in decisions beyond his control.

Michael settles into the couch and closes his eyes. His nerves settle as the pot mixes with the liquor in his system. He feels insulated from the outside world. Veronica's body is warm beside him. There is a sense of fulfillment. "Do you believe in fate?" he asks. The question seems to come from nowhere, but Veronica doesn't mind.

She touches his knee. "Belief is a funny way to talk about fate. But, I guess, if we're looking for a reason why you're here and why I'm here and why we're drawn to each other the way I think we are," she slides her hand up his thigh, "then fate is as good a word as any."

Veronica leans toward Michael, and they kiss. Her lips are full and lush. He feels her hands slide under his shirt, and her nails scratch into his back. He pushes her back on the couch and kisses her neck. She lets out a long sigh that bends toward a moan. She touches her lips to his ear. "I want you to fuck me," she whispers.

*   *   *   *   *

Susan's cheeks are numb, and the wind whips her scarf in the air. She digs her poles into the snow and pushes forward while skating with her skis. A moment later she is gliding downhill atop several feet of powder. She bends her legs and twists her hips to steer her way down the mountain. She picks up speed and loses herself in the motions. Her breathing syncs to the rhythm of her turns. Trees flash by the sides of her vision in a blur. It dawns on her that skiing at this speed could be dangerous, but she feels in control. Occasionally she hits mounds in the powder and she's lifted away from the mountain. She feels her heart and lungs rise in her chest and then drop when her skis return to the snow beneath her. Halfway down the slope, she turns off to the side to take in the view.

She glances back over her shoulder. She can feel the mountain's strength radiating around her, and she's tempted to lie back and let it hold her. A pair of skiers passes by, and something rustles nearby in the woods. Susan pans her eyes across the landscape. Mountains rise in front of mountains for as far as she can see. She wishes Michael were here. There is a tingling across her nose. Her eyes begin to water, and she blames it on cold.

When Susan was just twelve years old, her mother would take her skiing and let her go off on her own. At times Susan would relish this independence, but often she felt lonely. She remembers asking herself once, as she skied solo down a windy slope at the edge of the resort, if there was any point to doing something if no one was around to watch her. She imagined herself alone on a desert island sitting idly without any motivation to survive. The memory gives Susan a strange feeling. She tries to dismiss it as frivolous but her mind can't move on so easily. *I've never been satisfied when I'm alone.* She repeats the thought as a question and pulls her goggles back over her eyes. She bends her knees and then pushes against the slope. Her goggles give the scene an amber hue.

Susan watches Leah descend the final stretch of the mountain in short choppy turns.

Leah skates toward Susan. "Zoom zoom," she says, "you were *fly*ing up there. You have to teach me how to do that." Susan smiles. She's glad to see Leah happy.

The chalet Leah has rented for them is large and removed from the others. There are two large bedrooms, each with its own bath and extra beds. Five-foot tall windows offer a view of the snow-covered mountains around them. A waist high cedar counter with a granite top separates the kitchen from the main room. The furniture is comfortable to the point of luxury.

The sun has set, and the night is descending into deeper shades of blue. Susan sits on the large green recliner facing the windows and counts the stars as they appear. Leah stands behind the stove stirring melted chocolate and heating a pan of milk to a simmer.

"Leah, that smells wonderful," says Susan, turning slightly toward the kitchen.

"Do you want any whiskey in yours?"

"Maybe just a little."

Leah uncorks the whiskey bottle. With a quick turn of the wrist, she coats the bottom of Susan's mug and then adds a little more. She fills her own mug to just under halfway full. She tops off the drinks with a mix of chocolate and milk and then adds a crown of whipped cream.

She takes the mugs by their handles but hesitates before picking them up from the counter. She thinks of Marcel and what to tell Susan. The last time they spoke, she had nothing hopeful to say about her marriage. Recently, she has begun to warm to the idea of forgiveness. Marcel has repented, and he claims he's ended things with Annelies. Leah isn't sure she believes him but she wants to. Glancing around the chalet, she reminds herself of the type of life that Marcel is able to provide for her. *Women have endured worse for much less. I should be grateful.* Her thoughts have a taste of desperation. *We can still make this work.*

Susan sips her chocolate, "This is delicious."

"Thank you."

"You know this is the first time I've ever been out of the country?"

"Of course Suzie. If you'd been out of the country I'd have known about it."

"Well I just wanted to thank you for inviting me out here. It's really good to see you."

"Susan." They sit for a while in silence and drink their chocolate. Leah wants to tell Susan that she loves her, and that she's more than grateful she came here to be with her. "Susan," she says again, and reaches her hand toward her.

Susan stands and takes a seat next to Leah on the couch. She sets her chocolate on the table and wraps her arm around Leah. Leah nestles her cheek just above Susan's chest.

"So," Susan whispers, "Do you know what you're going to do?"

"No. I don't even know what I *want* to do. No matter what I do, I'll feel like a failure." She pulls away from Susan. "I've been thinking a lot about trying to make things work with Marcel. I mean…" she rolls her eyes, "he is my husband after all."

"But Leah."

"I mean just because he broke his vows doesn't mean I should break mine too. And he says he's ended things with his fucking whore and he's trying to avoid working with her when he can. And I'm his wife and she's just a fucking whore." Leah can see her and Marcel standing together on their wedding day. *I do*, he said.

"And you think you can trust him?"

"We promised to spend the rest of our lives together."

"I know."

Leah's voice begins to crack, "He promised."

"I remember."

Leah wipes the tears from her cheeks with her palms.

"I'm sorry I'm such a wreck."

"It's OK."

"I don't want to just sit around and cry about myself all night. Tell me about you. How are things with you and Michael?"

*   *   *   *   *

Michael and Veronica are sitting up in bed, naked, with their backs to the wall. A white sheet covers them up to their waists. They are sharing a cigarette. Snow piles on the windowsill, but the air inside is hot and thick with the smell of sweat. It's been four days since Michael dropped Susan off at the airport, and tomorrow morning he will return there to pick her up. The thought has hardly any effect on him at all.

The past few days, Michael has felt like he was watching his life through a kaleidoscope. He stares forward and the scenes unravel in his memory: At a club by Station Square strobe lights turn Veronica's movements into a series of stop motion photos, she averts her eyes as she dances, her shirt is damp to the touch, she cuts him a line of cocaine on the bar of an afterhours spot in the Strip District, he slides his hand up her skirt in the cab on the ride home, her naked body slides against his own, he finds math theorems written in lipstick on her bathroom mirror, she holds his hand while they listen to the bass solos on an Ornette Coleman album, he asks her about her family and she says that she is a child of nature, she tells him she'll never be in love, she tells him she's never felt as close to someone as she does to him, she asks him to split a cigarette, he tells her he has a girlfriend and she says she doesn't care, she says that he doesn't have to care either, they walk at night through Schenley Park and she stays two paces ahead of him, they smoke pot in the morning and watch movies through the afternoon, they buy vegetables in the strip district and she makes couscous in a tagine she brought back from Morocco, they drink liquor with lunch and dinner, he calls her name while she's writing and she tells him to shut the fuck up, they fuck on the floor just inside her apartment door, she asks if he wants to share a cigarette, he asks how many men have fallen in love with her, she says she doesn't believe in unrequited love, she tells him about how her brother killed himself, they drink red wine from the bottle, in the minutes before sleep he tells her she can trust him, she says that she hopes so.

The day is almost over, and they haven't eaten since breakfast. Veronica stubs out the cigarette in the ashtray by the mattress and announces that she's going to order Thai food. "You should pack a bowl," she adds.

Michael picks up the glass pipe and bag of pot from the foot of the bed, "Susan is coming back tomorrow."

"Then I guess our little holiday is coming to an end," she says from the other side of the room and then jumps into an order for vegetable pad Thai and green curry.

"It doesn't have to," says Michael. He takes a hit of the bowl. Veronica slips on underwear and a loose fitting cotton dress.

"No?" she says. She returns to her place on the bed, and Michael hands her the pipe.

"I can talk to Susan. I like being with you." Michael struggles to keep his tone from getting serious.

"I like being with you too."

"You make me feel alive."

"You shouldn't need me to feel alive."

"I know. That's not what I mean."

She squeezes his knee, and Michael understands that she doesn't want to talk about this right now.

"Do you want to split a cigarette?" she asks.

"You want me to crack a window?"

"Please."

Michael pulls on his boxers and walks toward the window. When he pulls it open, a wave of cold air pours into the room. He feels a chill on his feet and shivers run along his back. Veronica takes an exaggerated breath when the cold air reaches her toes. She lights a cigarette and closes her eyes.

After they eat, they watch an old French movie on her computer. The action is slow, but the dialogue is witty, and Veronica laughs out loud at several points. The theme of the film is the relationship between spiritual transcendence and submission before God. *But*, asks one of the characters, *is God without or within?* When the film is over, Veronica takes a bottle of wine to the couch and stares out the window. The snow and ice have etched designs across the glass. A steady stream of cold air continues to pour in from the opening at its base. Michael reads a few pages from a book of stories and notices that Veronica's expression hasn't changed. He walks over and sits next to her on the couch. She passes him the bottle of wine. He takes a gulp and she reaches for him to return it.

"I want to keep seeing you but I don't want you to break up with your girlfriend."

"Why not?"

"Because I'm fucked up and I can't make any promises and I don't want you to be hurt." She takes a drink of wine and looks down quietly. Michael can tell she wants to say something. "Can I ask you something?" she says and turns toward him, "Did you ever notice anything strange between me and Faraday?"

The question takes Michael by surprise. "No," he says and shakes his head slightly.

"Well," her voice continues in a detached whisper, "After the first class we had with him, the one where he said all that shit about beauty and truth, I followed him back to his office. I don't know what I was expecting. I know I had an idea to ask for more clarity on the assignment but I also remember having a crush on him. I had this fantasy of locking his office door. Obviously I didn't do that but I did flirt with him and when I mentioned I was going to see a concert a friend of mine was giving I said that he should check it out. I didn't expect him to say yes, but he did. That night he drove me back to my apartment, not this one, my old one, and on the drive he gave me some cocaine and I snorted it off the dashboard. When we got home he came in and we had sex and then he left to go home to his wife and kids, he had a fucking wife and kids." She presses her fingers into her forehead. "And then we started doing that type of thing every couple weeks and then every week and then twice a week. We'd do some coke and fuck and then he'd leave." She takes a long drink from the bottle.

"How long did this go on?"

"Off and on until a few months ago. Anyway…" She lights a cigarette but doesn't ask Michael to share. "Faraday sometimes talked about you. He noticed how you'd keep looking at me during class and later on he'd talk about it. He said that you wanted to fuck me. He said that you were smart but that your ideas never went forward they just spun around in circles one way or the other. He said that's why we were perfect for each other and then he'd make me promise never to fuck you. That's the word he used. Fuck."

Michael sets his hand on her knee, but Veronica brushes it away.

"That's why I approached you and gave you my number. I wanted to burn every promise I ever made to that asshole. But I didn't expect to actually like you. You're a good person Michael. It's been a long time since I spent time with a good person. But we shouldn't be together. You should pick up your girlfriend tomorrow and forget about me. Don't worry about me. I'm used to being alone."

"I don't think you're fucked up."

"I am. Trust me… Sometimes I feel like a spider watching its web get shredded by the wind."

Michael watches her close her eyes. He thinks she might cry, but she just sits still. After a while she stands and walks to the window. She opens it as high as it will go and then presses it shut. Clumps of snow fall and melt into the carpet.

*   *   *   *   *

Susan holds up a large green cashmere sweater for Leah to see. "What do you think of this one? I think Michael might like it."

"It's nice, I guess." Leah is not enthusiastic about helping Susan pick out a present for Michael.

"No," Susan trades the sweater for a blue one with a higher collar, "I think I like this one better." She slings it over her forearm.

"Do you really have to leave tomorrow?"

"You know I do."

Susan feels sorry for Leah, but she's looking forward to going home. She wishes that Leah could be as lucky as she is.

"Fine," says Leah, bitter but still joking, "go home to your loving boyfriend."

Susan smiles. Tonight she'll fall asleep in his arms.

Year 5
Michael

The room is colder by the windows where Michael is sitting. His eyes catch pairs of headlights as they cross his view. He is finishing a beer at a bar he found after getting out of the subway. In an hour or so, he'll walk up to Adam's Shakespeare party in the park.

Michael is remembering his first night in New York City. He met Derrick's brother on the back patio of a café in the East Village. Together they walked around southern Manhattan. He was taken, more than anything, by the sheer number of people. Block after block, the streets and restaurants were full of people. The wind hummed with conversation. Familiar looking faces flickered behind windows. At each corner he thought he recognized someone he knew. Of course, none of them were the people he thought they were. Out of place, his mind was trying to connect this new world with something familiar. That first night he met Danielle. She worked in advertising. They flirted in a bar and ended up going back to her place. For the next few months they slept together, and she showed him around the city, but eventually, he stopped returning her calls. He told himself that being with her was too easy. He hadn't moved to New York to settle into a relationship.

When Michael looks toward the bar he is startled. Veronica is standing there next to an empty stool wearing her same old leather jacket. He stares to make sure it's her and then walks to sit beside her.

"Hey stranger," he says, placing his hand on her shoulder, curious how she'll react when she turns toward him.

But when she turns, he sees that she is not Veronica. The woman smiles lightly as she leans back to reveal the face of the man sitting next to her. He is visibly irritated. Michael slides off his stool and steps away but the man is already in front of him staring him in the eye. Michael's first thought is that he's too tired to deal with this.

"What the fuck you think you're doing? You gonna apologize or what?"

"Look, your girl was—"

The man's fist crashes into Michael's face just below his left eyebrow. The room falls silent. The man punches him again in the stomach and then pushes him to the ground. Michael pulls himself onto all fours, and a kick snaps into his ribs. He grunts and falls on his side. The man grabs the strange women's wrist and leads her to the door. The next person Michael sees is Danielle. The real Danielle. She is standing above him. Her hair is longer now.

"Michael? Still a fucking bastard." She flicks what's left of her drink at his face and turns away. He feels the ice hit his nose and eye. The room is silent for his groans. After a few moments, the bartender helps him to his feet.

When Michael gets outside, he leans against the first cement wall that he sees. He can feel his eye swelling. Every breath stabs his ribs, and his fingers grow numb in the wind. He's not going to be able to go to Adam's party after all. He kicks the building with his heel.

Year 3
Michael and Susan

Michael sits at his kitchen table with a bottle of whiskey and a glass. He takes four shots and could take any number more, but instead, he pushes the glass away and decides to collect his thoughts. He rests his face in his hands and then combs his fingers over his head and presses them into the back of his neck. He curls his hands into fists, brings his forearms to rest on the edge of the table, and stays like that for a moment before taking a long, slow, deep breath. He relaxes his hands. Images of Veronica flash in his mind. He sees her writhing beneath him and filling the room with her voice. He can feel her pressing herself against him as he grips the hair on the back of her scalp. It's been less than thirty minutes since he left her apartment. Susan is probably beginning to wonder when he'll be over. His shoulders slacken, and he reaches for another shot.

Michael arrives at Susan's later than usual. He is wearing the sweater she bought him in France. She is happy to see him and asks how his day was but not where he's been.

Soon he is in the kitchen with her, asking to be useful and touching his fingers to her hips.

"Baby," she says, "can you get out the basil?"

When dinner is ready, they watch television and talk about their day during commercials. Susan is concerned about Michael. He doesn't seem to want to talk about where he's been and ever since she returned from visiting Leah, he is always either too affectionate or too distant but never anything in between. While they sit in silence, she takes his hand, and he slides toward her.

"You know I love you," he says.

"I know," she replies.

When they stand to go to bed, Michael's thoughts return to Veronica. His mood sours. He watches Susan straighten up the kitchen and prays that she won't find out what he's been doing. He can't bear the thought of it. For the first time, Michael thinks of Veronica with fear instead of promise. Susan loves him. This is not the type of person he imagines himself to be.

Susan turns on the light in the bathroom, and tells herself that she must be imagining things with Michael. She brushes her teeth and decides to wake up early to work on an article. She washes her face and rubs lotion into her arms and neck. She thinks of Michael waiting for her in bed and feels a ripple of desire pass over her. *I have a sexy boyfriend.* It's been almost a week since they've had sex.

Michael is reading without his shirt on when Susan enters the bedroom and curls up next to him. She places her hand on his chest and rests her head beneath his shoulder. Michael kisses her forehead and returns to his book. Susan paints lines across his chest with her fingers, and Michael sets down the book. She pulls herself toward his lips, and they kiss. As they slip off their clothes, Susan embraces the passion in Michael's touch. They continue through familiar movements with a fresh intimacy. Susan feels reminded of how completely loved she is. Michael's phone begins to ring. He glances at it lighting up and vibrating against the nightstand, and Susan turns her eyes. Michael wonders if she suspects what kind of phone call it might be. He looks away and pulls her toward him. Her body is warm against his skin.

The phone beeps, and Michael rolls away from Susan to silence the sound. He lies that the message is from Derrick.

"Derrick? That's strange," says Susan.

"I know. I'll call him back tomorrow morning."

"I hope everything's all right."

"I'm sure it is."

The exchange doesn't sit well with Susan. Michael seems nervous and evasive. If she were pressed she'd admit that Michael may be lying, but she'd rather not think that way. Instead she starts to tell herself that Michael loves her, and she should trust him, and any secret he might be hiding is probably not as bad as she would imagine it to be.

Michael is angry with Veronica for calling so late. She must have known where he'd be. The clock reaches midnight. Susan rolls away to try and sleep, and Michael lays flat on his back. He curses himself for spending the afternoon with Veronica. He's stupid for risking what he has with Susan. *Tomorrow I'll call her. This can't keep going on.*

That night Susan dreams she is alone in a large log cabin waiting for Michael to return. She grows nervous, and when she looks out the window, she sees hordes of large cats prowling and circling the cabin. She fears that Michael has been killed by the cats. She hears claws dig into the front door. A lioness brings her eye to the window and stares at Susan. A wooden roof beam falls and crashes next to her. "Michael," she screams, "Where are you?"

In the morning, Susan is still anxious. While Michael is taking a shower she picks up his phone. She tells herself that making sure the call was from Derrick will calm her nerves. Of course, she tells herself, she shouldn't have to check; she should trust him. She turns on the screen and looks at the recent calls. *V. Who the hell is V?* Susan's heart races, and her fingers begin to shake. She decides to listen to the message. The water in the shower cuts off. She holds the phone to her ear and hears Veronica's voice, "I can't stop thinking about what you did to me today. Try to break away from Susan. We can—" Hearing her own name sends a pulse of rage through Susan's nerves. She flings the phone away from her. It bounces off the foot of the bed and slides across the floor. Michael steps out of the bathroom with a towel wrapped around his waist.

"What was that?" he asks.

"Who the fuck is V?"

Year 5
Susan

The teakettle squeals across the room. Susan finishes typing the sentence she's working on and makes her way to the kitchen. She silences the kettle and waits a moment to pour the water. The steam rises, and the mug grows warm. Susan walks back to her computer and sets the tea down to cool. She is writing the intro to the paper's annual "Young and Restless" spread about people under 40 who are making an impact on the city. The task calls for flattering hyperbole and the impression of a city on the rise. It's the type of formulaic prose she's become proficient with over the past few years. When she finishes a draft, she reads it over and decides to add more specifics. She picks up a manila folder and begins to flip through the bios of the people who have been selected for this year's edition. There are lawyers, entrepreneurs, and non-profit executives as well as musicians, poets, and politicians. Some of the people are younger than she is. She makes note of the people she'd prefer to interview. The others she can delegate to junior reporters.

It's been two months since she spoke with Michael and told him she wouldn't be up to visit him in New York. If she had visited, she might be planning to move to New York right now. She'd be looking for jobs and talking with Michael about a place to live. The thoughts cloud her focus, and she feels a nagging doubt. She tests the tea and finds it's still too hot. She watches the steam rise above the mug and then disappear. She tells herself to concentrate on her work.

When the tea cools, Susan takes it to the couch and curls her knees up to her chest. She thinks of *Love in America*. It's been over two years since she pledged to write the book, and all she has are a dozen pages without any unifying theme. She's not even sure what type of book she's trying to write. The profiles for "Young and Restless" have put her in a sour mood, and a fog of inadequacy clings to her thoughts. She has never aspired to be the type of person who would be profiled in Y&R, but she doesn't like the idea that it seems like an impossible idea. She sets down the empty mug and returns to the bios on the table. She tries to focus, but she doesn't care.

Once, when Susan was a girl, she made her mother a crown of dandelions for Mother's Day. Susan was embarrassed by the gift. She hadn't even known it was Mother's Day until a friend told her while they were playing outside. Her friend had made her mother a painting. Susan panicked. She did the simplest thing she could think of and started picking dandelions to weave into a crown. She knew it was a lazy gift, but her mother loved it and praised her for her thoughtfulness. At first Susan was relieved, but as she thought more about the gift, she became frustrated with her mother. She didn't like the idea of being praised for something so simple. She wanted her Mother to expect more from her.

Again, she flips through the folder and one of the profiles catches her attention. It's for a chef in his early 30s who opened a restaurant last year in the Southside. She remembers reading a review of the place when it first opened and thinking she might want to go there. She decides to call him and set up an interview.

"Hello?"

"Hi, this is Susan from *The Boulevard*. Is this James?"

"Yes it is." His voice is friendly and relaxed.

Susan slips effortlessly into her professional cadence, "I'm sure you're aware that you've been selected to be profiled in our 'Young and Restless' edition, and I was wondering if I could schedule a time to come in and speak with you."

"Of course. When were you thinking?"

"Well, obviously not next week. Maybe early in the New Year. How does that first Wednesday look?"

"I should be flexible."

"One o'clock all right?"

"Sounds great. I'll be expecting you."

Susan says that she's looking forward to it, and they exchange goodbyes. The conversation leaves her in a positive mood. She takes her mug to the kitchen and washes it along with her plate from breakfast. She looks for life in the park across the street and finds a pair of tracks in the snow. She decides to take a walk and tucks a few strands of hair behind her ear. *I need to take control of my life.*

Holidays

"Look," says Veronica, "I didn't mean for that to happen. I was walking home and I wanted to see you so I called."

Michael doesn't want to aggravate her. He sits on the edge of his childhood bed. He can hear his mother in the kitchen downstairs. Veronica's voice seems far away.

"That's not what I meant. Anyway, there's nothing we can do about it now. It might work out for the best. I've been thinking about you a lot the past few days."

Michael fidgets with the sheets on his bed. The thread between them is growing taut.

"I've been thinking about you too."

"Have you thought about coming back for New Year's?"

"I have…"

"But you'd rather not."

"I would. I want to see you. More than I thought I would… But I should stay here with my sister. I don't see her much and I know she's looking forward to going out together. You should meet her sometime. I think she'd like you."

"Why is that?"

"Because she likes whatever I like."

"Very funny." Michael lies back in bed. "I'm looking forward to seeing you again."

"Me too… But, Michael, I think we should start out slow."

"That's fine," he says, facing the ceiling, "We can meet for coffee or something. I don't need to rush into anything."

"I like you. A lot. I don't want to fuck anything up."

"You can trust me."

"I know."

"And I'm not going to hurt you."

"Michael. You don't need to protect me."

"I'm not trying to. I just don't want you to be afraid of

me."

"I'm not afraid of you I just don't know what I'm able to handle at this point in my life."

"Do I make you happy?"

"Michael, I need to learn how to be happy in other ways."

"I know. I know. We can take things slow."

"I'm glad you called. But…"

"But what?"

"I need a little while before we talk again."

*   *   *   *   *

It's twilight on Christmas Eve and relatives from across the mountain have ascended for the evening's celebrations. Families gather for dinner and the hum of conversation carries between the homes. Derrick and Rosa are in the village center helping the children decorate. Emilio sits on top of Derrick's shoulders and hangs paper snowflakes in the trees while the other boys gather wood for the fire. Rosa helps the girls circle the nativity scene with luminaries. She shows them how to use a cup of dirt to make the candles stand up in their white paper bags. When Emilio hangs the last snowflake, Derrick lifts him from his shoulders and sets him on the ground. Emilio runs toward Rosa, tugs at her sleeve and points back toward the tree. Rosa places her hand on the back of his neck.

"Que bueno," she says. Emilio nods enthusiastically.

At the house, Rosa's aunts, uncles, and cousins are waiting for Rosa to return with Derrick. The room is small, and everyone stands within arms reach of at least two people. Everyone has a different idea of how they expect Derrick to be. Aunt Gabriela says he will be tall and arrogant, and Cousin Maya suggests he must be rich. Rosa's mother defends Derrick and says that he is kind and honest, but her brother Diego states plainly that he doesn't see the point of such a relationship. Rosa's mother starts to respond, but she's overtaken by a scraping cough, and Maya hurries to bring her a glass of water.

During dinner, Derrick feels lost. One-on-one he can carry a conversation in Spanish but with a dozen people talking he feels lost. He sets his attention to the food and compliments those who made it. He fills his plate more than once. There is paella, chicken stuffed with papaya, a jicama and orange salad, nacatamales, and fresh baked bread. Occasionally, someone asks him a direct question, but his responses are over-thought and his phrases lack rhythm. Rosa tries to help him. She explains that he's from Pittsburgh, and she tells stories about games he's done with the children in school and talks about how much they've learned since he came to the village. Derrick wishes he could add to what Rosa said in a way to make people laugh, but he's not sure what to say or how to say it. Instead, he smiles and nods.

When everyone has finished eating, Rosa and Maya begin to clear the table. Rosa's mother looks exhausted. In recent weeks she has spent more and more time in bed. Derrick watches Rosa joke with her family, and he feels suddenly out of place. They are outsiders in each other's lives. Soon they'll have to talk about what will happen when he leaves.

Outside the breeze is warm. A waxing moon brushes the air with light. The sound of bells and voices singing carries from the village center. Families file from their houses toward the music. People carry candles and shield the flame with their hands. Around the nativity, shadows from the luminaries flicker and pass over each other.

Derrick and Rosa walk side by side but he knows he can't take her hand. A subtle smile is etched on her lips and pulls at the corners of her eyes. Derrick leans toward her, "Me alegra estar aqui contigo."

"I'm happy you're here too," says Rosa. She leans toward him and lets her body brush lightly against his arm.

Derrick is impressed by the sight around him. The whole village is gathered in a swollen crescent around the nativity. Children from his class stand still and sing loudly with their candles clutched between both hands. Faces he's only seen picking coffee in the forest or carrying water are smiling broadly and joined in song. He feels as though he has stepped behind a curtain. At first, Derrick resists joining in the songs, but he soon realizes that he has no choice. Not knowing the words, he jumps in after the first syllable of each line, but he doesn't always guess correctly. Rosa is amused by his effort. She takes his hand. Her fingers are slender and strong.

*   *   *   *   *

Michael and his mother sing the last bars of "O Come All Ye Faithful," close their hymnals and sit down. The final chord of the organ fades into the steeple. Winter coats rustle against polished wood, and a baby cries from the back of the church. As the phases of the mass elapse, Michael speaks in union with the congregation.

When the priest begins to speak, Michael tries to picture the story that he tells. Mary watches Gabriel appear before her. She can feel the warmth of the Divine that clings to his form. His fingers settle just below her waist. He leans toward her and whispers, "You are with the child of the Lord." There is a flash of light and when Mary is able to open her eyes, Gabriel is gone. She thinks of Joseph. *I hope he'll understand.*

Michael's mind wanders to a girl he met two nights ago. They got drunk and ended up at her place in Queens. In the morning he dressed while she slept. He looked at her and felt annoyed that he would have to rush to the train station. He didn't remember her name. As he closed the door behind him, he asked himself when he had become such an asshole.

"We Christians," the priest continues with soft-spoken certainty, "understand that Christ's birth is God's way of showing that he is committed to his relationship with humanity. Nowadays, the story is so familiar that we rarely consider the power of its details. We don't take the time to contemplate the humility of Christ's surroundings. We gloss over the simple fact that this was the day when the divine entered this world as flesh and blood. It is easy to take the story for granted, to allow it to be obscured by modern distractions.

"But, when we settle our attention and consider the

beauty of Christ's birth we can feel the love of God glow inside us." The priest opens his arms in a broad, sweeping gesture, "We have gathered here today to remember God's greatest gift to mankind. Many of us have traveled here to be with family and we give thanks that this day allows us to be with those whom we love most. This is a time for finding comfort in tradition and for reflecting on the choices in our lives. It is a day for celebrating the Son of God and as we leave here, in the spirit of both tradition and reflection, I hope that we will take the time to consider our relationship with Christ and God the Father.

"Let us give praise to God for the sacrifice he made for us and rejoice in the birth of our Savior Jesus Christ. Let us remember that we are made in the image of God and that through his Son we may achieve salvation and everlasting life. Thanks be to God."

The church responds as one, and Michael surveys the faces in the pews. There are a few attractive girls, but no one he recognizes. He finds himself looking forward to going to his Aunt Mia's after Mass. She'll cook broccoli soup and honey baked ham. She'll make garlic mashed potatoes and spicy asparagus. For dessert there will be cheesecake and pecan pie. His cousins will be happy to see him. Again, a baby wails from the rear of the church.

As Michael imagines the greetings from his cousins, he notes a feeling of separation from himself. There is a tingling sensation at the base of his skull that spreads through his neck. The voice of the priest sounds thin, as if it's traveled a great distance. He remembers chasing and being chased by his cousins as children. He feels unlike himself. A subtle panic creeps into his nerves. He wonders if he is still the person he used to be. When it is time for communion, Michael stands. The lines stretch to the back of the church. He shuffles toward the altar two steps behind his mother. When he returns to his pew, he kneels down and clasps his hands to pray.

*   *   *   *   *

Susan holds a still packaged roll of blue and white wrapping paper. She is thinking about pressing it smooth across her gifts when she feels the pull of tears tighten her cheeks. Michael wraps around her thoughts like a blanket of sharpened nails. She remembers his look of horror when she asked about Veronica, and the pain that twisted through her lungs as she waited for him to respond. She knows she doesn't hate Michael, but she hates what he has done to her, and she wonders if she can still try to love him. *Michael.* His name runs through her like thread through a needle. Everything she does is stitched with its presence.

*   *   *   *   *

Leah finds James waiting for her beneath a stop sign at the corner of Walnut and Bellefonte. He stands with his shoulders slouched forward, and his jacket cuts a softly rounded silhouette. He is neither short nor tall, and his girth is spread evenly across his frame. A winter hat conceals his receding hairline. His cheeks are round and pale from the cold. When Leah approaches he waves brusquely and walks toward her.

"Thanks for meeting me here," he says.

"Of course."

"There's something I want to ask your help with."

Leah has always liked James. He has been charming towards her, and he makes Susan happy. The tip of her nose is numb.

"Well, what is it? Do we get to go inside?"

James laughs. He gestures to the storefront behind her. There is a green awning, and diamond necklaces displayed in the windows. "This is it," he says and walks past Leah toward the door. Leah feels short of breath.

Jewelry cases line the edge of the room and pull back over the marble floor in linear perspective. A well-dressed jeweler welcomes them and asks if he can be of any assistance.

"In a minute," answers James. He turns to Leah. "So, do you think you could help me pick out a ring?"

*   *   *   *   *

Susan lifts the brand new sewing machine and sets it on the desk in her childhood room. She takes a seat on the edge of her bed and stares absently toward the contraption. She tries to think of the steps she'll need to take to learn how to make a dress but she doesn't know where to start. Downstairs she can hear her mother and little brother in a minor squabble about whether he can borrow the car. Richie is a sophomore in high school and has had his license for less than a month. Warm air purrs from the vent in the ceiling above her.

Susan's room is small. The desk, dresser, and twin-sized bed nearly butt against each other. Her closet is stuffed with clothes she hasn't worn for almost a decade. A box of photographs sits in the corner. The girl who grew up here seems to surround her like a ghost.

Downstairs, she finds her brother watching a documentary about Jesus.

"Hey Richie," she says.

"Hey," he responds, his voice dejected.

Susan takes a seat next to him and sets her attention on the television. She enjoys being with her brother. When she left home, he was only eight and often more of a nuisance than a friend, but recently she's tried to strengthen their relationship. The documentary details the type of life Jesus must have lived before he was baptized by John the Baptist. It talks about the work ethic a young Jesus would have acquired as a carpenter's apprentice and identifies moments of injustice in Judea that would have framed his worldview. Susan wonders how much of a community figure Jesus must have been before he started his ministry. It only makes sense that he would have been well known for something. No one just appears on the scene when they're thirty and starts to change the world. She imagines interviewing Jesus for a Galilean version of the "Young and Restless." *Tell me, Jesus, how did you get started as a prophet? Well,* he'd reply, *I guess it all goes back to my relationship with my Father.*

Richie is restless, and when the documentary is over, he turns to Susan. She can tell he has been thinking about something personal. He turns off the TV.

"I haven't told you about Gloria," he says quietly.

"No," she says.

He slides his hand up and down his arm and glances toward the empty screen. Richie explains, with a kind of frenetic anxiety, that Gloria is a girl who kissed him at a party two weeks ago. She is beautiful, but she has another boyfriend. The other boy is a loner with a tough reputation. Richie doesn't know what to do.

"She kissed you?"

"Yeah."

"And have you talked with her since then?"

"She's been ignoring me at school."

Susan wraps her arm around his shoulder.

"Richie. I know this isn't what you want to hear, but I think maybe you should try and forget about Gloria."

Richie pushes her away. "I'm sorry I told you."

"No, you're not."

"I like Gloria."

"It's not so difficult to *like* somebody Rich."

Richie falls on the couch away from Susan and stuffs a pillow behind his head, "Why does life keep getting more *complicated?*"

The house is quiet. Susan turns off her bedside lamp, and the room goes dark. She snuggles beneath the covers and closes her eyes. She is enjoying her visit home. In a few days, she will meet Leah in New York City. She considered letting Michael know that she'll be in town, but she doesn't want to stir her emotions. Susan enjoys being single. She thinks of the sewing machine that sits on her desk. *It's going to be a good year.*

*   *   *   *   *

The past two nights, Michael hasn't been able to sleep. Again tonight, he lays still in the dark, but sleep does not come. Fear pulses in his chest. His thoughts tighten around the hope that Veronica will call.

Two days ago he talked with Susan. She asked him how he'd been and he didn't know how to answer. She said that she missed him. She said she wanted to know why he did what he did. Michael listened silently and said that he was sorry. His instincts pushed him to try and reconcile, but he resisted. He reminded himself that he had made his choice. He was going to be with Veronica.

After a while, Michael sits up and flicks the light back on. He walks downstairs to the liquor cabinet and pours a glass of vodka over ice. The wind rattles the windows and shakes snow from the trees. It's just after two in the morning when his phone rings.

"Veronica?"

"I don't mean to call so late."

"It's OK. I'm up. It's good to hear from you."

"I was thinking about something and I felt like I should let you know right away." Michael hopes she'll say she's coming back for New Year's. "I don't think we should see each other when I get back."

The words deafen his thoughts. "I don't understand."

"You don't need to understand. Look, I was clear about what I wanted from the beginning. I wasn't looking to get involved."

"You said that you wanted to be with me."

"Michael, I've liked being with you. But that doesn't mean that I want you to come into my life and try and fix everything."

"That's not what I'm trying to do."

"Yes it is. You want to fix me and tame me. You don't have to admit it."

"I just think you should give us a chance."

"It's better this way," she says. Michael paces in the kitchen. His eyes are wide and his breathing is sharp. "Michael…"

"Yes."

"Please don't call me anymore."

*   *   *   *   *

Derrick's Christmas has been tense. His father doesn't approve of the choices he's made over the past few years. At dinner he spoke directly about Derrick's irrational infatuation with 'some Nicaraguan farm girl' he hasn't seen in over two years.

"Almost two years," Derrick corrected. These kind of minor clarifications have been a staple of their larger disagreements for years.

"What the hell are you talking about?"

"You said, over two years," he tried to soften his tone, "but it won't be two years for another month."

"Jesus *Christ*, son. Aren't you at all interested in American women?"

His mother interceded, and his brother nudged the conversation toward sports. A few moments, later it was like nothing had happened. They passed bottles of wine amongst themselves. The family has become accustomed to its patriarch's fits of temper.

Hours later the exchange with his father still thunders in Derrick's mind. He is furious, more furious than he should be. The anger eats at him. He can't focus. He wonders if he's angry with his father, or if he's angry because his father brought his own doubts to the surface.

He takes a deep breath and wonders what Rosa must think when she's alone. He remembers the promises they made. *Rosa.* The thought of her name quiets his nerves. He knows that she loves him. Still, he feels vulnerable. Everything revolves around the promise of their reunion.

Year 7
Leah

Leah returns home from the drugstore and closes the door behind her. The apartment is quiet except for the sound of the furnace. *Susan must still be at James'.* She places a cardboard box on the kitchen counter and pours a glass of water. She wonders if James has proposed. It's been a month since they bought the ring together.

Leah is nervous. She scratches at her palms with her fingernails and paces in the kitchen. She fears her sense of control is slipping away from her. Over the past two years, Leah has worked hard to reinvent herself. She has pushed men to the periphery of her life, and focused on her career.

For over a year, she's been working as an executive assistant for a major foundation in the city. The work is demanding, and Leah has carved out the role of always being the person people go to for answers. She often boasts to Susan about how the foundation would be lost without her.

Leah finishes her glass of water and returns her attention to the cardboard box. She turns it in her fingers until she finds the directions. She hopes that Susan doesn't walk in.

On New Year's Day, Leah set up an online dating profile. She met up with two men over the same weekend and slept with them both. It was the first time she had had sex in almost a year and the rendezvous left her feeling satisfied. Neither of the men has had his calls returned.

Leah rereads the directions on the box and checks the diagrams once more. The furnace cuts off, and silence drops on the room. She opens the box, removes the slender plastic stick and walks toward the bathroom.

While she waits for the results, she wonders which of the men could be the father. The first one was sweet and shy and was taken by surprise at Leah's advances. Afterward he clung to her while she tried to fall asleep. The second one was younger and more aggressive. She remembers how his face growled while he fucked her. She tells herself that the father doesn't matter. *I don't even know if I'm pregnant yet.* She turns and glances at the test sitting on the bathroom sink.

Marcel flashes in her thoughts. She wonders what he'd think if he could see her now. *Maybe he has children of his own.* Leah is many steps away from the life she was supposed to live. *If I have a child I will love her every way I can. She won't need a father.* The plastic feels cold and smooth between Leah's fingers. She checks the display and then walks briskly back to the kitchen to double-check the reading. Her hands are shaking.

"I'm pregnant," she whispers. *I'm pregnant.*

Year 5
Derrick

Derrick has always had a habit of packing his things a day in advance. He centers his pack on the bed and glances at the piles of clothes stacked neatly on his cot. The room is hot. Derrick is wearing a green shirt and khaki cargo shorts, and he thinks of the northern winter that he'll find back home. *Home.* He lingers on the word with cool detachment.

Derrick is trying to stay calm. He folds a pair of jeans and pushes them into the bottom of his backpack. He pairs up his socks and shoves them to the side of the jeans. He wonders how long it will take for him and Rosa to be together again.

It was just five months ago that he arrived here. He remembers the rain that fell his first time on the tractor and how he thought of it as a baptism.

Earlier today he said goodbye to his students. They were more emotional than he expected, and at the end of the day they lined up to hug him goodbye. They walked one-by-one into his arms and then to the sundrenched path outside. Most looked over their shoulder before they turned out of sight. Afterward he sat at his desk in front of the empty classroom and stared for a long time at the far corners of the room. He thought of the girl who was here before him and wondered who would come tomorrow to replace him. A stack of student reports on his desk reminded Derrick just how much work they've all done since he arrived. He felt a swell of pride and tried to measure the weight of these feelings against his plans for back home. *What would my dad say if I told him I wanted to be a teacher?*

The trail to Rosa's house is familiar now, and he takes comfort in the rustle of the forest as he walks. A pair of students, Elena and Guillermo, call out to him. They run toward him and knock him off balance as they collide against his legs and throw their arms around his waist. Elena composes herself and asks, in English, where he is going.

"I'm just going for a walk," he says.

Guillermo giggles to himself.

"Que pasa?" asks Derrick.

"Creo que vas a buscar a Rosa."

"Te gusta Rosa?" asks Elena.

"Si," says Derrick, "Rosa is very nice."

"And," Gabriela continues, "when you leave, us miss will you?"

"Will you miss us," he corrects her, "And of course I'll miss you."

"Will we miss you also!" she responds and Derrick laughs.

"*Thank you!*" adds Guillermo, and the pair run ahead of him down the trail.

Rosa has always been a dreamer. As a child, she would

disappear into the forest after breakfast and not return until dusk. She would invent elaborate worlds and fill them with characters from her imagination. She loved the village and the mountain but sometimes she would pretend she was trapped and would plot elaborate schemes to escape. Once she invented a portal between the branches of a tree. The portal took her to an ocean kingdom off the coast of Brazil. Alone in the forest, she would climb through the portal and then higher to explore the kingdom. With each grip, she maintained a determined concentration. The ground drew further away, but that didn't matter. Once, when she reached as high as she could climb, she looked away to survey the kingdom and her foot slipped and she fell. She broke her ankle, and it was hours before anyone found her. Her next memory is of her father kneeling beside her. His eyes seemed large as moons. She told him what happened, and he promised that one day he would take her to find the ocean kingdom. But first, he explained, he needed to go away for a little while. He needed to go fight for the government so that she could have a better future. Rosa remembers this exchange often. It was the last time she saw her father.

After word of her father's death, Rosa bore a well in her mind and climbed deep inside of it. In that first week, there was a funeral, and that was the last time she heard his name in public. The silence around him seemed like a betrayal. She became the steward of a violent anger and nurtured an insecure determination to escape the village. When people would gather for a celebration, it took everything she had not to scream.

Slowly, her anger softened. Her body began to change. She told herself that she needed to come to terms with the life she would have to live. She took on the role of big sister to the younger children and would invent games for them to play while their parents were working. She talked to Ramon about building a school and was surprised when he took her seriously and began to organize the community around the idea. People she hardly knew began to compliment her and ask her to dinner. Rosa embraced the special role she was growing into but she never forgot that tragedy defined who she was. She never stopped imagining herself in a life far away from here.

To the boys in the village, Rosa was the ultimate prize. Each of them developed his own scheme to hook her attention. They left notes and flowers at her doorstep and invented reasons to take the tractor if they knew she would be riding. Rosa was always polite to them but never anything more. She had romantic feelings, but it was more important to her to be free. She was proud of her independence.

For a while, the boys respected her distance and spoke of her as someone who was out of their league. She wasn't meant for the same types of feelings as other girls. But over time their reverence corroded into frustration and then rejection. She was ridiculed and ostracized. Her loneliness became more acute, and she thought again of the ocean kingdom off the coast of Brazil.

When she first saw Derrick, she was intimidated by him. He seemed smart and reserved, and she was sure that he wouldn't like her. She didn't know how to act around him, but when he introduced himself, she could tell that she made him nervous. He smiled awkwardly and fidgeted with his hands. When she played with the children, she could feel him watching her and it made her blush. She began to joke with him, and the first time they laughed together it felt like something had been unlocked inside her.

There is a knock at the door, and Rosa stands to answer. She opens the door and greets Derrick quietly. A sheet hangs across the middle of the room. Her mother rests on the other side.

"Como esta tu madre?" asks Derrick.

Rosa scrunches her brow and shakes her head. "She is not good."

"I'm sorry."

Her mother lets out a dry cough and then wheezes for air. Rosa touches her fingers to Derrick's shoulder and then steps away to pour a glass of water. She disappears to her mother's side of the room. Derrick hears whispering, and Rosa reappears. "We should let her rest," she says.

As they walk through the twilight, Derrick and Rosa hold tightly to each other's hands. The wind is cool. Each step carries a feeling of consequence. Derrick wonders if it's absurd to try and make a relationship work with Rosa. She has more obligations than he can begin to understand. He is terrified that this could be their last night together and he is furious at himself for how it is going. *We should be having fun.*

"Rosa," he says, "Yo recuerdo que dijiste pero…" he struggles to find a phrase, "Are you sure you want us to stay together?"

Rosa turns toward Derrick and takes his other hand.

"Derrick, te promiso, yo voy a hacer lo que necesito hacer para estar contigo. I love you. Sabes que te quiero."

Derrick pulls her toward him. Her arms grip firmly around his back. He brushes the hair from her face. "I love you too," he says. He feels Rosa shake and knows that she's afraid.

They walk on in silence, taking the long way through the forest, toward the open fields. They cross over hills and back again. When they speak they move between English and Spanish. Derrick no longer needs to translate every phrase he hears. Often, he simply understands. His speaking is clumsy, but he spends far less time putting together what he wants to say than he used to. Rosa has taught him that the feeling of a phrase is more important than the particular words. He finds himself leaning into his Spanish with an enthusiasm that is still missing in his English. As they walk, they talk about the children and how Derrick's time here has differed from his expectations. Their faces are lit by moonlight, and their bodies form shadows on the trail. Before the final bend back into the village, they pause and kiss. Her lips are thin and firm. The forest crackles with the sounds of the night.

In the morning Rosa sneaks into Derrick's room while he is talking with Ramon. She carries slips of paper and a pen. She takes Derrick's bag and empties it onto his cot. On one slip of paper she writes, "Te quiero, I love you." She folds it and pushes it inside the back pocket of his jeans. On another slip she writes, "Remember when Emilio said we should be married," and sticks it in a pair of socks. Between the pages of his journal she puts, "We rolled together in the grass," and "Tu espanol ha mejorado." She smiles at the thought of Derrick discovering these messages. She is proud of herself for being so clever. Under the cap of his deodorant, she puts, "I miss you." She wraps his underwear around a series of exclamation points. She folds other messages into the pages of his books and the pockets of his bag. She opens his passport and touches her finger, tenderly, to the picture of his face. She hates the fact that he is leaving her. *Wait for me.* She writes out the thought and folds it into the passport. *Nos vemos pronto.*

Year 7
Michael and Derrick

Three types of king cake sit on the table surrounded by bottles of liquor, orange juice, and bloody Mary mix. A live brass band plays on the back patio, and people step to the rhythm as they walk. Everyone is wearing pink: pink vests, pink earrings, pink necklaces, pink tutus and pink feather boas. Pink hats, pink cups, pink jackets and pink flamingoes scattered everywhere. Shane, the geologist, shouts greetings as people enter. The softened blare of faraway speakers lingers by the open door. Michael pours more vodka into his cup of orange juice. He smirks toward Derrick as if to say, *This is fucking crazy.* Derrick raises his eyebrows in response, *No shit.*

"What time is it anyway?" asks Michael, "Ten-thirty?"

"Ten-fifteen."

"What time is the parade?"

"Noon."

Michael taps his cup against Derrick's.

"Happy Mardi Gras," says Derrick.

"Happy Mardi Gras."

Flocks of people in handmade costumes masquerade through the normally quiet streets. Michael notices a loosening in the muscles around his eyes and decides to slow down on his drinking. Derrick feels at ease with the crowd around him. They find a crew from Shane's at the corner of Spanish Town Road and Bungalow and decide to join them. Across the street people in pink t-shirts huddle around a keg set up on the sidewalk. Several blocks away the first float appears. It's speakers play funk music while its krewe throws green, pink and gold beads into the outstretched hands of the crowd. The world is simplified. Music. Beads. Life. Derrick catches a green tambourine, and Michael snatches a small Frisbee from the air. Their necks grow thick with plastic beads. The sky cracks, and rain pours down like gasoline onto a fire.

Michael feels fingers dig into his side. He turns to find Sasha from school.

"*Hey!*"

She's wearing pink and black striped tights under a polka dot tutu, a pink tank top printed with a flamingo dressed in a tuxedo, and large plastic glasses. Her bangs are wet and pressed to her forehead. Michael is taken by surprise.

"Hey! Funny seeing you here," he says.

"I *love* Spanish Town. This might be my favorite

parade." She is almost shouting and Michael is relieved to realize she is drunker than he is.

"This is my first Mardi Gras but I live just around the corner," he says.

"Of course you would live in Spanish Town."

A string of beads flies by Sasha's face.

"Yeah, I love it here."

"Are you heading into New Orleans at all? Lundi Gras this Monday! I love Orpheus. It's one of my favorite parades."

"Not sure," he reaches out to grab a t-shirt from the air, "possibly."

"Nice catch!" Sasha whirls around, but the float with the t-shirt cannon has already passed. "Anyway, if you come into New Orleans you should give me a call," she glances down the sidewalk and then back to Michael. "I need to catch up with my friends." She's halfway down the block before Michael realizes that he doesn't have her number.

After the parade Michael and Derrick head back home. They track wet footsteps through the house and pile their beads on the kitchen counter. Derrick puts Coltrane's *A Love Supreme* on the record player. The house purrs under the weight of the rain.

On the porch they sit quietly. Michael knows the celebration has diffused throughout downtown. At Shane's house people are probably making more food. The bars on Third Street are filling with people. Michael considers heading back into the rain, but the idea exhausts him. He pushes his toes against the ground, and his chair rocks gently back and forth.

Derrick is thinking about Rosa. She says she'll visit over the summer, but she also seems afraid. Sometimes waiting for her feels foolish. The doubt wears on him like a river against its banks.

"This was a good day," says Michael.

"Yeah." Derrick's voice is soft.

"I'm glad it rained."

The next morning Michael awakes feeling refreshed. Colors seem richer than usual, and he is uncharacteristically bothered by the clutter around him. He clears the clothes from his floor, starts a load of laundry, makes his bed, and clears off his dresser. He vacuums the rug in the living room, returns his books to their shelves, throws away random papers, collects the loose dishes, and heads into the kitchen. The water runs hot as he scrubs at dried red sauce, and hardened oatmeal. On the radio, upbeat voices list the parade schedules for the next three days.

Michael's momentum pushes him forward. He sweeps and mops the kitchen and uses a damp cloth to dust the furniture in the living room. When he's finished, he falls backward onto the couch. He feels accomplished and in control. A soft smile sits effortlessly across his lips.

Derrick walks directly from his room into the shower and back again. When he emerges Michael has put *Catch a Fire* on the record player.

"You cleaned," says Derrick flatly, "Looks good."

"You don't have to be so surprised."

"I just didn't think you knew how." Derrick is walking

toward the kitchen

"I've cleaned before."

He twists toward Michael, "Really?"

Michael hesitates. "Uhhhh... Fair enough. I can try to do a better job of cleaning up after myself."

Derrick turns back toward the kitchen and calls over his shoulder, "Seeing is believing, my friend."

"You don't really believe that."

Derrick's voice carries from out of view, "I do when it comes to cleaning. Coffee?"

"Please."

The cleaning trucks have come through, but broken and discarded beads are still scattered on the sidewalk. As Michael walks along, he conjures images from yesterday and meditates on the idea that he is the only one who has returned here today. Thousands of faces have all gone their separate ways. He remembers the day, almost seven years ago, when he ran with the bulls in Spain. Every breath he took was electric. He remembers the girl who invited him onto the roof and how she danced for him, and he imagines her now with a family in Spain raising her children, and he wonders if she has ever thought of him. He digs for other memories from that trip. He finds images from stories he's told over the years, but he digs deeper. He wants to find a memory that he hasn't thought of since it happened. When he steps out of Spanish Town, the canopy of shade disappears, and he turns his eyes away from the sun. A calico cat throws him a curious glance. By reflex he turns on the path into the park. He tries to remember being at the bullfight in Spain, but the scene is more impression than substance. He thinks of Lindsey from Paris, but he can't remember her voice. The sun pulls sweat from his pores. *Escape.* The word comes from nowhere. Michael looks over to a sundrenched patch of grass and squints his eyes. His back begins to ache, and a decisive exhaustion crawls beneath his skin.

Back at the house, he flips open the vertical mailbox and finds a thick envelope resting on the bottom. When he reads Susan's name, he thinks there must have been some mistake. He pushes open the door and sits on the edge of the couch. He flips the letter between his fingers and brushes his thumb across the stamp.

Michael,

I'm sure you're surprised to see this letter. I wasn't sure if I should write it, but the more I convinced myself not to, the more I thought about writing it. Just starting it now, I can already feel my nerves relaxing.

I'm writing mainly for two reasons. The first is rather awkward to say. I'm kind of writing a book about you. Or about us. Well, really about love and two people who are a lot like us. In a way it's the book I once told you I was going to write. Leah and Marcel are in it, too. It's not really a novel. It uses a lot of poetry. Truth is I'm not sure what I'm trying to do with it, and I don't want to go on trying to describe it. But if you can take a look at the pages I've worked through so far, I'd be curious to hear what you think.

The second reason I'm writing is to let you know that

I've gotten engaged.

Michael stops and rereads the first two paragraphs.

His name is James and we've been together for just over two years. He makes me very happy.

I'm not sure what to say after that. I love him very much but it's different than the love you and I had. It took me a long time to admit that.

I don't know why I'm saying this, but sometimes, when I think about you and me, I think about the monks who make art with colored sand in the Himalayas. Do you know about this? They close the doors to their temple and spend hours each day for months arranging grains of colored sand into these giant patterns. They're gorgeous. But when they're done, they open up the doors, and the wind from the mountains sweeps through, and after a few minutes, all the sand is gone. I saw a video one time, and I almost cried. Anyway...

I'd like to say we should try and be friends but... Maybe we can be friends. I'm not sure. But I really would like to know what you think of these first pages of *Love in America*. Your opinion means a lot to me.

-Susan

Spring

Year 7
Susan

    While James helps his parents prepare for the engagement party, Susan studies the pictures on the mantel. There is one of James as a round-faced toddler curled up beside a black Labrador puppy. Another shows his mother laughing in her wedding dress while the dark arms of his father's tuxedo wrap around her. The photo is overexposed, and the softened colors give the picture a kind of joy. Susan touches the frame and breathes a long, soft breath. A portrait of James with his brothers reveals a withdrawn expression that she hasn't seen before. James, maybe twenty years old, is the youngest and shortest of the four. His chin slumps into his chest, and his smile is unconvincing. He is the only one in a sweater instead of a tie. By the edge of the mantel is a solo picture of his little sister, Mary. She wears a white dress with pink flowers and is putting a lot of effort into her pose. The pictures continue: unknown faces in silver frames. Susan tells herself that she should make herself useful in the kitchen, but she hovers in front of the photos. She allows her mind to skip like a pebble across a lake, casting ripples as it goes.

The guests enter without knocking and are quick to offer Susan their congratulations. She shakes their hands while trying to remember if they've met before. A sense of anxiety builds in her throat. Middle-aged couples make labored jokes about Susan having her hands full. The wives lament their husbands, and the husbands are unified in their desire for beer. Susan feels like she is sinking. *Where is Leah? She should be here by now.*

Susan excuses herself, locks the door to the bathroom behind her and sits on the edge of the bath. The ceramic is cold and ungiving. Susan has always gotten along with James's friends and family, but there has never been anything approaching intimacy between them. Even with his brothers, she feels pressured to laugh at their jokes and ask uninteresting questions about their wives. Her grandmother's health took another turn this week and she told her mother and Richie that they should go to Florida, but now she longs for them. She feels confined. Her lungs are beneath the sand. She thinks of the letter she sent to Michael and wonders if he'll reply. The idea terrifies her, but she hopes for a letter. She opens her purse and checks her phone for a message from Leah.

Leah is running late and driving quickly over windy roads. She checks her makeup while slowing down for stop signs and blinking yellow lights. *I'm pregnant.* The phrase has become a symbol of possibility. The stores beside the road give way to houses, and Leah rehearses ideas for how she'll break the news to Susan. *Susan. I'm pregnant. Susan I have something to tell you. Susie, you're my oldest friend and I hope you can be happy for me. Susan, there's something I've been keeping from you. I'm not sure why I haven't told you. Susan, I know this is your day and I'm happy for you but I can't keep this to myself any longer.* When she turns into James's parent's neighborhood she teases her hair with her fingers and looks at her profile in the mirror. *I'm glowing.*

James notices his brothers standing by the liquor cabinet. Tom, the oldest, is on the left. He holds a bottle of bourbon by the neck and splashes generously into Paul and Ryan's glasses. They wave for James to join them. All of his brothers have been quicker to success than James, and they all have wives and children. Tom's oldest son is almost eleven. For most of his life, James felt eclipsed by the shadow of his brothers. In high school they each knew what they wanted to do with their lives. Their father never pressured James to do the same, but he didn't hide his satisfaction when Tom, Paul, and Ryan, set themselves on respectable career paths. When Tom got his first job at a law firm, their father, a judge, had the partners over for dinner. When Paul became an engineer, he received a new car. When Ryan graduated from medical school, their father sent him on a three-week vacation through East Asia. When

James graduated with a bachelor's in history, he moved back home and hardly spoke with his father for a month.

As a child, James had trouble fighting back when his brothers would punch him. He would swing wildly, and they would knock him to the ground and dig their knuckles into his ribs. He cried, and they called him names. He was angry but he also wanted to belong. He craved the times that his brothers would include him in their schemes. What they knew was all he wanted to know. They were his gatekeepers to the world.

When Mary was born, he enjoyed the idea that he would play a similar role for her, but it soon became clear that Mary was to come up in a completely different way. Mary became the darling of their mother. They went to church together and disappeared for entire weekends with hardly a word. James loved his sister and tried to get to know her better when he moved back home, but she carried herself with an aloofness that he couldn't understand. She buried herself in books and had little interest in her older brother. James often wondered if she had been warned against him by their parents. The idea would trigger his anger and set him pacing in his childhood room. He imagined himself a leper in his own house. When his brothers started getting married, the feeling got worse.

After two years of living at home, James enrolled in culinary school. His father congratulated him on "finally doing *something*." With his brothers, their father expected to be proud, but with James, it seemed he was content to not be burdened. Over time James became more and more comfortable in the kitchen. He thought less about gaining his father's approval and more about refining his craft. He would stay up at night remembering the heat of the kitchen, the clang of knives, the suspense and the reward of an edible creation. It was far more satisfying than James had hoped. He kept a notebook and filled it with descriptions of flavors and ideas for new dishes. Behind each new ingredient or technique, he found a dozen more to pique his interest. He became entranced by the notion that, even after thousands of years, cuisine still contained vast frontiers to be explored.

Still, his family did not understand. On three separate occasions when guests were over for dinner, his father contrasted James' work with one of his brothers in a way to make the guests laugh. The phrasing was innocent enough, but the effect was obviously intentional, and the barbs wounded James. He became more reclusive and set his mind on opening a restaurant of his own. He told himself that it was for his own creative freedom, but he often thought how such an accomplishment would impress his father. That was almost seven years ago.

Tom hands James the drink he prepared, "Well, I'll be damned," he says.

"Finally getting hitched," adds Paul, and slaps his hand against James's back.

Ryan gestures toward Susan and their wives circled beside the coffee table "I hope she's not giving them any crazy ideas."

The whiskey warms James's cheeks. He watches Susan and is glad that she seems to be getting along with his brother's wives. He notices how his brothers watch her and feels a flush of pride. "I wouldn't put it past her," he says.

"So, Tommy bought us a boat last summer but of course we haven't been able to take it out since the week after he bought it. It's a gorgeous thing. I don't remember how many feet but it's one of the bigger ones. It has a kitchen and plenty of room on the deck. I was worried because sometimes I get claustrophobic, but there's really plenty of room. We should use it more but you know how work can be. Anyway, it's a nice thing to have."

"Well, I'll tell you, I wouldn't put up with that from Paul. We've had our lake house for almost three years now and I always make sure we use it at least every few months or so. Even if Paul can't make it, I make sure to take the children up without him."

The wives laugh, and Susan grins politely.

"Maybe that's what you should do, have Tom show you how to take the boat out on your own," says Ryan's wife.

They laugh louder, and Susan's eyes break from the circle, searching for an escape.

"And what about you Susan? Do you and James have your eyes set on anything to help you relax?"

"Oh…" she tries to re-center herself in the conversation, "you know most of our money is getting tied up in the new restaurant."

"*New* restaurant," says Tom's wife, "No, I didn't know."

James warned her not to mention the restaurant. She curses herself for having said something. She twists her lips and prepares for the barrage of questions.

"Tell us more. Where will it be?"

"Isn't it a bit soon to open a second restaurant?"

"I shouldn't say anymore. Really I shouldn't."

"Oh my. Is it a secret?"

"No, of course not. It's just… I don't know much about the details. We don't talk too much about those things."

When Leah enters she's surprised by the number of unfamiliar faces. She sees Susan talking with a group of women and feels a prick of jealousy. All of the furniture is unusually nice. She feels people's eyes on her and is unnerved by the attention. "Oh, Susie," she cries and throws her arms around her. Susan is relieved. She introduces Leah to the wives and offers to show her where the food is.

"Have they seen the ring?"

"Oh, not nearly enough," says Ryan's wife.

"Let us have another look," adds Paul's.

Susan extends her hand and averts her eyes.

"I just love the ring," says Leah, "you know James called me to help pick it out." Susan has heard this story more than once. "You should have seen James, he was so helpless…" Leah continues while Susan looks around the room. She sees James talking with his brothers and notices his parents whispering to each other. *This will be my children's family.* She tries to smooth the edges of the thought.

When Leah finishes her story, Susan insists on getting her a plate of food, and they walk together into the dining room. They pile fruit on paper plates, and Susan suggests going to the patio. They sit in wooden chairs and watch the children playing in the back yard. The breeze is warm, and the light is gentle but clear.

"This is a pretty fancy soiree," says Leah.

"It's definitely more elaborate than I was expecting."

"Well you need to make sure you have more of a say in these types of things."

"I don't know if I'm ready to start disagreeing with James's mother."

"You'll have to eventually."

"Eventually." Susan bites into a strawberry and touches Leah's knee with her fingers. "Leah, I'm glad you're here. You know, sometimes I think you're the only real friend I have left."

"Susie, sometimes, I think you may be the only real friend I've *ever* had."

"That's not true."

"Well it feels true enough right now and…" emotion creeps into her voice, "Susan, I have something I need to tell you. I probably should have told you already."

Susan watches Leah steady her gaze. Her eyes shimmer, and her jaw begins to shake.

"I… I'm…" Leah is close to tears. Her hand moves toward her stomach and, with a shock, Susan realizes what she is trying to say.

"Leah," she takes her hand, "are *you*—"

"Yes."

"Oh my God. Are you sure?"

"I'm sure."

Susan feels James's hand on her shoulder.

"There you are," he says.

She twists her neck to look up at James and places her fingers on the back of his hand, "Honey, can you give Leah and I just a few minutes. I promise to be in soon."

James hesitates. His cheeks are red. "Alright. But I hope you appreciate how embarrassing it is for a man to go looking for his fiancée and return empty handed."

"I'm sorry love. I'll be with you soon."

Year 7
Derrick and Michael

Derrick squats between two rows of kale, clips the unbitten leaves and wraps them in bunches with the rubber bands from around his wrist. The shadows around him are long, but the sun clings stubbornly to its heat. He drags his forearm over his brow and dirt smears across his face. The steady rumble of traffic carries through the ten-foot tall grass behind him. The air shakes, but the ground is calm. Derrick straightens up and sees Lane wave to him from across the field. He is rinsing a crate of Brussels sprouts with the hose from the side of the house. Lane is a short man with a bulging stomach and an unkempt rim of white hair around the back and sides of his head. He has been working this small farm with his wife, Martha, for almost twenty years.

Derrick rolls his shoulders and pushes them forward to stretch his back. The soreness spreads from his back and into his thighs. His once white t-shirt sticks to his skin. It's time to head in, but he lingers amongst the plants. Thoughts of his already packed bags flash before him. *It'll be good to get out of town for a little while.*

Before he leaves Martha offers him a glass of tea. Derrick has made a habit of awkwardly avoiding Martha's hospitality, but today he is thirsty and especially tired. She invites him in, and he takes a seat at a small wooden table covered with a plaid tablecloth. The kitchen is separated from the main room of the house by three steps and a banister. In the three months Derrick's been coming here he's never been inside. He pivots in his seat to take in the room. The kitchen is small but clean and well stocked. The main room is spacious. A large blue rug covers most of the floor. Beside the back wall is a pair of upright pianos with books of music stacked on top of them. Martha takes a pitcher from the fridge and pours two glasses of sweet tea.

"You have two pianos?"

"Oh, that's something I do in my spare time." Martha's voice swings between her words in a way that underlines the casualness of what she's saying, "I teach piano to some of the children from town." She hands him his glass of tea and sits across from him. "Do you have plans for the weekend?" she asks. Her voice is gentle. Derrick lets himself relax.

"I'm heading out of town with a friend of mine. It's spring break at school, so we're going to make a trip."

"*Oh,* where to?"

"Savannah, Georgia. There's a concert out there and I've heard good things about the city." He sips his tea and nods to show he enjoys it.

"Yes, Savannah's a wonderful city. Of course it's been years since I've been there. What's the concert?"

"A guy named Dahntae." Derrick is never sure how to talk about music with people whose taste he doesn't know. "He does modern folk-type stuff. I'm looking forward to it." As Derrick finishes the phrase, he can see Martha's mind drift from the conversation. He listens to the ice clink inside his glass and wonders if Michael is waiting for him. Outside the window the setting sun casts an orange sheen across a small pond. Derrick's eyes settle on the bench that sits above the far bank and thinks of how peaceful it must be for Martha and Lane to sit there when no one is around. He imagines Rosa beside him, sitting there, watching the night pull up around them. *I wonder how bad the mosquitoes get.*

"So," Martha's tone is suddenly more consequential, "Lane tells me he's talked to you about how we're moving out west after the summer."

"Yes ma'am. We've talked."

"And have you been able to give it much thought?"

"I have, but I'm still not sure. It's a big change. I mean I've thought about doing something like this for a while."

"That's what Lane was telling me."

"But… You understand. And I need to talk more with my girlfriend. She's supposed to be moving here around then." Derrick inspects the ring of condensation on the table below his glass and takes his final sip of tea.

"I understand. But you let us know soon." Martha takes the empty glasses and walks toward the sink. The house is still, except for her movements. As Derrick watches Martha rinse the glasses and place them in the drying rack he feels a deepening envy for the type of life that she's crafted in this home. He stands from the table and looks to the door. The world seems to be slowing down.

It's a half-hour past dark when Derrick gets home. When he closes the door behind him, he hears Michael yell that he's almost ready. They load their bags into the back of Michael's car, and Derrick mentions he's tired from the farm. Michael offers to drive the first shift. They still haven't decided if they'll try and drive through the night.

"How long is it again?" asks Michael.

"I think about seventeen hours."

Outside of Baton Rouge, the highway becomes a tunnel of light through the country. The shadows of the bayou brush like an opaque fog against the edges of the road. There are no hills and few turns. The exits grow farther apart. By the time they reach Mississippi, Derrick is asleep. Michael's eyes grow heavy, but he resolves to drive for at least a few more hours. He doesn't feel like dealing with a hotel room. When they reach Mobile, Alabama, the lights wake Derrick up. He offers to drive when they reach Georgia and closes his eyes again as the lights of the city drift behind them.

Michael's thoughts circle around his letter from Susan. The pages of *Love in America* confounded him. They traced the most dramatic moments of their relationship together with an air of finality, but also of longing. There was no mention of her impending marriage. The last lines scroll through his mind:

Whispers, remind me of you.

Memories sing a siren song.

They echo,

Beckoning from rocky shores.

Like thunder before a storm.

Do you hear them calling?

I really would like to know what you think. Michael resists the temptation to read the pages as a love letter. *She probably just wants my OK to write about all this... Maybe it's her way of saying goodbye. Siren song. Do you hear them calling? Rocky shores. Whispers. Could she still be in love with me?* The thoughts float in front of him, suspended above the road. He tries to focus on driving. If it were daytime he would see that the ground outside has turned red. *She probably just wants to be friends. She needs to put this part of us behind her. We could be friends. We'll both move on but we can always be friends. We can share things with each other.* He notes a bizarre poetry in the fact that he's driving toward a concert by Dahntae. He remembers the image of Dahntae silhouetted beside the Cathedral. *Meaning is woven with passion.* Of course Dahntae didn't mean sexual passion when he said that, but that was how it seemed at the time. That was the night he began lying to Susan. Four years later, driving past midnight through rural Alabama, Michael is beyond regret. He is a different person than he used to be. *Me and Susan both.*

The stars fade away and the sky begins to lighten as the glow of dawn breaks over the horizon. Derrick awakes sluggishly, and Michael mentions that he's about to stop at a gas station. Michael is exhausted. Derrick straightens and flexes his legs as he steps out of the car. Michael does the same and lets out a sound that slides between yawn and growl. Inside they buy a large bag of chips, a pair of drinks and a newspaper. There is a two-person line, and each customer chats politely with the cashier. Michael tosses Derrick the keys as they walk back to the car.

"I thought you liked driving."

"If I drive another mile I'll fucking kill us both."

"Where we going?"

"East."

Derrick's beard is heavy and he can feel the dried sweat across his brow, but he is surprisingly rested. School and the farm seem very far away. He chides Michael for closing his eyes right away and not keeping him company.

"Shut up."

Derrick smiles. They never mention it, but they are both acutely aware of how important they are to each other. There was a time when Derrick felt inferior to Michael. He envied Michael's ability to draw respect from his classmates and professors, the way he could laugh with strangers, and how he felt comfortable around attractive women. For a while, Derrick wondered why Michael wanted to spend so much time with him. They would hang out for days at a time: shooting pool, splitting lunch, reading magazines, playing football, smoking pot, drinking at bars. They held no pretensions around each other, and it wasn't until years later that Derrick appreciated how rare that type of relationship would be. Michael seemed to have known it all along. Still, when they graduated, and Michael left for New York, Derrick was left feeling like he had drifted along without taking control of his own life. His ambitions quivered before him like paper in the wind. Michael suggested he 'do something crazy.' After Nicaragua, Derrick felt a change in himself. He stood on the other side of a line he hadn't known existed. His anxieties settled into a sortable pattern. When Michael arrived from New York, the dynamics between them changed. Derrick became the one who made plans for the weekends. Michael often seemed despondent, and the challenges in his classroom didn't help. Only in the last few weeks has Michael begun to seem like he's enjoying his life again. Derrick can tell it's taken effort. Driving along the highway, he takes comfort in the way that they can bond through silence.

Michael tries to sleep, but sleep does not come. The windshield magnifies the heat against his face. His limbs squirm restlessly and with a slight feeling of defeat, he opens his eyes and rubs at their corners with his knuckles.

"You up?"

Michael straightens his posture, "Yeah."

"How long you been awake?"

"I'm not sure I ever got to sleep. How long have you been driving?"

"About an hour. We're still over a hundred miles south of Atlanta."

Michael unfolds the newspaper and reads the headlines out loud. There's a story about artists moving into small towns in Georgia for the low rents and being welcomed by the residents. There is a story about memory that says the more people remember an event the more they change the memory. A bald columnist with a round face encourages people to talk more. He quotes data about the decrease in duration of the average conversation, and he worries about the world the youth are creating for themselves. There's an article about a pet store opening downtown. A picture shows a middle-aged woman with four small dogs cradled in her arms. The caption reads, "Shirley McMurphy and her dogs; Do, Re, Mi and Fatso."

Derrick sings: "Do, Re, Mi, Fat-*So*."

Michael folds the paper against the crease and flicks in onto the floor.

An hour outside of Savannah, Derrick decides to breach the subject of the farm.

"So, there's something I've been meaning to talk to you about...

"Lane and his wife are heading out west for a couple of years at the end of the summer to help take care of their new granddaughter, and they've asked if I'd be interested in moving in and helping to take care of the farm."

"Damn."

"I wouldn't have to keep getting the same yield that they're getting. I could try and go to school for agriculture in the evenings. And I think Rosa would like it. She's kind of intimidated by the idea of living in the city." Derrick feels relieved to finally say all this out loud.

"Have you talked to her about it yet?"

"No. We're supposed to talk next week."

"So, you'd work the farm and sell what you grow at market?"

"That's the idea."

"And then use that experience to try and break into farming?"

"Well it's not an easy racket to get into. I think I'd like it though and this isn't the sort of opportunity most people get."

"You going to do it?"

"I think so."

"Well, sounds like a plan. You're making me feel like I need to get my life together."

"I thought you said you're starting to enjoy teaching."

"I did." Michael glances out the window to the fields of corn and then back to Derrick, "I mean, I am... I am."

The hotel is nicer than they expected. The carpet in their room is plush. The windows look out over the city's historic district. The bathroom is sleek with a large waterfall style faucet. After they drop their bags, Michael collapses onto his bed and pledges not to move until the next morning. Derrick heads out into the street. The air is lighter than in Louisiana, and the breeze carries a hint of the ocean. At the corner of each block, he finds a large square shaded by oak trees and the Spanish moss that hangs from their branches. At the center of each square is a monument with a statue. People talk on benches, and young musicians busk for change. Their songs carry out of the squares and follow Derrick as he moves past them into the streets. He makes note of a used bookstore and a large coffee shop with hardwood floors and pre-vintage furniture. Small art galleries are sprinkled between bars and clothing stores. The atmosphere reminds him of New Orleans, and he pauses on the thought that living in the south has begun to feel like home. On his way back, he finds the theater where Dahntae will be performing tomorrow night. It's smaller than he expected. He stops to admire the antebellum mansions he finds every couple of blocks and reads the historic plaques in front of them. There is a faint recollection of a French architect in Georgia from one of his design classes. When Derrick returns to the hotel, he finds Michael at the bar talking with a married couple a few years older than them. They are on vacation from Atlanta and come here every year. Derrick declines to get a drink and heads back to the room to clean up. He takes his time in the shower. The water presses his hair over his forehead and drips from his beard. He lets his mind fall silent. The room fills with steam. Before he steps out, he shuts off the hot water and the chill shakes him awake. He feels refreshed.

For dinner, they walk down to the river and find a restaurant with a balcony. They order oysters and the second cheapest bottle of white wine. Michael talks about the couple from the hotel bar. They both work marketing jobs and have two weeks of vacation a year.

"I'd shoot myself," says Derrick.

"They seemed happy enough."

"They're on vacation."

"Fair enough. But not everyone can run off and be a farmer."

"True."

"Do farmers even get vacations?"

"I'm not sure how all that works. I guess I should probably figure it out."

"Probably. Teaching is tough but vacation time is definitely a perk." Michael raises an oyster shell in a toast.

"To spring break," says Derrick.

The waiter returns, and they order the salmon and the shrimp fettuccini with the understanding that they'll share. Before the dishes arrive, they ask for a second bottle of wine. They eat until full and then press on further. They order a chocolate soufflé with ice cream for dessert. They finish the wine while they wait for it to arrive.

"I can barely walk," says Michael, as they stand from the table. Derrick grunts.

They hobble heavy-footed back to their hotel.

"It's good to get away," says Michael.

"Amen to that."

The next morning, Derrick shows Michael the coffee shop he found the day before. Inside, Derrick picks up a copy of Savannah's weekly tabloid, and Michael grabs some loose sections of the daily paper. Michael compliments the atmosphere in the coffee shop, and Derrick says he likes the furniture. The room is large, and the floor is made of a dark brown wood cut into wide planks. Local art hangs from the walls. They order coffee and bagels with different types of cream cheese. When they sit down, Derrick opens the paper and scans the table of contents. He notices an interview with Dahntae on page seventeen and flips directly to it. He skims over the intro and learns that Dahntae grew up in a working class family in Chicago's south side. After studying at NYU for two years, he dropped out to dedicate himself to music. He has been traveling the country now for eleven years.

"There's an interview with Dahntae in here."

Michael looks up, disinterested in his own paper, "How long is it?"

"Not long."

He glances around to make sure no one is sitting nearby, "You want to read it to me?"

"Sure." Michael moves forward in his seat and starts to prep his bagel. Derrick takes a sip of coffee and then begins, "First Question: What's the longest you've spent in one place?

"Dahntae: You know, normally not more than a couple of nights, but once and awhile, I get caught up somewhere. I was in Denver for a few weeks not too long ago. Last fall I got caught up in New Orleans for almost three months. That might be the longest. Good music town. Savannah is nice. I could stay here for a week or so. I'd like to come back sometime.

"Question: How has traveling affected the type of music you write?

Dahntae: It keeps me focused. Don't get me wrong. It's tough a lot of the time. Tough in a way that it doesn't do much good to talk about. But it keeps me focused, forces me to refine what I'm doing. I don't plan on moving around forever, but I don't know when I'll stop, either. I'd probably write different music if I wasn't moving around, but then I'm not sure about that. No way to tell really.

Question: You're known for the weight of your lyrics. What questions would you say motivate your writing?

Dahntae: First of all, I don't think that's completely true. One song I just recorded, "Lumpy Grits," doesn't have much to it at all. The whole song is just, 'Stir that pot don't let'em sit / I don't want no lumpy grits.' It's got a good rhythm to it though, and recently I've been getting more of a positive reaction on that song than just about anything else I do.

But as far as my other stuff goes, it's been changing. I used to be real interested in that worn out question of how to life an authentic life. I'd sing about people being afraid to harmonize with the chords inside their minds, that kind of stuff. But lately I've been trying to get beyond that. I mean, I still think it's an important question, but I don't think it's as central to today's generations, my generation, as it was to the people who came up during the second half of the last century. I think the question for artists today is more about how to live deeply. How do you make sure that this personal set of likes and dislikes and morals and goals we build for ourselves is more than just a facade? I'd say that nowadays, it's easier than it's ever been for people to tap into their authentic selves, but it's getting harder to develop that self in a way that adds depth to your character.

Question: So, would you say your songs push against the influence of modern media?

Dahntae: No. I don't consider myself a Luddite. Obviously learning how to keep from just ricocheting from one stimulus to another is an important skill nowadays, but overall, all that media stuff is great. Very useful.

I've got a song now called *Company Store*. It's a riff off an old blues song called *16 Tons* where a man hauls coal every day, but all he gets is deeper in debt. Sold his soul to the company store, you know. I thought it would be interesting to take that idea and set it to modern themes. Make the

Company Store those things in our culture that tempt us into a self-contained world, you know, the modern branding stuff that asks us who we are and then tries to do all of our thinking for us. That can be a dangerous thing when you look at the power dynamics around it. But focusing on all that misses the point. The emphasis shouldn't be on judging what's happening around us. It's about how we react, you know, making sure we don't forfeit our creative potential to the path of least resistance. That's the issue for my generation, or at least it's one way of thinking about it.

Final Question: How do you spend your time on the road when you're not performing or writing songs?

Dahntae: Different things. I like talking with people I meet. I play go when I can. Mostly I fold shapes out of paper."

The rest of the day passes quickly. They explore the used bookstore and take a tour of one of the old mansions. They buy sandwiches for lunch and eat them on a bench in the square closest to the hotel. After some patience, Michael gets a bird to take a piece of bread from his hand. The bird flies off and a train of other birds follow behind. When they leave to return to the hotel, Derrick gives a few dollars to the man who was singing by the bench next to them.

Back in their room, Michael's thoughts settle again on Susan's letter, and he wonders why he hasn't told Derrick about it. The line about coming to know ourselves through learning how to love has been stuck in his mind since breakfast. Derrick steps out of the bathroom and lies down on the bed. Michael takes a breath, intending to mention the letter, but the words don't come.

"Were you going to say something?"

"No." The room's AC kicks in and fills the silence. "I'll tell you about it on the ride home."

"I'm going to try and get some rest before the show."

They arrive early because Derrick wants to be close enough to watch the guitar. They're on their second drink when the waitress comes around for a last order before the show. They order two gin and tonics and two beers. The room has filled to standing room only. There is a sudden change in lighting, and a middle-aged man steps onto the stage. He gives a brief introduction where he describes Dahntae as a bohemian troubadour. Dahntae walks to the microphone to the sound of chatter and polite applause. His thumb picks out a baseline and then his other fingers join in. The room becomes quiet. His left hand moves with deceptive simplicity. Derrick admires the way he can snap key notes as he plays to create a third layer of emotion that weaves between rhythm and melody. Michael is at ease. The lights go dim. Dahntae begins to sing.

Year 7
Susan and Leah

Leah stands naked in front of her bathroom mirror. The skin on her stomach is pulled tight over the small pillow-sized bulge that curves outward just below her ribs. She sets her palm above her almost protruding bellybutton and moves it up and down in long elliptical strokes. A set of stretch marks has appeared on the underside of her stomach. She frowns as she traces them with her middle finger. She turns sideways and then back again. Her breasts are swollen and patterned with a network of thin blue lines. She traces the veins with her pinky, and the sensation splits outward like a wake across her skin. She imagines what will happen to her nipples if she decides to breastfeed. Her apartment is silent. She takes her robe from the hook on the door, slides her arms through the sleeves and ties it closed around her waist. She feels a quake across the back of her neck and a sudden loss of breath. *I'm not afraid.* A now familiar nausea builds in her chest.

Deciding to make her own wedding dress seemed like a perfect idea at the time. Now, Susan is not so sure. Her sewing table is cluttered: three yards of fabric, a pair of scissors, a packaged bodice pattern with a sweetheart neckline, a balled up stretch of measuring tape, bound strips of corset boning, ribbon, a red pincushion, a three-inch ruler, fabric pencils and spools of thread all vie for her attention. The sewing machine presides above the scene with an air of disquiet. Beneath the table, layers of tulle in shades of pink and white billow from a cardboard box. A vintage petticoat sits folded beside them. Susan stares blankly at the array. She regrets not buying a pegboard to help keep organized. She tries to conjure an image of the completed dress. The vision is clear in its impression but elusive in its details. She looks away from the table and back again.

Behind her, on a second table, her laptop is opened to

the last page of *Love in America*. She's decided to follow her own character up through her wedding but has had trouble writing her as enthusiastic. The writer's block feeds into a growing apprehension she feels toward all things wedding-related. The steady barrage of decisions has pushed her into a bland indifference. Discussions with her mother are helpful but exhausting. James seems forever detained at the restaurant. When they are together, he is fully open with her, and she knows that he loves her. But more and more they are apart. She knows she should share the pressures she feels with him, but she worries it will poison the moments they have together. She sacrifices her piece of mind for his and she resents him for it. The wedding dress was meant as her locus of control, but now its pieces taunt her with their incompleteness.

Leah lies in bed. Her body aches. She feels alone. At work her colleagues have begun to treat her differently. They are overly polite and rarely come to her for help with anything anymore. Even her boss asks less of her. She knows the change is meant as a courtesy. She knows a gradual shift is necessary for when she goes on leave. Still, it frustrates her incessantly. Only a month ago, she was invaluable. She delighted in doing favors, solving problems, and connecting people. Now, she feels like another spoke in the wheel. In a few months, she will be gone altogether.

The responsibilities of being a mother rise around her like a wall. When she told Susan she was pregnant, Susan said she would do anything she could to help, but it's been almost a month since they've seen each other. Leah sits up in bed. For the second time today, she has a craving for fresh fruit.

Susan unpacks the bodice pattern and cuts it out into four pieces. She compares her own measurements to the pattern's dimensions and adjusts the outline slightly as she marks the fabric for the lining. She readies her scissors to cut, and her mind begins to wander. She sees a blurred image of her final dress, and then she's imagining a young daughter, and James combing her hair with his fingers. Her chin tilts away from the table, and Susan remembers sitting up in bed when she was a little girl and listening to her parents argue downstairs. They would never shout, but their voices were always heated, and Susan would strain to hear what they were saying. Sometimes she would slide off her bed and tiptoe down the hallway. She remembers being careful to step along the side edges of the steps to make sure they didn't creak. The voices grew more distinct. When she made it downstairs, she would stand just outside the doorway and listen while her heart raced. Once, she got on her hands and knees and crawled behind the couch where her mother sat. Sometimes the fights were about her father's desire to spend money the family didn't have. Sometimes they were about her. Susan isn't sure how many times she did this or exactly what she heard. The only words she still remembers distinctly were from her father. "If it wasn't for that damn girl I wouldn't have to..." The rest of the line is lost in her memory. *If it wasn't for that damn girl...* Susan hates these memories of her parents fighting. She sees a flash of a broken TV at the foot of the stairs and hears her mother whisper with a detached calm, "Your father just got mad sweetheart. It's ok, he's not mad at you." But Susan knew better. She had heard him say so.

Susan shakes her head. She presses her eyes closed and then stretches them wide. She refocuses on the paper and cloth before her. The scissors feel lifeless in her hand.

Leah leans against her kitchen table dipping cut watermelon and cantaloupe into a plastic dish of plain yogurt. Each bite is succulent. She empties the cup of fruit, finishes the yogurt with a spoon and briefly considers drinking the juice at the bottom of the fruit cup before she regains control and throws it away. She sits in front of the television and flips through the channels, pausing to watch commercials that catch her eye. It's the middle of the afternoon, and she is as bored as she has ever been. She turns off the TV. She tells herself she should enjoy the quiet while she can. She starts to hum an improvised melody and then loses interest. She looks down at the bump in her robe, "Do you like it when mommy sings?" She hums a few more phrases. "Mommy used to have lots of friends, but now it's just me and you."

Engaged to a chef and I still cook dinner four nights a week. Susan stirs a mixture of butter, blue cheese, herbs, and lemon juice. In her four hours of working, she barely managed to cut out the lining panels for the top of her dress and write a pair of lines for *Love in America*. She takes the defrosted chicken breasts from the refrigerator and sets them on a pan. She lifts the skin of the breasts with a fork and spreads the cheese mixture underneath. She presses the skin into the blue cheese, and smiles at the thought that James will be impressed with the meal. He should be home within the hour. She slides the pan into the oven, and boils a pot of water for the green beans. She texts James to make sure he'll be home on time.

Ninety minutes later, she hasn't heard back from him. The chicken is done, and the beans are cooling in a large ceramic bowl. Susan is restless. Her sense of balance had returned while she was preparing dinner, but now her emotions are swirling toward anger. She sits at the dining room table. She stands, paces, looks out the window and returns to her chair. She doesn't mind James keeping long hours at the restaurant, but she can't stand feeling like she's been forgotten. She stands, paces, looks out the window and walks into the bedroom. She decides to call Leah. `

Leah is watching a musical from the early days of Technicolor when her phone rings.

"Susie!"

"Hi Leah."

"I thought you had forgotten about me."

"No. I'm sorry. You must think I'm a horrible friend. How are you?"

"I'm fat and grumpy. I miss you. Why did you have to move into the country anyway?"

"I don't live in the country."

"You may as well. Why don't you and James invite me over for dinner sometime?"

"I would if I ever knew when we were going to eat,"

Susan's irritation leaks into her voice. "I've been waiting for James to come home for over an hour and I have dinner ready in the kitchen. He won't even return my texts."

"Have you eaten?"

"No."

"You should. Don't let him force you onto his schedule."

"But I've been looking forward to eating together all day. I feel like I never see him. And I made this new recipe... Leah, sometimes I doubt this whole thing. Am I settling? Is this what people mean when they talk about settling?"

"Oh fickleshit Susan," Leah's tone becomes harsh, "Some of us would kill to have your problems."

"I don't mean to complain. I just can't get out from under this cloud of forever. I thought the engagement would pull James and me closer together but it's like he's used it as a license to neglect me."

"Look, James loves you. Anyone who's spent time with the two of you knows that. He really, *really* loves you. It's not his fault if you're not com*municati*ng."

"I am communicating. He won't even tell me when he's going to be home. Why aren't you telling me I have a right to be upset?"

"Because I'm tired of this. You've a*l*ways done this. If you just realized the life you have you could be happy. Instead you talk yourself into this romantic discontentment, but there's nothing ro*mantic* about it. It's like you're set on sabotaging your own life and it's frustrating for those of us who need to pull all the energy we have just to believe we might one day be as lucky as you are." Leah's voice quakes, and she strains for breath. "I'm sorry," she laughs through her cracking voice, "I told you I was grumpy."

Susan breathes quietly on her side of the phone, absorbing the hurt in Leah's words. "You've always lived," says Susan, "like you've deserved to be happy. And I've always admired you for that. Maybe you're right... I don't know what's wrong with me."

"Nothing's wrong with you."

"Sometimes I feel like the only relationship I was ever happy in was when I was with Michael."

"Michael? You were with Michael for like four months."

"Longer than that."

"You get my point."

"I know. And I love James. I just keep coming back to this idea that I met him when I wanted to be single. It's like part of me is convinced being with him has stunted me as my own person."

"Susie, I knew you a long time before James. What did you want to do back then? You wanted to write, learn how to design and sew your own dresses and find someone who would love you for who you were. That's how you described the life you wanted to have. Instead of accusing him of things maybe you should be thanking him. Look, James helps you bring out the best in yourself. You know that. This is what I mean when I say you always try to talk yourself out of being happy."

"I want to be happy."

"Me too."

"You know there's not a woman in my family who

hasn't gotten divorced?"

"Divorce isn't genetic Susan. It's personal. *Very* personal. Trust me. And James is a good person."

"Leah," she brushes a strand of hair behind her ear and looks at the living room around her, "I think I'm most lucky to have you as a friend."

"Finally! Something we can agree on."

When James comes home, he's carrying a bottle of wine. Susan flings her arms around him and kisses him on the cheek. She presses her face against his chest.

"Hey there. I'm sorry I'm late."

"I've been waiting. But I forgive you."

"After we open next week things will calm down, I swear. At least a little bit." James grins.

"Dinner is ready." Susan walks toward the kitchen.

"Good. But just a small plate for me."

"Whatever you want love."

James goes to the bedroom to change. Susan prepares two plates and opens the bottle of wine. They sit together at the table.

"I started my dress today."

"I can't wait to see you in it." He takes a bite of the green beans. "Did you put salt in the water to boil these?"

"Yeah. Why?"

"It could probably use a little more."

"Honey, tomorrow morning, do you think you could help me pick out gifts for the bridal party?"

"I don't know. I was hoping to get an early start tomorrow. And you know I trust you."

Susan nods and her nerves tense up. She focuses on the meal. The chicken has dried out a little since it was first ready, but it is still delicious. She takes a sip of wine.

James takes a second bite of chicken, "How did you cook this?" he asks, less curious than concerned.

"*Oh for fuck's sake!*" Susan has never cursed in anger at James before, and the word drops like a bomb between them. She resists the impulse to throw her plate from the table. She stands up violently, and her chair falls backward. "It was fine two hours ago." She storms toward the back door and walks out to the patio. James sits dumbstruck.

Outside the air is fresh, and the spring air is soft against Susan's skin. Even in the dark, the plants and flowers by the patio sweeten the breeze. Susan sits in one of the two wicker chairs she bought last week and stares up at the sky. The clouds are moving quickly. A quarter moon rests just above the tree line. Crickets sing, and two birds chirp in a call and response. Susan breathes deeply. She picks a star from the sky and watches a cloud pass over it. She waits for it to reappear, and when it does, there is a smaller star beside it. The edge of the next cloud brushes just below them. She's not sure how long she has been sitting there when she hears the door slide open and watches James step onto the patio and take a seat in the chair next to her. The crickets count the beats of silence between them.

"I'm sorry," he says, "I know you have a lot going on. I spend all day critiquing food and I just wasn't thinking."

"It's not just the food. It's the wedding. It's supposed to be *our* wedding but I feel like you don't want to have any part in it. I know you're busy but have you thought at all about what your priorities look like to me? And, I'm not opening a restaurant, but I do have a job and I want to make my own dress, but it all gets to be too much if I feel like I'm doing it all alone."

"You're right." He reaches out, rests his hand on top of Susan's and presses lightly, "I guess part of me has been afraid of arguing over the whole thing. I know I haven't been fair to you."

"It's just this process is kind of like a rehearsal for the rest of our life together. I don't want to fall into a pattern where I have to make all the decisions that don't have clear answers. And… you have to let me know when you'll be coming home. I feel like a fool if I'm just sitting here waiting for you." Susan feels a weight lifting from her chest.

"I can do that." Susan turns toward him and slides her thumb across the back of his hand. "I'm glad we're talking," James continues, "I had been worried about you recently, like you were keeping something from me. I guess neither one of us has been as open as we should be."

"James. Since we've been together, for the first time in my life, I feel like I'm the person I've always wanted to be. I don't ever want to lose you." Her voice slides above a sheet of fear.

"More than anything," James turns, and Susan watches his eyes shimmer in the light of the moon, "I want to build a life with you."

Year 7
Michael and Derrick

Farhea looks left and right and then left and right again. The hallway is clear. Her heart suddenly picks up speed. She looks left and right for a third time and feels a prick of exhilaration as she realizes that she's going to put her plan into action. She sets her hand on the doorknob of the classroom in front of her. The door swings inward. She hears footsteps encroaching from around the corner. She rushes inside and turns rapidly to shut the door behind her as smooth and quiet as she can. She pauses and tries to take control of her breathing. Farhea has never done anything like this, but over the last several weeks she has become convinced that something absolutely must be done and this is the only idea she could come up with.

The rest of the eighth graders are in the gymnasium where they have been set free to greet each other with yearbooks and pens. They make promises to stay friends through high school and read each other's messages with wide eyes and unbridled grins. Groups of girls giggle as boys approach and posture awkwardly while suggesting that they should, maybe, hang out over the summer. Scattered in front of folded up bleachers and padded walls are solitary students who survey the scenes around them with contempt. They try to convince themselves that in high school, people will be more mature but they are less than optimistic. A pair of teachers stands at each exit. They exchange helpless looks when the noise starts to shake the walls. When students approach them with their yearbooks extended, they write brief messages of confidence and encouragement that stand out from the other handwriting on the page.

Michael watches the scene with an air of relief that is rich with layers of pride, exhaustion and the promise of two open months before him. It's been a long school year, and he's surprised to find himself looking forward to starting again in the fall. Bashyia, a large girl who once threatened to smack him with a broom if he insisted on standing between her and Chris, approaches him with a glow in her cheeks and wrinkles at the corners of her eyes. He finds an open space in the back pages of her yearbook and writes that she'll 'take high school by storm.' She thanks him and disappears back into the morass of exuberance. Michael's eyes skip from face-to-face. He remembers the first day of school when he came to this gymnasium to meet his homeroom class. All the same faces were here. They seemed eager to learn, and he was confident he knew how to help them. He was going to be a 'cool teacher.' By the middle of his second week, he was shouting his way through his lessons and picking up piles of incomplete worksheets after every class. Each day seemed longer than the last. His emotions became hard and fragile, like a layer of thinning ice. His students weren't learning, and he heaped blame generously upon himself. By Christmas his ego was shattered. He gave into the idea that he had no idea what he was doing. He began to rethink his most fundamental assumptions about how learning works.

Over the next few months, Michael began to see himself more as an organizer than an instructor. He embraced the creative potential built into his profession. His whole demeanor changed. He created individualized expectations for every student, reorganized his classroom into stations, and stayed late creating materials to stock them with. He decorated the classroom. He met with families. He made a point to not be frustrated when students resisted his instructions. The same problems persisted, but they became more diffused. The average grades on quizzes shifted from Ds and Fs to Cs and Ds. More students approached him for help, and he dug into research about curriculum and pedagogy. Even Sasha began to notice. Two weeks ago she stopped by his classroom to tell him how Deiby and Bashyia had started to rethink their opinion of his class. "Might be too little too late," he joked. She hesitated before leaving, and the subtle pause left an impression on him. Sometimes the moment gets stuck on a loop in his memory. There's a knock on the door behind him.

"Farhea? What are you doing out there?"

She seems surprised to see him. "Nothing. I mean the bathroom. I had to get a drink of water." Her rail thin limbs slide against the edge of the door as she sidesteps inside the auditorium and then runs away toward no one in particular. *Farhea? I don't think I've ever seen her lie before.*

Derrick grips the tip of the corduroy strip that runs around the edge of the bulletin board in his classroom and pulls outward. The border peels off with a succession of muted pops as the staples break away. He yanks outward, and the far tip swings away and sends a wave riding back down the strip to his hand. He tosses the border into a growing pile in the center of his room and reaches for the next piece. He should be in an end-of-year data meeting down the hall, but he doesn't see the point. Besides, Rosa is supposed to call at some point during the day.

He finishes clearing the bulletin board and stands above the pile of torn paper. It is heavy in the middle with construction paper, chart paper, folders, and bulletin board paper. Loose-leaf worksheets and ruler paper with pencil marks fan out at the edges. The significance that each sheet carried at some point over the last ten months seems decisively irrelevant. He takes a pair of large black bags from their box in the corner and checks his phone again. A mouse steps cautiously out from under the cabinets in the back of the room, looks up at Derrick and continues sniffing the ground. The room is thick with heat and lingering body odors. Derrick lowers his hands from his waist and stomps his foot. The mouse retreats back under the cabinets. As he fills the garbage bags, Derrick notices Sasha cross in front of his door twice in each direction.

When the phone rings, he is quick to answer.

"Rosa?"

"Hello Derrick."

"Como estas?"

"I am good."

Over the last year and a half, they have made a point to speak every other week, but the last two times Rosa has called, their conversations have been brief. This time Rosa assures Derrick that she has time to talk, but her voice is hesitant. She tells him about the children and how they're becoming more mature, and she says that Ramon is doing well. Every time she speaks, Derrick fears she'll break off her plans to visit in the summer. He tells her about working on the farm and how it reminds him of Nicaragua.

"Derrick." There is anxiety in her voice. "I am afraid to travel. People tell me that it is not safe to travel alone for me."

"No…" he begins, but he isn't sure how to continue. "Do you want to travel alone?"

"I want to see you, but I am scared."

Derrick scolds himself. Of course she shouldn't be expected to travel alone. "Claro. I can come and get you. I will fly to Nicaragua and we can travel back together."

"De verdad?"

"It will be good to see everyone. They can remember that I'm a good person and that you'll be safe with me." Rosa laughs. The last bell of the school year rings, and the floors begin to shake.

"Que pasa?"

"It's the last day of school. The students are excited."

"Oh," the noise carries across the line. In Nicaragua the mountain is silent. "Derrick. I hope I like Louisiana."

"Me too."

"Derrick. What if you are disappointed when you see me? What if I am not how you remember?"

"Rosa. Te quiero. We just need to see each other. That's the most important thing."

"Sometimes I cannot understand how this happened. How am I in love with an American who lives in Louisiana?"

Derrick looks out the window and watches the students

skip off the curbs as they file into the buses and cross the street away from the school.

"Tomorrow night I'm going to play guitar at an open-mic."

"Open-mic?"

"When anyone can perform if they want."

"Are you going to sing too?"

"Maybe."

"I wish I could be there."

"Me too."

They settle into a weighted silence.

"Rosa," he kicks at a piece of paper on the floor, "you should know that I'm scared too. I know I want to see you but I'm scared."

Rosa laughs, "*Good*. I don't want to be the only one."

Sasha is agitated. She paces nervously between the students as they file onto buses and start their final walk home of the year. They brush past her without noticing her concern. She returns to her classroom and looks again in every corner and every cabinet. She stares dumbfounded. She refuses to accept the idea that someone could have stolen her purse. *And I finally had a decent year.*

Sasha leaves her classroom. She checks the stalls in the student bathrooms and looks beneath the liners of trashcans. She begins to work her way down the hall, inspecting other people's classrooms. Most of the faculty is gone. She tells the few that she finds that she is looking for a student's backpack. They wish her luck and she tells them to enjoy their summer. *It's gone. What am I even doing?* Still, she continues the search. Her thoughts jump to Michael's classroom at the end of the hall, and she hopes that she can run into him one last time before the summer. A sudden fear that he may have already left briefly eclipses the concern she feels for her purse. The fear startles her. She tries to brush it aside, but instead she walks directly to his room, looks inside and pushes open the door. He's not there, but his leather bag is sitting on one of the student's desks. She starts to move around the edge of the room like she's done in nearly every other classroom along the hall, but here she moves more slowly. Every few steps she glances toward the doorway. She picks at the skin at the base of her fingernails with her thumb. Normally at school there is a constant a sense of having to be inside a persona, but at the end of the year, people let down their guard. She feels decisively unprofessional and can't shake her desire to linger here to wait for Michael. Her purse is slinking away from her thoughts when she notices a green strap under Michael's desk.

She sits in Michael's chair, reaches under the desk for her purse and sets it in her lap. Lying on top is a note. The letters are neat with broad curves, and while not on lined paper, the words run across perfectly straight. She recognizes the handwriting immediately. *Farhea?*

Mr. M,

When you give this purse back to Ms. J you should ask her on a date. I think you would have a good time. Ms. J is very nice and so are you. I know because I see you both

EVERYDAY. I'm sorry I took this purse. But something had to be done!!! I hope you're not mad at me. I'm glad you were my teacher. In conclusion, I think you and Ms. J should go on a date.

P.S. Please don't be mad at me!

Sasha reads over the note twice more and laughs. She folds the sheet in half and slides it into her purse. When Michael returns, she is sitting on the counter by the windows.

"Hey," he says, trying to sound natural.

"Hey. Are you about to head out?"

"Yeah. I just came back to get my bag."

"I was wondering if you wanted to get a drink or something. You know, celebrate."

"Um, uh," Michael picks his bag up off the desk, "yeah, OK," he slings it over his shoulder, "You mean right now?"

"Sure. Why not."

Thirty minutes later they are seated on stools at a tall square table in the bar of a Mexican restaurant. The lights are dim. The pair of TVs above the bar play the same college baseball game on slightly angled screens. The bar is empty, and the dining room tables are sparsely populated. The waitress takes her time to arrive. Michael and Sasha comment on the paintings of Chihuahuas and Mexican wrestlers hanging around the restaurant. They alternate reading the names of drinks on the specialty margarita menu: "Loco y Libre," "Horni Gringo," "Hijo de Patron."

When the waitress arrives, she slides a plastic basket with tortilla chips and a dish of salsa between them. Michael and Sasha both order classic margaritas with salt. Sasha asks for hers on the rocks.

"Frozen always gives me a headache," she explains.

"Me too. But I drink too quickly if I get'em with ice."

The conversation settles into a lull. They eat chips with salsa and glance around the bar. Michael is worried Sasha will regret asking him out for a drink, but she seems to be enjoying herself.

"So," she says and her face begins to brighten, "I was getting ready to leave school today when I realized I couldn't find my purse."

The waitress returns, "Two margaritas. One frozen, one on the rocks. Will you two be ordering any food?"

They glance at each other. Sasha shrugs. Her lips narrow and eyebrows rise. Michael looks back to the waitress, "No, I don't think so. At least not right now."

"Alright, just let me know if you need anything."

"Anyway…" She tells the story of panicking and looking everywhere and finally coming to terms with the idea that her purse was gone. "And then I looked in your classroom," she picks up her purse, and takes out a sheet of paper, "I found my purse, and I found this." She slides the folded note across the table.

Michael is visibly amused as he reads, "I guess this was all Farhea's idea then?"

"I guess so."

Michael hands the sheet back. He considers saying something like *Remind me to thank her,* but he doesn't want to be overly flirtatious. He hesitates, and Sasha is glad to see the note has made him a little uncomfortable. "Farhea. I knew she was up to something mischievous when I saw her in the auditorium. She's not the greatest liar in the world."

"I'm just glad I found my purse," she says, almost playfully.

Suddenly, Sasha's eyes jerk over Michael's shoulder and she waves with a flick of her wrist. "I think one of my old students just came in."

Michael turns over his shoulder to see a group of teenagers, one of whom is breaking away from his friends to walk toward their table. He is tall with thin facial hair and walks with a self-conscious stride.

"*Wyson*. How are you?" Michael is impressed with how fully she commits her attention to him. *No wonder the students love her.*

"Hey Ms. J. I'm good." His smile is broad and proud.

"Last week did you…"

"Yes ma'am. I just graduated. And I got a scholarship to go to Loyola next year. I'm going to major in engineering."

Sasha leans back, "Oh Wyson. Congratulations." She turns to Michael, "Wyson here was one of my students my first year teaching. He gave me a lot of trouble but he was one of my favorites. Very smart. God. I can't believe you're already graduated."

Michael extends his hand, and Wyson shakes it firmly.

"Wyson, this is a friend of mine, Michael, he was one of the new teachers this year."

"Right. *Friend.* I got you Ms. J." He bends to nudge her with his elbow but thinks better of it and clumsily straightens his posture. Sasha blushes. "Anyway," he glances over his shoulder, "I gotta run and I'll let you two get back to, whatever. It was good seeing you. And nice to meet you."

"Good to meet you too."

Sasha drinks liberally from her margarita. When Wyson is seated with his friends on the far side of the bar, they call the waitress over and order another round.

The conversation flows smoothly, and at times Michael is amazed by how comfortable he feels. Sasha has always been kind to him, but he had always assumed that she didn't fully respect him as a teacher. When they spoke he was shy and often embarrassed by the exaggerated problems in his classroom. None of that seems to matter now.

Michael asks about her past, and Sasha explains how she taught for two years right out of college before going to law school. "But it didn't feel right, and after a year I knew for sure I didn't want to be a lawyer and I was building all this debt, and I started to have these panic attacks so I left and went back to teaching. I love teaching; I really do." Her family doesn't approve of the decision. Michael says he's not surprised, and they talk about the goals and expectations of their parent's generation. They toast, half-jokingly, to the fall of the baby boomer's value system. Michael talks about his time in New York and arriving in Louisiana just before the hurricane. They realize that they both went to Houston for a couple days when the power stayed out and may have been at the Museum of Fine Art at the same time. "Did you go see the bats?" He hadn't. "Next time you should see the bats. There's a giant colony under a bridge, and you can watch them swirl into the sky when they go out for the night." Michael tells the story of the time he and Derrick went to a party at a barn, and Derrick went bat fishing and ended up falling off the barn into a bush.

Sasha laughs, "Bat fishing? You can do that?"

"Apparently."

"When was this?"

Michael thinks for a moment, "Damn. Must have been almost seven years ago."

Wyson and his friends are getting up from their table. He waves again as he leaves.

"God. I can't believe my babies are all grown up."

"Well. He's not quite grown yet."

Sasha takes another sip of her drink.

"You know," Michael continues, "when I was his age I was getting ready to head on a trip to Europe with my friend Adam. We had saved up over the year and then we spent almost two months traveling all round." He traces a sideways parabola in the air with his finger. "It was a lot of fun."

"What was your favorite part?"

"Probably running with the bulls."

"Sounds scary."

"Well, I was invincible. So that helped."

"I bet it's hard to feel invincible when you're being chased by a bull."

"Maybe. But I did feel real grown up at the time. I felt real in control through the whole trip. I had the time of my life just feeding every impulse I had. I remember thinking that I had discovered the type of person I was meant to be."

"And now?"

"Well, now I look at people like Wyson and realize I was just a kid. To be honest, it probably took me much longer than it should have to realize that the person running around Europe wasn't some sort of true self I should be fighting to return to. He was just…"

"Just a point in time."

"Yeah. Maybe."

Again, the conversation lulls. Michael finishes his margarita and takes a long sip of water. He mentions having to drive home and gestures to the waitress for the check. A crowd has been trickling in, and the once-quiet dining room is alive with conversation. Michael looks into the open kitchen and listens to the sounds of water, fire, and metal against metal pour over the chest-high counter toward them. The check is on its way, and Michael insists on paying. When Sasha protests, Michael says that Farhea would never forgive him if he let her split the bill. Sasha smiles, happily defeated. Michael is rehearsing what he'll say when they're outside. He wants to invite her to see Derrick perform tomorrow. The question twists into a knot at the bottom of his throat.

The waitress thanks them and tells them to have a good day. "We'll do our best," says Michael.

They stand from their stools and head to the door. Outside, they squint beneath the light of the sun. Across the parking lot stands a row of magnolia trees in bloom, and the scent carries in the breeze. They walk toward their cars with patient steps. Michael's heart thuds against his chest.

"So," he begins, "tomorrow night…"

Year 7
Leah and Susan

Forgiveness waits while feelings pace.

    In the night they link their hands

From his touch, a breath of grace.

    Her ring flashes beneath the stars

A promise made, a leap of faith.

    "More than anything," he says.

Through our love we build our life.

    "I am bound to you."

Through our love we build our life.

Susan reads back over the last two pages and saves the file. She likes how it is coming. Soon she'll be able to share the pages with James without feeling awkward about where it leaves off. Behind her, her nearly completed wedding dress hangs on a dress form. She picks up her cup of tea. The teabag steeped while she wrote, and the taste is slightly bitter, but she doesn't mind. She drinks and stares above her computer screen. Since her fight turned conversation with James last week, Susan has been suspended in a feeling of contentment that is almost jarring in its stability. Tonight is the restaurant opening. She plays with daydreams of showing up with Leah and imagines the flush of pride she'll feel when James greets them and takes them to their table. She knows the night will be a success. *And when it's over he'll be all mine.*

Leah opens the passenger door and places her shopping bags onto the seat. At the first stoplight, she whisks at her hair with her fingers and contemplates the shrinking distance between her belly and the steering wheel. Once on the highway, she calls Susan.

"Susie!"

"Hey Leah."

"I'm driving home from the store and just wanted to check-in about tonight."

"What did you get?"

"*I got. Two* dresses: one for tonight, and one to motivate me for after the baby. It's gorgeous; I'll show you. But I have a lot of work before I can fit into it. *Oh*, I also bought a camera, one of those nice ones. I really need to take more pictures, especially for when little Bella gets here. You'll love it. We can take pictures at the restaurant tonight."

"I don't know if I want to show up snapping pictures."

"Or not. All I'm saying is that it's a nice camera. I might try and get into photography as a hobby."

"Whatever makes you happy... I'm really looking forward to tonight. James has been working practically nonstop."

"I'm just excited I get to go to a fancy restaurant as a

friend of the chef. I was telling my mother about it this morning."

"How's your mother?"

"She's good. She wants me to move to North Carolina to be near her."

"What did you say?"

"That I don't know anybody in—*Ahhh*. Some people can't drive. This *dinglewad* just cut me off."

"Do you want me to let you go?"

"No. I'm ok. Anyway, I don't know anyone in North Carolina and I told her that you and James are excited about helping out with the baby. You are, *right?*"

"Of course."

"Right. So now she's talking about moving back here. Says she can probably get transferred back if she asks."

"That's exciting. I haven't seen your mother in years."

"She sends her love, says she's looking forward to coming up for the wedding."

"Good."

"How's the dress?"

"It's coming along. I finished the bodice and the skirt. I really like how the tulle worked out. All I really have left to do is the straps and figuring out what type of trim to do. I'm thinking about lace and playing around with fabric flowers."

"Can we do a fashion show before dinner?"

"Maybe. I still need to attach the bodice to the skirt. First you'll have to help me get a final measurement."

"Susie. Listen to us. We're all grown up."

"I know. Who would have thought?"

"Not me. That's for sure."

There's a beep on the line.

"This is James. I should probably take it."

"Alright. I'll see you in a few hours."

Leah hangs up and opens her sunroof. She pulls into the passing lane and listens to the wind lick through the inside of the car.

"Hey hon. I'm just calling to let you know I'm going to come home to change before the opening."

"When will you be here?"

"Soon. I'm leaving now."

"How much time will you have?" Susan layers her voice with insinuation.

"I'm not sure," he says, playing along.

"Will you have *enough*?"

"I just might."

"Then I'll see you soon."

"I'll hurry home."

Susan decides to take a shower and greet James in her robe. She runs the water hot and can feel her pores breathing in the steam. She thinks about undoing the buttons of his shirt, and how he'll still be able to feel the warmth of the water on her skin. She turns off the shower and grabs a towel. The bedroom clock reads 2:30. James should be home at any minute. She smiles at her reflection and lies down in bed.

When she hears his car pull up, she walks to the living room. James is flipping through the mail when he enters.

"You've got a fat envelope here forwarded from your old address."

Susan wants him to drop the mail where he stands and kiss her, but when she sees the envelope in James's hand, her thoughts turn cold.

"Says it's from somebody named Michael," James's mood is still lighthearted.

When Susan didn't hear anything from Michael after two months, she assumed that he wasn't going to reply. The realization brought a sense of relief.

When James looks up, he sees the panic in Susan's eyes. "Who's Michael?" he asks, his voice stern and not expecting an answer. James is disgusted. He turns his back to Susan and starts toward the bedroom. His index finger tears at the seam of the letter.

Susan tries to call for him not to open it, but the words don't come. Her feet are nailed to the floor. Blood rushes from her face.

Alone in the bedroom, his heart pounding, James skims through the pages, dropping them to the floor as he goes. Susan has told him she's not ready to share her book but here it is. The name Michael is on almost every page. When he reaches the last page he slows to read it line by line. *"Whispers," writes Susan, "Remind me of you."* His thoughts are poisoned by betrayal. There is a brief note from Michael at the end. He says that he likes the book so far, and he assumes she'll get around to changing everyone's names. He says that it's probably better if they stop writing letters. He wishes her luck with her marriage and says he's started to see someone he might be falling for. He says that Susan has talent as a writer, and that she'll always be a part of him. James drops the note into the scattered pile of papers at his feet.

He sits on the edge of the bed and stares into the wall. Susan steps to the doorway.

"I can explain."

"Last week I told you I felt like you had been hiding something from me."

"James, I'm sorry."

"You made it sound like it was my fault for pushing you away. Now *this*. What the fuck is *this*?"

"Michael is just an old friend," her voice is small and scared.

"Just an old friend? What? 'It's not what it looks like,' is that it?"

"I love you James. More than anything. I should have told you. You have every right to be mad. Please let me explain."

"Not now. Just leave me alone. I need to think."

Susan hesitates and then sulks away from the door and walks back into the living room. When James emerges from the bedroom, he's dressed in his new chef's uniform with his apron clenched in his hand. He walks directly to the door and then turns to her.

"You can come tonight if you want, but just know that I'm going to be busy."

He slams the door behind him, and the whole room shudders in his wake.

Leah stands on the roof of her apartment building on the slopes of the Southside taking photos of clouds. The sky stretches around her in shades of blue, white, pink, and grey.

She enjoys taking pictures. In the distance, rows of bridges string across the Monongahela and gesture toward the skyline as it fans back from the river's point. She enjoys the way the city is made up of rivers and the hills which rise around them. Someone once told her that Pittsburgh has more bridges than any other city, even Venice. She takes pictures of the riverboats and tries to play around with the camera's different exposure settings, but the pictures turn out blurry. *I need to get a tripod.*

She whispers toward her belly, "Would you mind if mommy spent your clothes money on a tripod?"

She returns the settings to their default positions and focuses on the skyline. She likes how the sun reflects off the buildings. She zooms in on the pictures after they're taken and is impressed by their level of detail. After every shot she grows more pleased with her camera. She walks to the building's edge and takes shots of the flowering bushes sprinkled between the trees along the slope. Heat rises in waves from the roof. Sweat beads and slides down her face.

"How are you doing Bella? Do you like taking pictures with mommy?"

When Leah is ready to go back to her apartment, she is exhausted. Her feet drag beneath her and thud down the metal stairs that connect the top floor to the roof. The narrow stairway echoes with each step. She takes the elevator back to her floor, leans on the door as she opens it and collapses onto her coach. The bing and buzz of her cell phone calls from the kitchen counter, but she's too tired to check the message.

"Bella," she whispers, and falls asleep.

Three hours later Leah awakes with a start. She shuffles over to her phone. There are seven missed calls from Susan. They're going to be late to the restaurant. Leah doesn't want to explain that she hasn't started to get ready, so she decides to shower and dress before calling Susan back.

It's almost seven o'clock when Leah rushes out of her apartment with her phone to her ear.

"Leah. Where have you been?" Susan is more worked up than Leah expected.

"I'm sorry. I fell asleep. I'm on my way now. They're serving dinner until eleven right? We should be fine."

"James and I got into a fight. I don't even know if we should go."

"About what?"

"It's bad."

"Listen. I'm coming over there right now. I want to hear exactly what happened, and then I want you to be ready to go to the restaurant. Later you'll make up from the fight and he'll resent you if you weren't at the opening."

"Maybe."

"I'll see you soon sweetie."

"I'll see you soon."

Leah fires the ignition and accelerates down the slope toward East Carson Street. She catches nearly every red light in the Southside and growls in frustration. She speeds up over the Liberty Bridge, but her progress slows when she has to cross through downtown. She is worried about Susan. It's not like her to sound so defeated. Leah crosses the Allegheny River and turns up the radio to distract her thoughts. She follows the expressway along the river and watches the skyline shrink in her rearview mirror. *Hartwood Acres. Hartwood Acres. Where do I turn?* She takes out her phone and programs the address, trying to keep her vision on the road and the screen at the same time. The river beside her shines like a mirror angled into the sun. She looks into the rearview mirror again and wipes at the lipstick at the corner of her mouth with her pinky. *Everything will be OK. Susan is probably overreacting.* When Leah pulls off the expressway, the scenery changes. Hills flow into the roads and then continue below them. Stores appear in clusters every couple of miles. Houses are further apart. Thick shadows blanket the road through long stretches of wooded land. Leah is glad to be away from traffic and accelerates through the woods. Yellow signs warn caution through the winding turns ahead. Leah puzzles over whether this is the same way she came the last time she visited Susan. She envies Susan for having a proper family home away from the city. Leah takes a sharp right and checks her phone again to make sure she's on the right track. The phone's tracking system takes a moment to reset. She looks back to the road. A large deer stands in her path. Its knees tremble. Its black eyes shine in the light of her headlights. Leah jerks the wheel to the left and stomps on the brakes. The front corner of the car clips the deer with a dull thud. The tires burn a pair of dark lines across the road. The front wheels drop from the asphalt and onto the slope below. Leah twists the wheel back and presses on the gas. The right side of the car pulls away from the ground. The rear wheels slip off the road. The car flips and rolls twice. On its third turn, the driver's side door crashes against a tree. Leah gasps for breath. The smell of burnt rubber rises in the air. Blood runs down her face and wets her hair. She can't breathe. Her vision becomes dim. Leah touches her hand to her stomach and the world goes black.

The nurse is young, maybe younger than Susan. She speaks with measured phrases. The accident is very serious. Leah is in surgery right now. The doctors are doing everything they can.

"What about the baby?"

"I'm sorry I can't give you more details right now. I will let you know everything as I hear it from surgery."

"Thank you."

Susan sits back down and readies herself to call Leah's mother. Less than an hour ago, she called Susan to tell her Leah had been in an accident, and Susan rushed to the hospital. Susan looks around her. The scene is unreal. *Leah... Leah. You have to be all right.*

When James gets Susan's message, he announces to the kitchen that he has to go. He throws his apron into a basket of linens and walks through the dining room. He does not look at any of the guests that he greeted so warmly just a few minutes before. Outside, he turns his back to the crowd of people and jogs down the street to his car.

Susan stands and paces and then sits back down. She considers other people to call but doesn't want to worry them. The fluorescent lights hum. Metal carts rattle as they roll by. Susan tries to take comfort in the fact that everyone here knows what they're doing. The nurse approaches and takes a seat next to her. Her eyes are comforting but somber.

"How are you feeling?" she asks.

"I'd like to know what's going on."

"The situation is still very serious."

"How serious?"

"Leah has suffered a strong blow to the head that fractured her skull. Her collarbone is broken and, unfortunately, the impact of the steering wheel against her abdomen was quite severe. The doctors don't think that her pregnancy will survive the surgery. I am very sorry. They are doing everything they can to bring Leah into a stable condition."

Susan can't speak. She turns away from the nurse, and her eyes gloss over. She won't believe that Bella is gone. *Bella will make it.* She clings to the thought with an uncommon fierceness. Her blood quivers in her veins. *Bella.*

Leah lies on a bed beneath bright lights. An inner and outer ring of surgeons and nurses surround her. A mask is strapped to her face. Her skin is pale. The sounds of doctor's voices, monitors, air suction and metal instruments create a blanket of white noise. There is a long gash in the middle of her chest. Gauze thick with blood is cleared from her scalp. Her heartbeat is weak and getting weaker.

James rushes into the hospital. He finds the stairwell and takes the steps two at a time to the third floor surgery center. He searches the floor and finds Susan sitting against the far wall with a line of empty seats on both sides. He watches a nurse approach. She sits next to her. Susan asks a question and the nurse speaks for a while. She places her palm on Susan's hand. James begins to approach and sees Susan pull her hand away. Her body folds forward and she sets her face in her hands. The nurse stands as James takes a seat and places his hand on Susan's shoulder. Susan turns toward him. Her eyes are bloodshot and streaked with tears. Her shoulders begin to shake. James pulls her close. He strokes his hand across her back. Susan's tears soak into his shirt. He holds her tight. She feels frail beneath his hand.

"Susan. Honey, you can talk to me."

Susan pulls away. She wipes at her eyes with her fingers and then with the palms of her hands.

"I can't. I can't say it. She was on her way to see me. We were going to go to the restaurant and then... and now... they did what they could but... oh god, she's *gone*... First they told me that Bella wasn't going to make it and now..." She takes a deep breath. "God. I need to tell her mother." She picks up her phone, "I need to call her..." her hands tremble, "I can't do this. I can't..."

James reaches for the phone, and Susan looks away. The noises fade. A fissure opens up inside her. Susan knows that nothing will ever feel complete again. Nothing will be as it's supposed to be.

*   *   *   *   *

The next few days pass in a haze. Susan barely rests. She doesn't notice when night bleeds into day. Leah's mother arrives and Susan insists that she stays with her and James. She says that Leah was lucky to have friends like them. Leah's mother is a small woman with dark eyes and short dark hair. It's easy to see the lines of Leah's face in her nose and the curve of her jaw. Together they ride out to the site of the accident and place a cross beside the road. Susan glares at the skid marks and forces her reaction into the gulf that has grown inside of her. James goes with Leah's mother to the church and funeral home to support her through the decisions that need to be made. Susan cooks dinner but doesn't eat. She reaches out to old friends who have scattered across the country. She assumes Lillian will fly in, but Lillian says she can't get away from her job and sends a wreath of yellow roses to the funeral home instead. The note is brief. "Leah, you were taken far too soon. I will miss you forever."

When James encourages her to sleep, Susan retreats to the dining room and works on Leah's eulogy. She writes by hand and fills pages with stories and quotes. Single words are followed by thoughts that lead into sketches of dialogue and memories of specific days they were together. Susan loses herself in the writing. At times, the fact that Leah is gone is far from her mind. The house is silent except for the scratch of her pen. Occasionally she hears the creak of Leah's mother above her and wonders if she's sitting up in bed. By the end of the second night, the notepad is almost full. She flips through the pages but finds nothing that resembles a speech.

Just after dawn, Susan empties the downstairs closet into the hall and carries a crate of old photographs to the kitchen. She stands at the counter and sifts through them, sorting out pictures of Leah. There is a roll from middle school when Susan went on vacation with Leah's family to their lake house in New York. There is a roll from their first trip to Beam's Rock with a picture of Leah standing, triumphant, above the forest. A stack of pictures shows Leah on her wedding day. She is the soul of youth. The pictures continue jumping back and forth in time, but they skip over more years than they touch. There is a shot of them together beneath a large maple tree, and Susan has no recollection of the day it was taken. A subtle fear begins to take hold of her. She feels the moments between these photos already beginning to dissolve. Her vision grows heavy, and Susan realizes that she needs to get some rest. She straightens the pile of pictures with Leah in them and sets it on the kitchen table for her mother. She returns the rest of the pictures to the crate and carries it back to the closet. Upstairs she slides under the covers and pulls close to James. She sets her head on his shoulder, and he turns to wrap his arm around her. His heartbeat keeps a steady rhythm. His body warms the space between the sheets.

"How are you doing?" he whispers.

"I'm tired."

James strokes her hair and kisses the lines at the corner of her eye. He remembers their fight about Michael's letter, and the thought seems profoundly insignificant. He can feel Susan's body relax against his own. He had a right to be upset, but he is still embarrassed by his reaction. Susan brushes her cheek over his chest and lets out a long sigh. James knows that she needs him. His life is rooted in their love.

The morning of the funeral, a light rain brushes the sidewalk in front of the funeral home, and silences the birds in the nearby trees. Susan and James arrive with Leah's mother. The staff welcomes them. Their greetings are warm and somber. The priest arrives and again offers his condolences to Leah's mother. He is a grey-haired man with a round face, and he listens with sallow eyes as Susan takes his hand and introduces herself. His manners are practiced but dignified.

A short while later, people begin to arrive in pairs. Leah's aunts and uncles are the first. They circle around Leah's mother and then form a line beside her. When Susan's mother arrives, Susan greets her at the door, and they hug each other tightly. Groups of Leah's friends from work arrive. They move awkwardly and seem unsure of where to stand or what to say. Friends of Leah's mother filter in with their children. Susan recognizes a few but doesn't remember their names. Just under twenty people have arrived when it's time to begin.

A silver urn with Leah's ashes sits on a purple cloth atop a dark wooden table. There are too many seats, and the different groups of people sit apart from each other, giving the room a sparse appearance. The ceremony is brief. The church pianist plays an instrumental of "Ave Maria." Leah's mother reads a short prayer. Her voice cracks when she looks toward Leah's urn. The priest offers a reading that speaks of how all life and death is for the Lord. He talks of Leah with flattering generalizations and concludes with a reminder that Leah is looking down on us from heaven.

When Susan is introduced, she stands up slowly. The room is quiet. She walks calmly to the podium with the pages she has prepared. She looks out at the faces looking back at her and notices a tightening above her heart. She considers announcing that she can't do this and walking toward the exit, but instead she straightens the papers in front of her and begins to speak in a voice that feels like it is coming from behind her.

"I met Leah… I met Leah when we were in sixth grade. I was wearing a pair of bright pink shoes and she said that she liked them and that she wished she had a pair like them. This was strange for two reasons: first, because no one had ever said anything like this to me before, and second, because my mom had bought these shoes without my consent and I thought they were ugly and had been horribly embarrassed by them all morning. But after Leah said that she liked them, I saw them differently. I walked a little taller and by the end of the day I was showing them off to my friends on the bus.

"It's a simple enough story, the type that happens everyday. But in this case it was the beginning of something special. Within a couple of weeks Leah and I were inseparable. We talked nearly every night, and nearly every night, she told me that I was so much more than the person I thought I was, that I deserved to do the things I wanted to do; she told me that the two of us were the most beautiful and lucky people in the world.

"Leah taught me how to hope with courage and how to love with all my heart. She taught me that we don't have to live according to the plan that life offers us. She taught me to stand up for the life that I want.

"I'd like to say that Leah would want us all to move on, to try not to think about her, to find some other way to fill the place she held in our lives, but anyone who knew Leah knows that wouldn't be true. Leah would want to be remembered. She'd want to be missed. She would want thoughts of her, and thoughts of what she might say to us, to help us through our daily lives. She would want her death to be a challenge to us to love as fiercely as she did. She would want us to remember her. And if we were going to pray, she would not want us to pray for her, but for Bella, her baby girl.

"Leah, we'll miss you. And Bella, you'll never know how lucky you would have been."

Susan looks up. She steps out from behind the podium and walks slowly down the center aisle toward the exit. There is still silence behind her when the front door creaks on its hinge and she steps outside.

Susan squints beneath the sun. A chorus of birds chirps on all sides. James follows and stands quietly beside her. A few minutes later, people begin to exit to the sound of a piano. Several of them walk over to Susan. They shake her hand, and thank her for her words. Susan turns her eyes to a nearby tree. She sees a bird's nest and watches a robin fly to its edge and bend to feed the neck-stretched babies inside. She looks away and up to the cotton-colored clouds. She remembers the pictures they found on the camera Leah bought the day that she died. Pictures of the sky.

Wedding Day

Wedding. The word weaves between the nerves of everyone involved and tickles them with anticipation. A thin dirt road leads into the twenty-acre estate. A row of weeping willow trees marks the southern border and draws compliments from the stream of guests as they arrive. Above the road, a pack of uniformed staff are busy unfolding chairs, setting tables, pouring water, stringing lights and piecing wooden squares together into a dance floor. They place purple roses into white vases and set them at the centers of tables.

At the far end of the field, an outdoor chapel stands in front of a curved hedge of pink rosebushes. The guests glance at the scene with nods of approval as they mingle, drinks in hand, beside the long wooden building where members of the wedding party mull about, straightening their clothes and keeping anxious watch over the time. A small side room has been converted into a makeshift beauty salon. Susan stands in her plum colored bridesmaid's dress and turns her head gently from side-to-side, playing with the inch wide curls in her hair. Leah watches her in the mirror. The makeup artist brushes her cheeks and then announces that she's done. Leah is sure that she's more beautiful than she's ever been before.

"Thank you," she says, "you're wonderful. Susie, what do you think?"

"Leah. You look gorgeous." Her words are wrapped in the same playful sense of consequence that has marked all of their conversations over the past few weeks. "You look like you're about to get married."

"*I know*," says Leah, almost in a whisper, her voice brimming into a high-pitched but muted squeal.

There is a knock at the door, and Leah's mother enters. Her eyes broaden to take in the sight of her daughter. Her shoulders are pulled back with pride; her face is softened by disbelief. She takes Leah's hands and holds them in front of her.

"My baby girl."

"Mom. I know this isn't easy for you."

"I'm just glad to see you happy. You look beautiful. Are you ready?"

"I'm ready."

"Ok. I'll let them know."

Susan watches Leah walk toward her down the aisle. She marvels at the crowd around them. The seats are filled and dozens more stand behind them. Everyone wears their finest clothes and sets their attention on Leah and Marcel. As the ceremony continues, Susan feels a swell of emotion in her chest, jaw, and around her eyes. She forces back the tears as she watches Marcel slide the ring onto Leah's finger. And then it is over. Leah and Marcel walk back down the aisle. The guests rise and begin talking to each other. In a moment, a milestone is past. *Leah is married.* Lillian pokes Susan from behind. "Walk," she whispers, "You need to walk first, *remember.*" Susan shakes herself from her daze and realizes people have turned their attention in her direction. She follows the footsteps Leah set in the grass. Swirls of bubbles float around her and pop in the light of the sun.

An hour after dinner, the air of maturity that had tempered Leah's friends before the ceremony has vanished. Extra bottles of wine are smuggled to the tables. The dance floor pours past the first row of neighboring tables. Bands of high school friends head to the barn where group photos are being taken. Beside the barn, one of Marcel's groomsmen slides his hand up the leg of a friend of Leah's from literature class. Steven excuses himself to the bar, and Susan watches him walk away. She tries to ignore the fact that she can't imagine spending the rest of her life with him. On the dance floor, Lillian cuts loose. She sways her hips and runs her hand across the chests of unfamiliar men. Leah and Marcel crisscross through the crowd greeting family members and accepting congratulations. Marcel jokes in French with a group of friends, and Leah wraps her arm around his waist. Steven is on his way back to the table, but Susan pretends not to notice. She stands abruptly from her seat, takes down the last of her wine in a decisive gulp and starts toward the dance floor. Her steps keep rhythm with the music. When Lillian sees Susan approach, she pushes away the pair of men beside her and takes her hand. Susan leans forward and shakes her shoulders. Lillian lets out a long "*Ooooo!!!*" and spins under Susan's arm. Susan hikes her dress up a few inches with her left hand and waves the other in the air. The rest of the dance floor becomes a blur. Her worries dissolve. Lillian leans toward her and yells above the music, "*Finally*. I thought you were going to leave me to celebrate all alone."

Leah lies next to Marcel in the suite that overlooks the

grounds. Marcel held her for a long time, but now he is turned away, and his breathing is deep and steady. It's after midnight, but the rumblings of the party outside still whisper through the windowpane. Moonlight shines through the blinds, and casts shadows across the bed. Leah is exhausted, but she can't sleep. She turns to her side and slides her fingers along Marcel's shoulder. His skin is smooth and warm. She wants to wake him but decides to let him rest. The sound of their vows echo in her mind. *I do.* She remembers the soft press of his lips against hers. Leah closes her eyes. She feels herself floating upon a sea of bliss. A distant light warms her skin. *This is the beginning.* On all sides, the ocean bends toward a clear horizon. Waves roll beneath her. *I will always be loved.*

- THE END -

ACKNOWLEDGMENTS

My most fervent thanks is for my first and final reader, my wife Elizabeth. Without you I wouldn't have had the strength or inspiration necessary to finish this novel. Thanks also to my mother. You have made me the person I am today. I never would have developed the skills or confidence to write this book without the support of three teachers who laid gave me the guidance I needed to become the writer I am today: Janet Koza, Deborah Jordan, and Janet Kafka. Many thanks also to everyone who read early drafts of this book: Paul Kennedy, Sarah Payne, Scott Engholm, and Xander Subashi. Your criticism made it stronger and your support helped me embrace the often trying process of editing. To my poet friends, Xero Skidmore and Donney Rose, working alongside you inspired me to pick up my pen again and start this whole process in the first place. Thanks to Adam Aleksander for your spirit of adventure. A special thanks to Elaina Barna for your help with editing and for giving me the idea for the title.